Her Price for N

Book Two of The Noble Love Series

Amy Curiston

Contents

1.

2.

3.

4.

5.

6.

7.

8.

9.

10.

11.

12.

13.

14.

15.

16.

17.

18.

19.

20.

21.

22.

23.

24.

25.

26.

27.

28.

29.

30.

31.

32.

33.

Prologue

1816

Lillian removed the ring from her finger and placed it in the young woman's hand; the daughter of the friend who betrayed her years ago. Now she must swallow her pride for the sake of her son's happiness. Lord knew she had not been much of a mother, but she could do this for him.

The ring had been on her finger since the day she became the Duchess of Hawthorne, the title she had wrapped around her as though it could protect her from her past. The look in Andrew's eyes when he thought he lost the woman he loves was devastating. It was time to let go of the pain and find some peace in his happiness.

Her son came to her a short time later, kneeling before her in the parlor of his country estate. A haven he had created for his two daughters after the death of their mother. Lillian had chosen Patricia to marry her son, but the lady had proven unworthy, running off to London to live her life of lavish parties and young lovers. Andrew had chosen well for himself this time. Laura Parsons obviously loved her son and his children. Despite the past, she would accept Laura for who she was rather than hold her accountable for the actions of her mother in their youth.

Andrew took her hand and brought it to his lips. "Thank you Mother, your blessing means a great deal to both of us. Not because we need it, only that we wish you to be a part of your grandchildren's lives." She looked upon his face, the deep blue eyes and firm jaw with a small dimple in his chin; so like his father. Was that why she had kept him at arm's length? Certainty that he would be like the man that sired him? He had since proven himself a loving young man with a sound head for business, a credit to the Hawthorne legacy.

She gave her son a tight smile, still uncomfortable showing the affection she had so seldom received in her own childhood. His sincere words had an impact, dislodging another piece of that wall around her heart. Once young and carefree, she had hoped for a happy life filled with love and family. So much had happened since those days at her family home, so much betrayal and loss had caused that hope to wither and die. Could she resurrect her heart and embrace her family? Julia would soon have her own first season now that Andrew was happily married. Her daughter deserved better than the cruel circumstances that had hardened her to her own children. She would endeavor to open herself up to the love that surrounded her. She only hoped she had not waited too long.

Leaving Andrew with his betrothed and his children, she decided to go for a ride. Something she rarely did, though it had been her greatest joy in her youth. Perhaps it was a way to begin.

Chapter one
1782

Lillian's heart soared with the wind on her face as her horse raced over the field, the stable master's son close behind. As she crossed into the yard, she threw her head back, laughing. She rarely won when racing Noah, making it all the sweeter when she did. "If only you could ride so well in a sidesaddle," he taunted. She dismounted, leading her horse to the water-filled trough. "I see no reason to be placed at a disadvantage in a race," she retorted as she scrunched her nose at him.

Noah laughed as he slung an arm around her shoulders. She was four years his junior, and he had looked out for her as much as he teased her. They had been friends her whole life, although she was the earl's daughter. Lillian spent much of her time in the stables and at the Reeves' kitchen table, avoiding the glowering expressions from her father and her mother's ill health.

The pair entered the small kitchen through the back door, drawn in by the scent of roasting meat and baked apples. Bread cooled on the well-worn table at the center of the room, one loaf sliced, and he snatched a piece from over his mother's shoulder and took a large bite. His mother swatted him with her towel. "Give Lily a slice; where are your manners?" Noah took another bite then spoke with his mouth full, "She knows where it is," he said around a mouthful. "She's not a guest." His mother rolled her eyes heavenward. "Perhaps the army will teach you some manners, seeing as I could not." He kissed her cheek before handing Lily a slice of the warm bread.

The girl added a generous spoonful of strawberry jam to hers and took a bite, a bit of the sticky red sweetness smearing her cheek. Noah shook his head, taking out his handkerchief and dabbing at her cheek, making a tsking sound. "Goodness, my lady," Noah said, mimicking his mother's tone. "However, shall we present you to society in such a state?" Lillian, or Lily as only this family called her, brushed his hand away. "I still have far better manners than you, sir." She looked at him with sadness in her pale blue eyes. "Why must you go off and join the army?" she pouted. His Uncle Thomas had graciously bought him a commission, having the funds but no children of his own.

"It is a fair living for men of few prospects, little Lily." She detested when he called her that, and he knew it. "You could stay here and work with the horses like your father. You are wonderful with them." Her voice pitched higher with her pleading, and he was in no mood to hear her protests yet again.

"It is time for me to make my own way if I am ever to afford a wife and family. Your father would never pay another stable hand. He hardly pays the ones he has." His mother swatted him again, her grey eyes glaring at his remark.

"It is quite alright Mrs. Reeves. I know my father is rather tightfisted with his money when it comes to running Martin's Nest. I wish I could convince him to make improvements and hire more staff. This place could be much more productive, we could have extra help in the stables."

Noah chucked her under the chin, "You are a sweet girl my little Lily." She gazed up at him, her features softening at his tone though it was short-lived. His next words had her blue eyes flashing.

6

"I am off to say my farewells to Angelica. I will be home for supper," he said to his mother, giving her a peck on the cheek. Lillian ran after him, grabbing the sleeve of his worn coat before he could swing up onto his horse. With a glance over her shoulder, she tugged him toward the stable beside the house. Flustered, he pulled from her grasp and turned his angry silver gaze on her.

"What is it Lily? I am expected." He was eager to enjoy a few stolen moments in the lovely blonde's arms, not standing in a stable dealing with an impetuous child. Prepared for another plea for him to stay, he found himself at the receiving end of a rather frantic kiss. He froze for a moment, her arms about his neck and her lips pressed to his. Coming to his senses, he pulled her arms away, holding them at her side. "What on earth are you about, Lily?"

"Marry me, Noah," she pleaded, tears welling in her eyes and spilling onto her freckled cheeks. "Wha…"

"Then you could stay; we would be happy here. Papa would have to give us my dowry so we would have an income... please, I could not bear it if you died in battle." He raised his eyes to the heavens, then looked down at the child that had just proposed to him and chuckled. "You are a dear to worry, so for me, my little Lily."

"Don't call me that," she ground out, stomping her foot ineffectually on the straw covered floor. "I am not a child; I love you and I would be a good wife to you." She reached for him again, but he held her away. "You are very much a child, and you will marry a nobleman someday. ot be the wife of a soldier or a horse groom. Besides, you are like a little sister to me."

She was shaking her head, tears flowing freely now. "You don't mean that. I know you don't. You love me. If you cannot marry me

7

now, wait until I am of age, stay here with me." A smile touched her lips as his face descended toward hers, but rather than kissing her lips as she hoped, he brushed a kiss on her forehead.

"I'll hear no more of this nonsense," he said with a shake of his head. Turning on his heel, he left her there and went to mount his horse.

Lillian ran toward the house, entering quietly through the servant's entrance, hoping to avoid her father. She could not bear one of his tirades about her running about in men's breeches. When she reached her room, she threw herself on the bed and allowed her tears to flow. Noah had been there her entire life, teaching her to ride, fishing in the stream or running through the fields. Then, as she had grown, she saw him differently; the gentle way he had with a skittish horse, the kindness he showed the young children in the village, and the way he spoke of his plans for the future. She would watch his handsome face, wisps of his dark hair playing about his face as they escaped from the binding that held it back in the breeze. She could conjure his face so easily now, strong features with a squared jaw, and those silvery grey eyes beneath his dark brows.

Sharing his dreams with her had made her feel a part of them, as though he had every intention of being with her always. She had been certain of it, yet he had turned her away. Called her a child, going off to pay court to that blonde chit, Angelica.

Drying her tears on her sleeve, she rose to wash and change before supper. She braided her sweat damp chestnut hair and dressed in a simple blue gown. Looking down at her feet, not a hint of a bosom to obscure her view, she sighed. The tightest corset would have no hope of giving her the illusion of a figure. Of course, he saw her as a child. He likely thought of her as a boy as well. Her face was still round and her cheeks and nose covered in freckles. There was no hope of turning his head and tomorrow he would leave her. She would likely never see him again.

Tears threatened again, but she fought them, knowing she could not appear at the table with red-rimmed eyes. Her mother sat at the foot of the table, though her father had yet to arrive. She gave Lillian a concerned look. "Are you unwell, dear?"

"Only tired, Mama. I was riding with Noah today." Leticia Martin knew her daughter cared deeply for the young man and was likely upset about his leaving.

"Do not worry so for him, he will do well in the army and I am certain he will come to visit as soon as he can." Lillian simply nodded, keeping her eyes down, as her father came into the room like a storm cloud. Her mother dropped her gaze as well when Edmund Martin took his seat, bellowing at the cook to serve.

Her father held up his glass, waiting for Rose to fill it, then went back to eating. Meals were a tense, quiet affair in the Martin household as family and staff alike tiptoed around the earl. There was a clatter of silverware when he startled the ladies by speaking. "Saw the Reeves boy as I returned; off to London tomorrow to report for duty. Fine choice for him, the army will make a man of him."

"He should stay here and work with his father, not get himself killed. Why can you not offer him a position?" Lillian had felt bold when the words came into her throat, but her resolve quickly vanished under her father's withering gaze. "Best he leaves now. Mayhap you will stop running about the fields with him and learn to be a lady. Before long I will expect you to marry and take your place in society."

"I will wait for Noah or not marry at all." Lillian was unsure where the words of defiance had come from, but they were out now and there was no coming back from them. For a moment she thought her father was having an apoplexy, his face nearly purple as he glared. His chair fell back with a crash on the oak floorboards as he lunged forward and grabbed his daughter by the arm. "Have you been making a spectacle of yourself with that boy?" Drops of spittle showered her as her father raged. "How dare you throw yourself at the likes of him, son of a stable hand. I should allow it, it would serve you right, you ungrateful chit." He yanked her from her chair, stumbling as she begged for her release. "Out of my sight," he thundered as he shoved her out into the foyer. She sprawled on the polished marble, striking her cheek on the cold, hard surface.

Her mother was on her knees beside her, shielding her from the earl's rage. "This is your fault Leticia for indulging her; letting her run wild with that boy." He leaned down over Lillian as her mother cradled her. "You will learn your place and you will marry who I say when I say, do you understand me?" He spoke in a low, menacing tone that had her cowering against her mother's skirts. The Earl of Banbury returned to his meal as though nothing had occurred, his chair back in place when he entered the dining room again while his wife and daughter huddled on the floor in the foyer.

Leticia smoothed a hand over her daughter's tear-stained face, pausing at the curve of her cheek where a bruise was already appearing. "It will be alright my darling girl, you'll see. You are my lovely smart girl and you bring me so much joy."

"Yet Papa hates me." She felt heat rising within her as she recalled the way Noah had dismissed her feelings and now her father. Men had all the power in her life, and they all found her lacking. Envisioning her future, she could only see the loveless, shallow existence of her mother.

Chapter two

Smoke billowed around him, obscuring his regiment from sight as he pulled himself from the ground. The cannon volley was deafening, but the tide seemed to turn in their favor. "Sergeant, gather your men and fall in with Garrett's line," Noah called out, summoning them into formation as they moved to the left. He wiped the sweat and soot from his brow with a sleeve as he quickly stepped into position. His Captain had fallen early in the battle. A cannon ball rolling across the field had taken his leg and someone had pulled him to the rear. Noah wasn't certain he still lived, but now was not the time to consider such things. The general had tasked him with leading the regiment and he would see his men through.

"Fix bayonets," came the order from Major Clark. Noah's heart raced as the time to charge arrived. Both men looked at the general and hollered, "Forward," as his arm dropped. He was rushing into the fray, slashing as the French came at them. He took down three men before he felt a saber catch his left arm above the elbow. There was a sting, then he no longer felt it, caught up in the heat of battle. Cannons fired, cloaking the field in another cloud of smoke as men hacked and pushed their way through the line.

The heat was stifling, sweat pouring over Noah's face, obscuring his vision. This may have explained how he missed the man charging from his left. There was a cry from Corporal Reynolds to his right as the bayonet flashed and Noah turned, avoiding the full thrust, taking a slash across his ribs. He brought his sword hilt down on his attacker's head, then thrust the blade through his gut.

Pulling his sword free, Noah continued forward, though his side was on fire from the gash that bled freely. He stumbled and Corporal

Reynolds grabbed him under the shoulder, "Ye need to head back sir, you'll do us no good dead." Noah was struggling to regain his feet, but he was done in. He leaned forward, retching as the edges of his vision blurred. He was being dragged, his legs bumping over the rough ground as the fighting went on around him, though it seemed to be nearly over. They had pushed back the French and Dutch forces, leaving only a few small skirmishes toward the front of the line.

The stretcher bearers hoisted Noah up and carried him rest of the way to the surgeon's tent. A young man with streaked spectacles and loose strands of damp hair falling wildly from his cue forced Noah to move his hand from the gash. The surgeon dropped a wad of filthy looking cloth over the gash and placed Noah's hand back over it. "Press down, it will slow the bleeding, I will come back when I can to stitch it up." The young man left him, running off to deal with the man beside him that was missing an arm. Noah leaned over the edge of the cot and vomited again before blacking out.

When he came around, pain seared down his left side. He nearly sat upright, but a hand shoved him back down. "Easy lad," a gruff voice said. "Have to clean this out before we stitch you up." The stocky man shoved a piece of leather between his teeth and poured what smelled to be whisky over the gash again and he gritted his teeth, certain he would bite through the leather. Once that finished, the man poured some of the liquid in his mouth; definitely whisky, very raw whisky. He coughed as the burning liquid hit his throat. "I prefer a good scotch if you have it," he joked as the surgeon threaded the needle. The man's pock-marked face lit with a smile. "Perhaps when this madness is over, we'll lift a glass. Bite down now, son," he said as the smile morphed into a look of concentration. Noah felt the needle pierce his flesh, grunting as he bit down before blissfully passing out.

He spent a week in the infirmary or what passed for one in this place. His regiment shipped out to assist in the offensive against French and Dutch interference with the East India Company. Far from a glorious path. But there had been much he did not understand when he joined the Army. At least here they were winning; General Cornwallis' defeat at Yorktown, in the colonies, sent the British troops packing.

Corporal Reynolds found him sitting up on his bed swatting away the incessant flies and stood before him saluting, "As you were corporal." He motioned to the rickety wooden chair beside him. "What news today?"

"Things are going swimmingly sir, there's even talk of a promotion for you after the fine job ye did when the captain fell." Noah shook his head at the idea. He had only done as ordered. He couldn't very well leave the men to fend for themselves. "Oh, nearly forgot, sir. There are some letters that found their way to us." Reynolds pulled a small pile of envelopes from his coat and dropped them on the bed. "Is there anything else I can get you, sir?"

"No, that will be all, thank you." He gave the young man a salute and anxiously turned to the stack of letters. They were all from his parents, he noted with a slight pang, though he had given up on hearing from Angelica after his first year away from home. He read the usual news of home and his mother's prayers for his safe return. Opening the third letter, he found a folded piece of fine paper and quickly opened it. Smiling, he took in Lily's curling script. Her father likely would not allow her to write to him and so she would occasionally tuck a note in with one of her parent's missives. It had been three years since he left for the army, though it seemed like a lifetime now. Her sweet tales of life in the country still charmed him; how the horses were faring, the people that came to visit. He chuckled softly as she spoke of how she loathed her etiquette tutor. "No one strolls about with a book on their head," she had written and he could imagine the furrow of her brow as she groused. She no longer professed her love for him, though he could almost read it in between the lines as she begged him to return home safely. He folded the page and placed it back in the envelope with the others, his mind conjuring the image of the spirited freckle-faced girl that had proposed to him with tears in her eyes before he left.

He hoped the earl at least attempted to find her a caring man. She deserved that much, though Noah had his doubts. The brutal man would be certain to angle for the best advantage for himself rather than care how any man would treat his only child. It made his blood boil, the way Martin treated Lily and her mother. Never a kind word, spending all his money on the mistress he kept at his other estate.

Noah had seen it once, traveling with his father to deliver two mares to the grand stables at Banbury Hall. The estate was still lacking compared to other peers, though it was obvious where the man spent his money. His mistress was a rather spoiled vapid blonde, barely three and twenty, who lorded over the staff as lady of the manor despite not being the current Countess of Banbury. She had flirted with Noah unabashedly, flaunting her ample bosom and batting her lashes while the earl met with his father in the stable.

Infuriated on behalf of the Martin ladies, he pushed past the harlot without so much as a "by your leave."

Noah shook away the memories of his time at Martin's Nest, not wishing to drop further into a foul mood. He pushed down the burning in his gut at the thought of Lily being married off to some man that could never care for her as he would. The thought caught him off guard; it was not as if he wished to marry her and yet the idea of some selfish arse that behaved like her father marrying her, left him uneasy.

"What has you looking so glum, having more pain?" The surgeon who had tended him in the field hospital stood over him, inspecting his handiwork beneath the linen bandage. "Good day Dr. Dresher. I am fine, only tired of lying about." He glanced over at the stack of letters. "Good word from home, I hope." Noah nodded, placing a hand over the letters. "You should be heading back to England before long. Any chance you will have time to visit? Perhaps see your sweetheart?"

"One can only hope, but there is no sweetheart." Noah said, that ache in his chest returning unbidden. Dr. Dresher's bushy brow lifted, "Fine-looking lad as yourself with no lady waiting for him, I can scarcely believe that." Noah chuckled at the man's mischievous look. "Only a dear mother and father and, of course, the young girl of the manor that proposed to me before I left," he huffed out a laugh as Dresher replaced his bandage. "Be careful, little girls grow up and steal your heart sometimes."

"Consider me warned, sir," he said, laughing as heartily as his stitches would allow. As the older man departed, Noah thought of Lily. The way she laughed as he splashed her with cold water from the lake, the sight of her hair streaming behind her as she rode ahead of him. If he was being honest with himself, he missed her and was looking forward to seeing her upon his return.

Chapter three

Tears spilled over Lillian's cheeks as she held her mother's frail hand. The fever had come upon her suddenly and they had summoned the physician to no avail. It was only a matter of time now. Leticia's unfocused gaze settled on her only child. "You must be strong, my darling girl," she whispered. "I will be with you always."

"I love you, Mama," Lillian sniffled, gently blotting her mother's damp brow. The fever continued to rage, and she wished the heat coming from her mother's skin would burn away the pain in her own heart. Guilt swamped her as she wished it was her father being taken rather than her dear momma.

The Reeves had come early the day after Leticia died to pay their respects, Noah's mother embracing Lillian tightly then wiping the tears from her cheeks.

"You come to me for anything you need, dear girl," the woman soothed. Lillian wished Noah was here, but he likely had not even received the news of her mother's illness as yet. She knew he would have wanted to be here in the end, but there was no help for it. When Leticia Martin drew her final breath, Lillian was alone with her, holding her hand and whispering softly the simple childhood prayer her mother had taught her. For the next several days, people she barely knew came to pay their respects to her father, their eyes filled with pity as they looked at Lillian in her simple black gown as her father held court in his study. Her jaw tightened when she heard him laugh as he shared a bottle of whiskey with two other gentlemen. *At the least, he could act as though he cared she* died.

One face bled into the next as the hours slowly ticked by and Lillian had no desire to speak to anyone as she sat beside her mother's casket. Feeling empty and alone in the world, she knew her father planned to send her away at the end of the week. She would not even have the Reeves to visit for company and with Noah so far away she would likely never see him again. She was to live with her Aunt Rowena, her father's sister, with instructions to learn what it is to be a lady.

"You are of no use to me if you can not make a good match and lord knows who would take you as you are." Her father's bitter words rang in her words as tears threatened to flow once more. A handkerchief appeared before her and she looked up into the kind face of Mrs. Reeves. She handed Lillian the handkerchief, then sat beside her, a plate of food in her hand.

"You must eat something, dearie. Your mother would not wish to see you making yourself ill over her loss. She wanted only the best for you." The older woman's hand made soothing circles over her back as she took the plate, attempting to take a few bites, though she tasted nothing. Would the pain ever end she wondered?

"I do not wish to leave my home. Why must father be so awful," she sniffled, setting the barely touched plate aside.

"Oh, he likely feels he cannot provide the care a girl needs. Men are helpless in such things." Mrs. Reeves shook her head as she said this. They both knew it was not the truth, but Mrs Reeves was not one to disparage anyone, especially in sad times such as these. "You'll see. Your Auntie will be pleased to have you with her now that her own daughter married two years ago. Ladies are always wanting someone to care for. You will settle in just fine before you know it, and after a bit, you can come for a visit. Mayhap Noah will return and you can come for a visit then."

The thought of seeing Noah was bittersweet. She still cared deeply for him, but she knew he could never be hers. She would ma someone that could pay her father's debts and that someone likely could not compare to Noah.

Unshed tears stung Noah's eyes as he set aside the letter from his mother. By the time news of Lady Martin's death had reached him, it had been nearly two months. Lillian likely left for her aunt's some time ago. He wondered if she would still write to him, feeling a strange pang at thought of not hearing from her again. Of course, she was young, but he looked forward to her stories simply to know how she was. He told himself this often, though he longed to sit beside her by the pond, talking about trivialities. He had always felt happy and at peace with her, but of course, she was a child. Her mother had shielded her from her father's wrath as best as she could. Without the woman's love and concern, he worried the girl would founder in the harsh world of London society, with her father deciding. He could only hope that Lillian's aunt, Baroness Northrup, was a kind woman.

"Beggin' yer pardon Captain."

"Yes, what is it, Reynolds?" Noah tucked the letter away and looked up at the young corporal.

"I mustered the men as ordered, sir," he said, giving a crisp salute. Noah returned the salute and stood, fastening the top button of his coat.

"Lead on corporal." Placing his tricorn hat on his head, he hastened to the parade ground. They had arrived in Scotland over a month ago, but he remained unaccustomed to the icy rain that fell so often here. He swore his clothes were never dry, even when he first dressed in the morning, and he marveled at the fortitude of the Scots who seemed unaffected by the chill. He thought of his mother and father, nights seated before a fire with a mug of tea as they laughed and spoke of the day's events.

He hoped he might take leave and return to England at Christmas, though that was still six months off. He turned his thoughts back to his men as he moved along the lines, nodding or pointing out deficiencies. The general was to arrive this afternoon, and he wanted everything in order by them. He gave instructions to Corporal Reynolds and turned in search of Major Colson for his orders.

*** Lillian dropped her embroidery in the basket with a frustrated expulsion of breath. She longed to take her mare out for a run in the fields; the day being sunny and mild. Instead, her lessons trapped her inside. Her embroidery skills had not improved, as she was far too easily distracted from the tedious work. At least her music tutor would arrive shortly. She enjoyed playing the pianoforte in the conservatory. The instrument belonging to her aunt was a much finer instrument than she had grown up with.

Everything at the manor was grander than she was accustomed to. She had a personal lady's maid and new gowns, as they expected her to change her clothes several times a day for various activities. She was fluent in French and had been receiving instruction in Italian and German as well, though she was not yet proficient in the speaking of them, she could read and comprehend much of it.

"Lillian, will you join me in the parlor for a moment?" her aunt asked, appearing in the doorway. The older woman wore a simple yet elegant grey gown, her hair styled high atop her head. Lillian glanced down at her own burgundy silk gown that flared wide at the hips, making her corseted waist appear smaller than she had ever imagined. She met her aunt on the veranda and took her arm as the two ladies began a leisurely stroll along the fragrant path, taking in the roses and lilies so carefully tended by the gardeners.

She was so pleased to be outdoors that she became lost in her own thoughts until her aunt spoke. "The Baron and I will attend a dinner party in town tomorrow evening and we would like for you to accompany us. We will remain in town for the week so that you might become better acquainted with some people in our circle." Lillian was a bit startled by this news and felt a fluttering in her belly at the thought of spending time in London. It was a sense of excitement and dread rolled into one. She did not know how she would be received by the members of the *ton* having spent her entire life in the country.

Aunt Rowena noted her silence and stopped, taking in her tentative expression. "I thought you would be excited to go to London. I always told your mother it was not good to keep you cloistered in the country. You're young. It is time you enjoyed all the delights that London has to offer." She cupped Lillian's cheek, giving her a motherly smile. "All will be well, my dear girl, you'll see." Lillian returned her smile, though it did not reach her eyes.

"I am certain it will be wonderful, thank you Auntie."

The next evening, Lillian gazed up at the imposing stone edifice of the London home of the Duke of Hawthorne. The dinner party was being thrown by his mother in honor of his birthday and there appeared to be an extensive guest list. Baron and Baroness of Northrup flanked her as they ascended the steps to the door, held open by a footman in burgundy and gold livery. The large windows glowed and as they entered, she was in awe of the large chandeliers filled with candles, their light reflecting off of gilt mirrors and marble floors. She had seen nothing so grand in life. Even her aunt and uncle's lavish home paled in comparison.

The Dowager Duchess of Hawthorne received them as they entered and Lillian curtsied slowly, praying she would not lose her balance and make a fool of herself. She had been practicing, but still lacked the grace that seemed to embody the woman before her. "Baroness, I am so pleased you could attend," she crooned. "Is this your niece? She is lovely." Lillian bowed her head slightly as her aunt nudged her forward.

"Thank you, Your Grace," she said, overwhelmed by the woman's mere presence. "Thank you for your invitation." She blushed furiously as the dowager duchess reached out, lightly touching her face to take in her features.

"Yes, a beauty indeed." She turned to the man on her right, beckoning, "Hawthorne, you must meet our lovely guest." The Duke turned and Lillian lost her breath. His was a most handsome face, piercing blue eyes with dark brown hair that waved back from his forehead. She wanted to reach out and touch him, certain he could not be real. He beamed, a dimple playing at the corner of his mouth.

She felt heat creeping up her neck and over her cheeks as he fixed his gaze on her.

"Lady Martin, a pleasure to meet you." He held her hand, bowing elegantly. "The baroness has told us of your time with them and your impending season. I have no doubt you will be well received."

"Th-thank you, Your Grace," she finally stammered. He held her hand a moment longer, his thumb brushing over her knuckles lightly before he finally released her. The butler ushered them with the other guests into the salon for refreshments. She moved about the room with her aunt as her uncle moved off to speak to another gentleman across the room. Fine paintings adorned the walls, still life works mostly. Heavy silk draperies hung over the tall windows that overlooked the garden, which was lit with lanterns for those that might wish to take the air.

After a bit of mingling, the butler ushered the guests toward the dining room. Lillian found herself seated to the duke's left. A fact she found surprising given they were strangers, and her stomach fluttered as he looked upon her again. She was in doubt that she could eat a bite, being in such proximity to the dashing man. After several minutes, it pleased her to discover he was a charming conversationalist, quickly putting her at ease as he asked about her plans while in town and about her home.

"It saddened me to hear of your mother's passing, as I recall, she was a lovely woman."

"You are very kind, I miss her terribly." She dropped her eyes to her plate, where she continued to move her food around rather than eating. Lillian appreciated the duke's kind words. However, it brought the oppressive sadness back into her heart. She felt a large, warm hand take hold of hers beneath the table as he leaned closer.

"I apologize if I have said something to upset you," Hawthorne whispered.

"No, you have done nothing wrong, I…" Lillian fought for control as tears threatened. "Please excuse me," she said as she leapt from the table and made her way out to the garden, hoping the night air would bring her emotions to heal.

"Lady Martin." The deep voice sent a shiver down her spine before he touched her. Hawthorne took her arm gently, turning her toward him. Handing her his handkerchief, their fingers touched briefly. She felt dizzy in his presence, unsure of these sensations she had not experienced with anyone other than Noah. She knew she could only dream of having the affection of a man such as him, handsome and charming, with an estate worth a fortune that would appease even her father's expectations. What could she offer a man such as him? Giving him a weak smile, she handed him his handkerchief with a whispered thank you, then followed him back inside.

On the carriage ride home, she found her aunt staring at her, her expression unreadable as a smile played in the corner of her mouth. "The duke seemed to enjoy your company this evening."

Lillian gave a small shrug of her shoulders, "He has a lovely home and was a genial dinner companion." Aunt Rowena nearly burst with laughter as Lillian looked on in question.

"My dear girl, the man is the most eligible bachelor of the *ton*. There were several young ladies that were quite envious of the attention he paid you this evening," she remarked, laughter still in her voice.

Lillian did not believe her mood could get any lower, but she was wrong. "Then no one will wish to be in my company? My season shall be a disaster!" She covered her face with her hands, devastated at the thought of being cut outright by the members of London society. The seat beside her dipped as Rowena moved to her.

"On the contrary, you will be the envy of all if they see you as the next Duchess of Hawthorne. You would not need to worry over anything again." Lillian blinked up at her aunt in disbelief.

"You cannot possibly believe that the Duke of Hawthorne would have any interest in me as a wife?"

"And why would he not? You are lovely and accomplished, and he is an acquaintance of your father. The two have had many business dealings. It seems to me there is much to be desired in a match between the two of you." Rowena patted her hand with a kind smile. Lillian did not feel her aunt's certainty in the matter, especially given the remark that Hawthorne had dealings with her father. She thought a tie to the Earl of Banbury was nothing to brag about.

Chapter four
1817

Lillian arrived at Merveille, her son's estate after a two-day journey over difficult roads. There had been a day of rain that turned the packed dirt to mud, causing several delays, and it was a relief to exit the carriage. She was certain the smell of mud would not leave her nose for a sennight at least. Weariness quickly fled when her granddaughters rushed toward her, all smiles and curls. She fought the urge to scold them for their unladylike behavior, though she still found it difficult.

Charlotte and Rachel were lovely girls, but their father was fond of chasing about with them acting like a growling beast and they had taken to growling along with him. Charlotte was out growing some of this behavior, though her younger sister continued to embrace it. Looking down at the girls, she asked, "Have I missed it?"

"No Grandmama, the baby is being stubborn," Rachel pouted. Laura, her very pregnant daughter-in-law, waddled down the steps toward them, a hand over her round belly as Andrew kept a protective arm about her waist.

"Laura, there was no need for you to exert yourself so, I would come to you in your room," she scolded as she approached. "You should be resting." Waving the comment away, Laura took Lillian's hand.

"Nonsense, I rest far too much. Besides, I'm hoping I can walk the baby out of me. I am quite ready for him or her to make an appearance." Andrew placed a hand on her stomach lovingly as he smiled at his wife. Lillian found herself unsure where to look, being uncomfortable with such displays of affection. She directed her attention to the girls and followed them toward the house as the footman gathered her bags.

She had made the journey so that she would be present to welcome the next Duke of Hawthorne. At least she quietly hoped for a boy. It was high time Andrew had an heir, and he wasn't getting any younger. Once settled, she joined the family in the parlor for tea.

The room was not grand as her own parlor was. She preferred to display her collection of art and fine furnishings to her guests, whereas her son rarely entertained here. Still, the room was pleasant, filled with larger furniture that fit his tall frame and there were toys and such entertainments as the small family enjoyed together. She knew this house was for his family, not for show as Hawthorne Manor was.

A tea cart arrived as Lillian moved about the room, looking at the various items that Laura had added. Her father had built a successful shipping company that was now run by her brother Robert, now partnered with Andrew, who had taken an interest in the business' expansion. They had lived a far simpler life. Though her mother had been born to nobility, she had turned away from it to marry Robert Parsons.

Lillian felt a slight ache at the thought of Mary Bingham, or Parsons, she supposed. The woman had died in childbirth some time back, but she recalled the lively young lady she had been. Laura favored her mother in face and stature, though she had her father's auburn hair and green eyes. There was a small portrait of the Parsons on the fireplace mantle and Lillian stared at it for a moment. Her memories remained bittersweet when she thought of Mary, the end of their friendship so abrupt and painful. Looking back, she knew the woman had not been responsible, yet the fact that she had hidden things from her had been unforgivable in Lillian's eyes and she had never seen her again or answered any of the correspondence she had sent. She had tossed each letter in the fire without being opened. She would admit that she now harbored some regret at her actions.

"Are you certain you do not mind having visitors tomorrow, darling?" she heard Andrew ask his wife. "I know you are happy to have Minerva. I just did not feel I should invite her without her guest."

"You know I don't mind in the slightest. I am happy for the distraction. Minerva has been like a mother to me and I am looking forward to meeting her nephew. It was good of him to visit. She is always speaking of how much he travels with his business ventures. It will be wonderful to hear about the places he has been. When will they arrive?"

Lillian turned her attention from the conversation to sit near Charlotte, who was busy drawing in a large brocade chair in the corner. When she looked over, she could see the form of Laura coming to life. "My, your talents have blossomed, Charlotte," she said with admiration. "Do you have others?" The girl opened her book and removed an excellent likeness of her father and her sister. "Once the baby is born, I can draw him as well. I will have the whole family. I did one of Auntie Julia as well, but that is upstairs."

"I would like to see that." She looked over at her other granddaughter as she pretended to pour tea for her doll. The green ribbon was limp and partially askew in her blonde curls, as often occurred with Rachel. Somehow her dress always became wrinkled and a smudge of dirt would be on her cheek. Lillian shook her head as she took in her mussed appearance, but she chuckled to herself, recalling she was often in the same state as a child.

She retired shortly after dinner that evening, still weary from her journey. It was odd, but she often found that she slept well in this house. It could be the presence of others besides staff, but she often felt that she had escaped the ghosts of her past when she was here. The rooms of the manor so often spoke of sadness, the harsh words spoken between Hawthorne and herself, the room that had been Jonathan's, her eldest son, long vacant with his loss at such a young age.

She had placed all of her hopes and dreams on his shoulders knowing he would inherit his father's title and estates. She had groomed him to be a gentleman, worthy of all that lay in his future. Yet here was her second son, the one she had set carelessly aside that now held the title. She had underestimated him as much as she had overestimated Jonathan. His death in a duel over a married woman had destroyed all she had worked for in an instant and she had lashed out at Andrew for not stopping it. She knew in her heart that no one could have saved Jonathon from his own foolish actions and prideful ways. He had looked much like her, but his father seemed to have had the making of him.

Chapter five
1786

Over the following fortnight, Lillian and her aunt remained in London while the baron attended to business at his two estates. The ladies attended teas, where Lillian became acquainted with many other young ladies that would come out during the season. At the musicale the previous evening, it surprised Lillian when, once again, the Duke of Hawthorne approached her. Her memory had not deceived her. He was just as handsome as she recalled. She felt the same thrill down her spine when he smiled at her before placing a kiss on the back of her hand.

He remained close by, even sitting beside her during the various performances. She remained unsure what to make of his attentions, certain that there were other ladies with substantial dowries and more impressive pedigrees than herself. He was witty and charming, making her feel at ease as they became better acquainted. Lillian was feeling comfortable in her position as a young lady of the *ton* under the sponsorship of her aunt and uncle. She was thriving.

With the season to begin in two months, she established herself in the finer salons of London. Her wardrobe was fashionable, and she was familiar with the lineage of most of the marriageable gentlemen and her competition. She had one dear friend she felt she could speak with freely, and the two of them would sit together at the various functions, heads together as they sized up the other ladies and gentlemen in attendance.

Mary Bingham was a spirited girl, petite in stature, with dark silky curls and luminous hazel eyes that were often with mirth. She often had Lillian in stitches with her observations of the other girls that

31

were quick to pass judgment on others if they did not meet some unattainable measure. She was the daughter of the Earl of Devon, and her brother Anthony was among the young men looking for a wife during his sister's first season.

Anthony was currently leaning into Lillian's side as she finished her dessert at the intimate dinner the Baron and Baroness of Northrup were hosting before she returned home for a brief visit with her father. Edmund Martin was returning to his small country estate and wished for her to be present, as he would have several guests for a week of hunting before the season began.

Lillian realized this may be an attempt on his part to steer her toward whoever his choice of husband was for her and attempted to prepare herself. She had not seen him since he sent her away after the death of her mother, and she was not looking forward to this reunion.

Though it upset her at first, she now saw the benefit of being sent away. She felt confident and attractive under her aunt's care and the attention of a few gentlemen, including the dashing Duke of Hawthorne. Her father had made her feel insignificant all of her life, the treatment worsening after the death of her younger brother, Andrew, at ten.

One would think she had been responsible for the morbid fever that took him, leaving her father without an heir and only a worthless daughter he must support. The brush of Anthony Bingham's shoulder brought her attention back to the dining room. "You look especially lovely this evening, Lady Martin; your gown is exquisite," he remarked as his gaze slid down to her decolletage. She straightened in her chair, hoping to gain some distance from his intrusive gaze.

Being highly sought after for his future title and fortune, she could not bring herself to encourage his suit. It was not only his thinning hair or soft middle. She knew too much about his proclivities from his sister. He was a wastrel with his funds much like her father, and she had no intention of living in fear of poverty again. She would see herself well set up like her Aunt Rowena, doted on and provided for by a man like her uncle. Affection was fine, but she would not allow herself to live as her mother did; cast aside in a dilapidated estate, afraid of her husband.

Noah drew in a deep breath as his horse trotted along the narrow road that wound through the fields, green with spring growth. He was on his way home, not for Christmas as he had planned, but spring, which was just as well being a far more pleasant time to be in the country. There had been many small skirmishes with disgruntled highland Scots through the winter as food and shelter became scarce, making for a difficult few months.

Since the failed Jacobite rising in 1745, the clans had been broken and the lairds were forcing tenants from their lands to make way for cattle and other livestock that could bring in funds. Without land to farm and lacking shelter, there had been violence and Noah had been loath to battle these poor souls that only wished to feed their children. These sentiments had made his job far more difficult, and he was thankful to have leave at last to escape the sadness that had settled over him. He entered the town of Shere, where his mother grew up. It was only a brief ride from here to Martin's Nest, and he planned to spend the night in his aunt's home before completing his journey tomorrow.

It had been some time since he had visited his mother's sister and her husband. Uncle Thomas was a good man, generous and kind to his neighbors, especially the children. He and Aunt Minerva never had children of their own, but they often filled their home with the laughter of children that needed a meal or a place to play.

The sun was low in the sky when he arrived at the old stone house and he noted the new fence that held several goats that bleated loudly as he approached the door. The door opened at his knock and Ginny, his aunt's maid, immediately embraced him. "Aren't you a sight for these eyes? Come in dear. You are just in time for supper." He could hear chatter from the back of the house and found several children seated at the table. Minerva, dressed in deep blue, rose from her chair to embrace him.

"It is good to see you Auntie, I am sorry I could not return sooner." He could see the gleam in her blue eyes as she looked up at him with a small smile.

"You are here now. That is what matters. I know my sister is beside herself with joy to have you home for a time. It was kind of you to break your journey here." He took her hand, giving it a firm squeeze. She was thinner than last he saw her with a touch of grey in the light brown curls that escaped her cap. "Come meet Prudence and Ezra." She gestured toward the boy and girl seated at the table. They could not be more than eight years old, but they each jumped up and greeted him politely. "Poor dears lost their mother two months ago and their father is often late in the field so they come to share dinner with me." Noah was pleased to see that nothing had changed here. Once his uncle returned an hour later, they all sat down to dinner.

The meal was simple but hearty, and he noted they set a plate to the side to be kept warm for the children's father when he came to fetch them. Prudence was six and her brother eight. They spoke of their day assisting with the goats, which they had learned to milk, as they scraped plates and assisted Ginny as she cleaned up. Aunt Minerva and Uncle Thomas led him to the parlor for a glass of port, wishing to hear of his time in France and Scotland.

The place was not grand, but it was warm and inviting as they sat by the fire sipping the sweet wine. "You look tired, my dear boy. Was it an arduous journey?" Minerva asked as she set her glass aside.

"Not as such. This posting has been difficult, despite not being outright war, there is much unrest. Circumstances have displaced too many and those unable to take ship elsewhere are having a rough go." He glanced over his shoulder toward the kitchen, where the sound of laughter rang out. "Too many children are starving and there is very little I can do for them."

"That is the true cost of war, and it is always the innocent that seem to pay it," his uncle stated thoughtfully as he drew on his pipe. The scent of his tobacco was soothing as it brought forth memories of other times seated by a fire with the pair.

His aunt reached out, taking hold of his hand. "You have always had a good heart. I know it can be difficult. We do what we can, but it is not always enough."

"You have done a great deal for the children of this town. It is a credit to you both. Has business been good for you, Uncle?"

"Yes, all is well. I am representing several of the larger estates at present, and they are all turning a hefty profit. It is a pleasure to have a bit to pass on to others who require our assistance."

"Thomas works so very hard. Many of the farmers have him to thank for the price they garner for their goods." Uncle Thomas gave her hand a pat as he smiled at her.

"Always singing my praises, this one." The two shared a look of such devotion that Noah marveled at them. He could only hope to find someone to love, as his parents and his aunt and uncle had. It was a thing to be treasured.

Minerva offered him a plate of almond cookies, and he happily took one. Brushing crumbs from his coat, he asked if there were any tasks he could see to before his departure. "All is well. Mr. Cooper, the children's father, built us that fine fence for the goats last month and made repairs to the front steps. Such a good man."

"I am certain he appreciates you caring for Prudence and Ezra in his absence."

"It is always a pleasure to have children in the house." Her eyes turned wistful, and he found his heart aching for his aunt. She should have had a house full of little ones, though he knew the lord worked in mysterious ways. Had they had children of their own, mayhap these children would not have had a place to go for a meal... who was to say? The children's father came in through the kitchen and they could hear Ginny fussing over him, insisting he sit and eat the dinner she saved for him. It made him smile, listening to his aunt's little maid. He had always wondered that she had not married

36

herself, having been with Minerva since she was a young lady herself. Ginny was loyal and often said she had no need of a husband when she had such joy as she gained in this household.

Noah bid his aunt and uncle good night shortly after the Coopers left. He would leave after an early breakfast, eager to see his parents, but promised to visit again on his return trip. Lying back on the small bed, he listened to the sounds of the night with the window as he often did when one was available. After many nights sleeping in a crowded barracks or on the ground surrounded by his regiment, the luxury of a solitary room was welcome. As his eyes grew heavy, he found his thoughts drifting to his little Lily, and he wondered if the girl still lived with her aunt. It would be strange to be at the estate without her.

He had not received a letter from her in several months and reminded himself that it was for the best. She needed to become like the other ladies of London society if she was to survive the life her father expected of her. His mother had mentioned that Martin's Nest had been quiet, the earl remaining absent since sending Lillian away. It would be strange indeed, but it pleased him to be returning home.

After breakfast, he said his farewells and turned his mount for home. He gave Baylor, his chestnut stallion, his head and enjoyed the wind rushing over his face. He made the town market at Benson before noon and slowed to look about the small hamlet that sat a mile from the estate. People rushed about, seeing to their errands, and he noted several young ladies giving him appraising looks in his uniform. He had received no correspondence from Angelica in the years he had served in India. She was likely married by now. The thought did not trouble him as he had once thought it would, and he realized she had been a diversion in his youth, nothing more.

Seeing a cart filled with many varieties of flowers, colors bright as the day itself, he thought to stop and purchase a posy for his mother. Once he dismounted, another horse passed by the cart. Looking up as the lady rode by, he could not take his eyes from her, seated tall in her saddle. Chestnut curls tumbled from beneath her bonnet with ribbons of honey where the sun touched it. She was beautiful, and he felt a stirring at the sight of her curves, hugged gently by her tailored forest green riding habit. His eyes followed her as she passed, her chin lifted regally. He thought to follow her, learn who she was, but she had disappeared from view before he could mount his horse. He knew at that moment he would make another trip to town to find the young lady again.

An hour later he was in the stable with his father, seeing Baylor rubbed down and fed as his mother prepared lunch. She had nearly crushed him in her arms when he arrived, and he lifted her off her feet with his own embrace. His father could not seem to stop smiling at him as he moved his hands over the soft chestnut coat of his horse. The image of the woman in town came to him, her hair nearly the same color. He would see if his parents needed anything from the village tomorrow and hope that he saw her again.

When the men approached the house, the sound of women's laughter came through the partially open door. "Ah, Lillian must have arrived," his father said as his already present smile grew wider. "Your mother will be in heaven now that both of you are home."

"I had not realized she was to return," he remarked as he picked up his pace. He would be glad to see the girl again.

"Suppose the earl wanted her here to play hostess for the hunting party that is to arrive in two days. Man has been keeping us busy making the manor presentable for his fancy London friends." Noah raised a brow at this.

"I wonder if our little Lily is up to such a task."

"Not so little anymore, our girl. Come along, let's say hello." They entered through the kitchen door, taking in the scent of baking apples, sweet in the air. His mother sat across from someone whose back was to them. She was too tall to be Lily and his heart pounded again as he recognized the spill of curls, now fully visible without the bonnet the woman had been wearing when in town. He stepped closer, excitement building as his mother rose to make an introduction.

"There they are. Come see, our Lily girl has returned as well." The woman turned and Noah took in her lovely face, shocked when he saw her blue eyes flash. It was Lily and not little anymore. His powers of speech seemed to leave him as she smiled.

"It is good to see you again, Noah. I had heard you were returning. What good fortune that Father summoned me home." His eyes continued to take in her womanly curves, her ivory complexion with no hint of the freckles she once had.

"Y-yes, it is good to see you looking so well." He did not recognize his own voice as he croaked out the words and her eyes danced as she giggled.

"Are you alright Noah?" she asked sweetly. "Sounds as though you are parched." She turned back to the table and poured a glass of the lemonade his mother had made, passing it to him. He drank the whole thing down as he attempted to collect himself. They all sat as his mother bustled about collecting plates and a knife for the cinnamon cake she had made that morning.

His father finally broke the silence, "Since your father is not to arrive until tomorrow, join us for dinner." Lillian smiled graciously.

"Why do you not all come to the manor for dinner? Sally is preparing a feast for my return and by the look of it, there will be far more than I could eat on my own. I should like to have the company of all of you this evening."

"A lovely idea, that. I know we are all so happy to have you home, dear," his mother said, the gleam of unshed tears in her eyes. "I could not ask for better than to have my son and you sitting here at my table again."

"Keep the jam away from her, though. Now that she is such a fine lady, we can't have her smearing it over that lovely face." Lillian blushed at his words and he realized he had just said she was lovely. Now his face heated. He took another drink of lemonade as a thought came to him. Clearing his throat, he asked, "Lily, would you care to go riding tomorrow?"

She looked thoughtful for a moment. "It would need to be early. I have much to see to before my father arrives." Noah marveled at the way she held herself now. It seemed all traces of the lanky girl he had left behind vanished. "I should be going. I have a few matters to address today before our supper. Shall we say seven o'clock?" She rose elegantly from her chair as his parents agreed to the time. He quickly stood, offering to escort her back to the house.

When she took his arm, he felt a small shiver at the contact. What was happening to him? It was still just Lily, but he found himself tongue tied like a besotted fool in her presence. It had surprised him to find that he had missed her, their long talks by the lake. She had a sharp mind that rivaled most of the men of his acquaintance, and he had longed for the easy companionship they had shared. Seeing her after all of this time, it was difficult to reconcile the woman that she had grown to be with the girl he remembered, and he found himself drawn to her in a way beyond the friendship they had shared.

"It is so good to be back." Lillian's voice broke into his thoughts.

"Yes, quite. Much warmer here than in Scotland," he said lamely. She tugged at his arm, halting him just before they reached the door. She dropped her gaze to her feet as her cheeks colored before she spoke.

"I must apologize for my behavior when last we spoke. It was quite forward of me, I can only claim the ignorance of youth." She kept her eyes cast down, but he reached out and lifted her chin to meet his eyes.

"There is nothing to forgive, I assure you. I enjoyed your letters. I admit I was sad when I no longer heard from you." He nearly kicked himself for how petulant that sounded, but she only gave him a smile.

"Then I shall apologize for not writing. There were many distractions in London between dress fittings and teas. So many people, it was overwhelming for a country girl like myself."

"Did you enjoy your time at least?" he asked as he felt a now familiar pang of jealousy in his chest.

"Aunt Rowena has been kind, and the baron was most generous. They are sponsoring me for my first season and they are quite certain I will make a fine match, though I am not as optimistic."

The thought of another man courting her made his collar feel tight, but he pressed on. "Men will flock to you. You must not think poorly of yourself." She was quiet for a moment and he could not read her expression, though he had a feeling he knew what she was thinking.

"Your father never saw you for who you truly are." He reached up, stroking his finger down her soft cheek. "Mayhap I was blind as well." They stood there a moment longer, and he felt a pull toward her, the desire to hold her close. Those feelings that had blossomed at the memory of his time with her, the ones he pushed aside as he continued to think of her as a child, were resurfacing and merging with this grown woman that now stood before him. He touched her shoulder, allowing his hand to move down her arm, then taking her hand in his. She looked down at their linked fingers and he felt the pressure as she squeezed gently, keeping her gaze lowered. He tugged her closer until there was almost no space between them and began leaning down, the desire to taste her lips taking over.

Lillian pulled away suddenly, dropping his hand as though his touch had burned her.

"I should see to the arrangements for dinner." Then she disappeared, the door shutting loudly behind her. Noah took a deep breath, attempting to slow the beating of his heart. Turning back toward the stable, he thought to take comfort in the company of his horse. He stroked Baylor's silken nose slowly as his mind wandered to that day in the stables. The proposal made by his little Lily had shocked and flustered him back then, but now... Mayhap it had not been the right time then. She had seemed so young, but now... could she still want to be with him?

Lillian looked around the table at the people she saw as her family. The small house staff and the Reeves had cared for her just as her mother had and she felt herself relax in their company. Life was very different here now and, guiltily, she thought it was due in part to her father's absence. Everyone was at ease without his scowling countenance looming over them. Sally had outdone herself, creating a sumptuous meal, and it was wonderful to have everyone together before the earl returned tomorrow.

They hired two temporary maids to care for the needs of the four gentlemen that would arrive the day after tomorrow. Lillian was not looking forward to having strangers moving about the house, disturbing the tranquil setting of her childhood. Of course, her father never would have asked her to return had it not been for his need of a hostess. For tonight, she would enjoy the peaceful joy.

She glanced up to find Noah watching her, and he gave her a smile. She was still attempting to make sense of his behavior today. He had made his feelings clear when he left, yet today he had been attentive in a way she had never experienced from him. The way he was looking at her now had her stomach fluttering. She could not allow him to distract her before her season began. She had plans for her future and they no longer included Noah Reeves.

If she married well, she might make improvements to Martin's House, the home her mother adored. Given her father's lack of interest in the place, she would make it a retreat for herself and her children one day. All she needed was to make an advantageous match and her life would be on the proper path at last. Noah would leave before long, and no longer a concern.

After the meal, Mr. Reeves brought out his fiddle and played a cheerful tune that had everyone's toes tapping. Noah took his mother's hand, and the pair danced around the parlour. Mrs. Reeves was laughing as her son whirled her off of her feet. "Take Lillian for a spin. I am far too old to keep step with a young man like you." Noah came toward her, extending a hand.

"Shall we?" Lillian hesitated a moment, but the sight of Noah's mother smiling at them had her taking his hand. He took her waist and spun her to the tune, and before she knew it, she was dizzy and laughing. Catching her foot on the edge of the carpet, she fell backward, but Noah pulled her hard against him, righting her and stealing her breath. Their eyes met, and she felt the color rising in her cheeks as he held her longer than was necessary.

She stepped from his embrace, turning toward Hodges with an outstretched hand, "Will you show this young man how not to trip his partner?" The old butler cleared his throat as he rose stiffly from his chair.

"It would be a pleasure, my lady."

The evening ended with everyone in a jovial mood, full after a fine meal and breathless from dancing. Lillian hated to see it end, however, she knew everyone would need to rise early to prepare for her father's arrival. Noah was the last to leave, just behind his parents.

"Will seven o'clock suit for our ride tomorrow?" It startled her, then she recalled his invitation from earlier.

"Um, yes, that would be agreeable." She looked everywhere but in his eyes until he wished her good night and walked back across the yard. It was only a ride, just as they had done nearly every day as children. There was nothing untoward about it, and her father would not arrive until the afternoon. She could take an hour and look over the property.

She hugged herself, suddenly chilled as she realized she had been standing outside watching Noah's retreating form. Shaking her head, she stepped back into the warmth of the house. Looking around, she took in the faded rugs and outdated furnishings. This was still her home and she would do all she could to keep it. She would not allow her father to let it fall into greater disrepair.

The next morning she strolled into the stables, which were clean and well cared for thanks to the hard work of Mr. Reeves. Lillian knew he took great pride in the place and had no worries that the few horses were well cared for. The scent of fresh hay and oats came to her as well as the pleasant animal smell. This was one of her favorite places at Martin's Nest. She spied Noah beside the last stall, saddling her palfrey. He looked up at the sound of her footsteps.

"I saw you in town riding her yesterday. I assumed she was yours."

"You would be correct. Ivy was a gift from my uncle." She moved closer, brushing a hand down the horse's long black nose.

"She is a fine girl," Noah said, patting Ivy's neck before moving to saddle his own mount.

Morning mist shrouded the sun as they rode over the dew drenched fields. The cool air was a balm to Lillian's spirit, easing the worry she harbored at seeing her father again. Noah spoke of his time in Scotland and the hardships of the people there. She noted he was avoiding any mention of his time in France. His mother had told her of his being wounded, but when she asked him about it, he brushed it away as no great matter.

"Others were far more gravely injured and many good men died." His voice dropped away, and he appeared to withdraw. Eager to improve his mood, she suggested they stop at the small pond they frequented as children. They had already been away longer than she had planned, but she hated to see him this way.

Now that the sun was higher in the sky, the mist had burned away, revealing a beautiful day. Noah sat on the old fallen tree that made a perfect bench beside the water. They sat, faces raised to the sun, each lost in their own thoughts, until she felt his fingers brush against hers. She had removed her riding gloves, and the contact made her shiver.

Unnerved by her body's reaction, Lillian lept from her seat, pulling her hand away and rushing to her horse. Noah seemed stunned for a moment, then gave chase, capturing her arm before she could mount.

"Release me," she gritted out as he attempted to pull her closer.

"There was a time you craved my touch. Have you outgrown the love you proclaimed to me?" he said with a devilish grin. She pushed at his chest, stepping back as she regained her breath.

"I seem to recall you had no interest, wishing to seek your little harlot from the village." She fought to keep the hurt from her voice as he looked at her, his eyes traveling the length of her body before resting again on her lips. With a huff, she turned back to Ivy, placing a foot in the stirrup and mounting quickly. It would disappoint her aunt to see her riding without a sidesaddle, but Noah had already saddled her horse, and she had no wish to correct him. He likely still saw her as that little girl that chased him and was now making sport of her feelings. It was a situation she knew all too well because of her father's cruelty.

She kicked Ivy into a run down the path back to the manor before Noah had even mounted his own horse. She reached the stable, handing the reins off to Mr. Reeves, who gaped at her abrupt arrival and immediate departure into the house.

In the security of her bedchamber, she threw herself onto the bed, fuming at Noah for being so arrogant. How dare he make fun of her? Had they not been friends once? She heard hoof beats approach and glanced out the window to see Noah return. He dismounted, chest heaving as if he had made the run rather than his horse. He said something to his father, who pointed in the house's direction, sending the young man in her direction with ground-eating strides. She could make out raised voices downstairs as he entered with a soft knock on her door a moment later.

"My lady, Mister Reeves wishes to have a word." Rosie was ringing her hands as she spoke. "He seems a trifle upset over something."

"Tell him I am not receiving visitors as I am quite busy with preparations for my father's visit at the moment." Rosie bit her lip,

47

pulling on her fingers as she glanced over her shoulder, obviously not wishing to deliver that news. "Off with you," she said, waving the maid away before closing the door.

She quickly washed and changed into a simple day gown and was relieved to see Noah back by the stables, taking the horses back inside. He glanced up toward her window as he reached the door frame, then shook his head and continued inside. She released the breath she had been holding and made her way downstairs to prepare for her father's return.

He arrived in the late afternoon barely saying two words to her and ordered Sally to have supper prepared as soon as possible, as he planned to retire early. The two of them ate their meal in the dining room in silence, nothing like the lighthearted evening she had shared with the household the night before. Lillian pushed her food around her plate, glancing up at her father as he held out his glass to Hodges to be refilled. He fixed his gaze on her. "I see your time with my sister served you well. Seems she made a lady out of you after all," he said smugly. Lillian felt a chill down her spine as he examined her. He behaved as though he was buying a horse rather than looking at his own flesh and blood. "I expect you to be an attentive hostess this week and mind your manners. No racing about the fields with that boy. I had not realized he would be here, have a mind to send him on his way except that he will assist with the horses while my guests are here."

The bite of venison Lillian had finally taken immediately caught in her throat. "Papa, Noah is here on leave. He fought for England and now you wish to treat him as a servant?" His watery blue eyes narrowed at her as he set his fork clattered onto his plate.

48

"Have you been making eyes at the boy again? Should have known there was no way to make you respectable," He grumbled. "I will not have it. If he offers his help for free, who am I to turn him away. Besides, he is staying on my property." Lillian sagged in her chair at his harsh words. Taking a deep breath, she drew her shoulders back and nodded assent to her father. If Noah wished to be a stable boy while he was here, that was his affair. She would likely find him in the hay with a girl from the village before long, just as she had found him with Angelica when they were younger.

She felt a tightening in her chest at the memory, then brushed it away. What he did was his business. She needed to concentrate her attention on finding a proper husband. After finishing their meal, her father moved to his study, where he looked over the expenses from the estate and those for entertaining in the coming week. He had grumbled under his breath about the cost, then said it would be worthwhile. Unaware of what he was on about or even caring, she moved past the door to his study and went up to bed, not bothering to wish him good night.

Noah lay awake, the memory of Lily by the water, her face turned up to the sun, her eyes closed with the hint of a smile on her. She had been impossible to resist, yet when he touched her she had fled, would not allow him to speak to her. He had thought she would welcome his attention given the sentiments she had expressed before he left for the military. Tossing and turning an hour later, he left his bed and walked to the window. Looking out into the dark, he could see the lines of the manor house, smoke rising in the moonlight. He knew Lily's window, finding it even in the shadows. There was no light at present, though he often recalled there being a single candle burning late into the night when they were younger. She would read stories of heros in far-off places wishing to escape her limited existence under her father's constant scrutiny.

He stood there staring off into the night, wondering how to approach Lily again. Mayhap he was being a fool. He had nothing to offer her as a soldier. He would be away for months at a time and his pay was insignificant compared to the gentlemen who would court her in London. Knowing this, he still could not leave again without her knowing how he felt. He had been a fool to dismiss her so cruelly. He could not recall a time when he was not at ease and happy in her presence, except when she had run from him today.

He would seek her out tomorrow, tell her how he felt. He had to know if there was any hope that she might accept him. His enlistment would end in a year. If only she would wait for him, he would provide a good life for her. Resolved, he finally returned to his bed, drifting into dreams of Lily in his arms.

Chapter six

Lillian stood with her father, greeting Viscount Mortimer and Baron Le Claire. They had arrived shortly after The Earl of Devon, who had retired to wash and change after his long journey from London. "We have one more guest arriving a bit later," her father said to the new arrivals. "Best take time to refresh yourselves. We will convene for drinks in the parlour at six." The Viscount bowed to Lillian, then turned to her father.

"Capital idea, if you will excuse me, Lady Martin." She curtsied to both gentlemen.

"I will see to things in the kitchen," she said to her father, then turned down the hall, relieved to be done with her hostessing duties for now. She passed the kitchen door, knowing Sally had things well in hand, instead she wandered out the back door to the small garden. She strolled along the rows of herbs and early spring vegetables that were sprouting forth in the sun's warmth.

Lost in her own thoughts, she was unaware of Noah until he touched her arm. She nearly lept from her skin, afraid it was her father, cross that she was not in the kitchen as she had said. Hand to her heart, she scolded Noah.

"You nearly scared the life out of me. What are you about creeping up on me in such a way?"

He chuckled softly, "I did not know you were so unaware. I could never surprise before. It was always you catching me unaware, often dropping some slimy thing down my shirt." Lillian found herself unable to stifle the giggle that bubbled up at that memory.

"I warn you I am not above hitting you if you attempt to slip a toad into my gown," she laughed before leveling her sly blue eyes on him.

"I wouldn't dare ruin such a fetching gown." His eyes moved down, taking her in, down to her slippers and back up to her face, and she blushed under his scrutiny. He took a step closer, and she lifted her chin, not allowing him to see how he affected her. She would not give him the satisfaction. His grip on her arm loosened and his hand moved to her waist, holding her gaze.

"I wish to speak to you about yesterday, I…"

"There is nothing to speak about. You felt the need to mock me about my silly behavior when I was but a child. I suppose I deserve that, though I do not appreciate it as I thought we were friends." She attempted to turn from him, but he kept her in place, his hold tightening on her waist.

"That was not my intention, Lily. I find myself at a loss, seeing you this way." Words seemed to fail him as he looked down at her lovely face, her cheeks still flushed. He wanted only to kiss her, here and now, though he knew he could not out here in the yard. Grasping her hand, he pulled her toward the stables, then recalled that his father was at work, mucking out stalls. He had been assisting, but when he saw her come into the garden, he knew he needed to speak to her while the opportunity presented itself.

He turned, moving behind the cultivation shed as Lillian stumbled behind him. He turned to capture her, pulling her close. His hand rose to tuck a lock of hair behind her ear as she brought her hands up to his chest, attempting to push him away.

"This is unseemly. You must release me this minute. I have guests to see to." Her aristocratic tone only strengthened his resolve.

"What have they done to you, my sweet little Lily?"

"I am not little and I most certainly am not yours, now let me go." He could not turn her loose until he said his peace and yet words continued to fail him. Instead, his hand came to her cheek, sliding around to the back of her head. He dipped his head, taking her lips with all the frustration and passion he had been feeling since he had set eyes on her again. He felt her hands pushing at him, but he did not relent. Finally, her lips softened beneath his as her hands slid up to his shoulders.

"Lily," he whispered against her lips. "I was a fool before." His mouth continued to move over hers, then he kissed a trail to her ear. "I love you Lily." She jerked back at his words, her stunned eyes looking up at him. He smiled at her expression, "Tell me you still love me, we can..."

"Miss Lillian!" Sally shouted from the back door. Lillian struggled again.

"I must go, please." She stepped away, but he caught her hand again.

"Meet me in the stable tonight," he pleaded. "Midnight. I will wait for you until you can get away. Please say you will come." He looked at her anxiously until she finally nodded, and then she scurried away. Noah leaned against the rough wood of the shed, his heart beating wildly. He could still feel her mouth on his, taste her sweetness. He knew she felt the same. She must. Smiling broadly, he walked back to the stable to finish the stalls with his father. He would make something of himself, with his Lily by his side, anything was possible.

Sally was ringing her hands when Lillian came around the corner. "Guest arriving, Miss. The earl is lookin' for ye."

"Thank you Sally." Lillian patted her hair, then smoothed her skirt. Taking a deep breath, she prayed her heart would slow. She was certain anyone near her could hear it. Could she believe Noah's words; did he truly love her? What had changed? Her father was waiting, impatience in the scowl on his face. A carriage was pulling into the circle and as it made the turn, she recognized the Hawthorne crest. Her breath caught as he emerged from the carriage, his thick dark waves cued back elegantly with a deep blue ribbon that matched his coat. He smiled, that dimple playing in the corner of his mouth when his gaze fell on her.

"Hawthorne, so pleased you could join us." Banbury slapped him on the shoulder. "I hear you have made the acquaintance of my daughter."

"Lady Martin, always a pleasure," he said as he bowed over her hand. "I should like to look at the estate on horseback if you would be so kind as to guide me?" Her father turned his eyes on her.

"I am certain she could make time for that Hawthorne. Please make yourself at home." The earl motioned him inside as the newly hired footman carried in his bags toward the guest rooms. The duke offered his arm.

"Mayhap we could begin with a walk in the garden." Lillian looked up into his smiling face, the feel of Noah's kiss still tingling her lips. She placed her arm in his and they set off around the manor toward the gardens. Theirs could not hold a candle even to his smaller London garden, yet he was gracious, asking her about various plants and flowers and inquiring which was her favorite. He plucked a daisy from the long green stem and reached out, tucking it behind her ear.

Lillian giggled as the soft white petals tickled her face when he slid it into place. She glanced around the garden, feeling as though there were eyes on them, but there was no one that she could see.

"I am to convey a greeting from a friend of yours," the duke said as he brushed the grains of pollen from his coat. "I made the acquaintance of Lady Bingham two nights past at a musicale and when I spoke of my coming journey, she bid me to say she is eager for your return to town." Lillian missed her friend. She would have been a welcome companion during this rather trying visit. "She is a lovely girl," the duke mused. As a wistful expression crossed his face, Lillian felt a tightening in her belly.

Mary was lovely and quick to smile, and Lillian was aware of the attention she drew from the gentlemen at each event they attended. Had she caught the eye of the duke in her absence? She stood, worrying her bottom lip with her teeth.

"Is there something amiss, my lady?" He looked down at her with concern.

"No, I only... I have some things that require my attention."

"I realize I am monopolizing the hostess. Forgive me, I could not help myself. I shall take my leave and allow you to see to the household." He bowed, giving her his most charming smile. "I look forward to seeing you at dinner." Lillian stood a moment longer, then straightened her skirts. She took one last look behind her and saw Noah in the doorway of the stable, watching her with an unreadable expression. The weight of his stare seemed to freeze her in place until he turned away from her.

Annoyance rose at his behavior. He had no right to behave in such a way. She had offered him her heart, and he had trampled it. Now he thought a few pretty words and a kiss would bring her to her knees? Her father had spent years telling her she was worthless to him, then he sent her away, expecting her to return as a perfect lady and hostess. She did not know what Hawthorne expected of her. Unaccustomed as she was to such attentions. Her father had made it clear to her that no man would want her unless he offered a substantial dowry, and that was certainly not possible in their reduced circumstances. Letting out a frustrated breath, she straightened her already smooth skirts and stomped back toward the kitchen door where she could escape the men that seemed to wish to complicate her life.

The company at dinner was lively as the men ate and drank, telling stories of previous hunts or the success of their latest business venture. Lillian sat quietly, her fork moving gracefully as she took small lady-like bites of her meal and feigned interest in the various conversations swirling about. She sat beside Hawthorn, noting her father's eyes shifting to them often. It was clear why her presence had been necessary. He expected her to charm the duke, garnering his vast fortune to lift her father out of the hole he had dug for himself.

The duke leaned to her ear, and she took in his spicy scent, his cologne exotic, unlike the simple male musk of Noah when he had held her. "This must be a rather shocking display for a lady to witness," he chuckled, gesturing at the other gentlemen of the group.

"I am not as delicate as you may think, Your Grace." His eyebrows lifted slightly as a wolfish smile curled his lips.

"You seem at home in these rustic surroundings, my lady. I must say, I find you intriguing." Lillian felt warmth bloom in her chest as his bright blue eyes locked with hers. She could not allow him to fall for Mary. Despite their friendship, she knew well that Mary had a significant dowry and family not tainted by the poor choices her own father had made. She must do all she can to keep Hawthorne's attention on her.

The gentlemen retired to the parlour to play cards, and she prayed her father would not suffer further losses, though she knew her prayers would likely go unanswered. Happy to be back in the quiet of the darkened garden. Lillian sat on the rough wooden bench her mother had loved, memories of her easing some emotions of the day. She supposed there had been a small hope within her that her father had missed her and that was why he asked her to return home. Of course, that had not been the case.

As the hour grew late, she recalled Noah's plea to meet him. Bringing her fingers up to her lips, she recalled their kiss, the desire in his eyes as his arms held her tight against him. Would the duke's touch burn the same? Yet she did not know that she could trust the man she desired to stand by her, provide her with the security she needed.

After asking herself these questions, it surprised her to find she had already crossed the garden and taken the path to the stable. There was a soft glow coming from the last stall, and she felt her heart flutter at the thought of him waiting for her. Despite her concerns, the thought of being in his arms again drew her forward.

As she moved through the shadows toward his lantern, she heard low voices, one decidedly a woman.

Her pace quickened, and she peered around the edge of the stall. Noah was leaning back against the wall, his hand on the shoulder of Violet, one of the temporary maids as she leaned in close to him. He wore a lazy smile as his grey eyes took in the pretty blonde girl before him. Looking over the girl's shoulder, Noah caught sight of Lillian standing at the edge of the soft circle of light. His eyes widened, and he drew in a sharp breath. "Lily," he said, his voice horse with what she thought was likely desire, she silently begged her legs to move.

Her vision blurred by stinging tears, she turned as her legs finally did her bidding. She ran toward the door as she heard heavy footsteps behind her. "Lily, please wait." She couldn't stop, couldn't look at him. She knew better than to trust him, and yet she had foolishly wanted it to be true. That he wanted her, that anyone could want her as she was. Not a perfect lady with a large dowry, just Lillian.

Back in her room, she dashed the tears from her eyes as anger at Noah festered in her heart. Never would she allow him to deceive her again. He had given chase, but she had slammed and locked the door before he reached her. She would not listen to the lies that so easily fall from his lips. The memory of those lips on her came unbidden, but she pushed them away with the vision of his hands on Violet. She let that thought ignite a fire to burn him from her heart as she dried the last tears she would cry for any man.

Chapter seven

Noah watched as a light ignited in her window. He had been angry when he saw Lillian in the garden with the tall, well heeled gentleman. The way he had touched her, tucking a bloom behind her ear without so much as a by your leave to her. The way she smiled at him, damnable woman. When Violet had sought him out in the stable, he was well aware the girl found him attractive. She had made that quite clear through flirtatious glances and touches, and tonight had been no exception.

He had been waiting for Lillian when Violet appeared. Perhaps she thought he was hoping for a visit from her. She had moved close, making it clear she was his for the taking, yet he had held her back. Laying a hand on her shoulder and telling her that her attention flattered him. Unfortunately, that was when Lillian had arrived, drawing her own conclusions about the scene before her.

The look in her eyes had destroyed him, the desolation that turned so quickly to anger. He wanted to explain, to tell her she was the only woman he wanted, but she would not yield when he called to her. Now he stood once again, looking up at her window. Silently he begged her to look down and see him, open the pane and allow him to speak his heart as though she were Juliet in Shakespeare's play.

The window darkened a few moments later, dashing his hope. The only course left to him was to corner her tomorrow and force her to hear him out. She belonged with him. He felt it in his bones. That fancy gentleman could never make her happy, not the way he could. It known that the marriages within the nobility were seldom loving unions. He could not bear to see the light within her extinguished by such a match.

Early the next morning he was back in the stable, feeding the horses, when his father called out, "Noah, ready Dancer in the third stall. His Grace wishes to take an early ride. I'll saddle Ivy." Noah set aside the oat mixture he was stirring, then wiped his hands on his work apron.

"Ivy belongs to Lily. I doubt she would wish her to be ridden by one of the guests."

"Tis Lily that's takin' her." Noah's stock seemed to strangle him as he saw the man from the garden striding toward him, riding crop in hand. His Grace, he thought. The man was a duke, likely her father had a hand in this. He had to speak to Lily before she rode off with the man. She had not yet emerged from the house and he hoped it was because of reluctance on her part to take an unchaperoned ride with this gentleman. His father greeted the duke at the entrance to the stable, so he moved toward the sleek black stallion known as Dancer. He was a beauty with his shining black coat with a single white star on his forehead. He poured feed into the trough before him, then set about gathering the tack and saddle.

"You are a fine beast aren't you." he heard the man's deep voice greet Dancer as he allowed the horse to take his scent. The enormous head dropped back toward the trough again and the duke smoothe a hand over his neck and side. Noah stepped up, laying the blanket and saddle on the horse's back, allowing him a moment to finish his breakfast before placing the bit.

"He will give you a fine ride, Your Grace," Noah commented as he took in the man's fine dark blue riding coat. It had velvet lapels set off by the snowy white linen of his shirt and perfectly tied cravat.

The Duke settled his gaze on Noah as he worked, "I was told you are on leave from the army. What is your rank, if I may ask?"

"First Lieutenant, sir." Noah continued to cinch the belt, adjusting the stirrups as he took in the man's substantial height.

"Your father speaks highly of you, saying they promoted you after your heroism in France." The duke spoke as though it impressed him, though Noah doubted it truly did. He thought it highly unlikely this gentleman would sully his hands in defense of his country. He only nodded at the comment as he brought the halter over Dancer's head, glancing up to find Lily approaching.

"Good day Lily," Noah said out of habit. This garnered a glare from her and a censorious look from His Grace.

"You are addressing a lady of nobility, young man."

"My apologies, Lady Martin," he said, his jaw tightening. He thought Lily might speak of their long acquaintance, but she remained quiet as she turned toward his father, who was leading Ivy forward, properly set with a sidesaddle. Once out in the yard, he moved to assist Lily up, but the duke was there before him, touching her again as heat rose from his chest at the sight. Again, Lily smiled at the man, who moved to his own mount. Feigning concern for her stirrups, Noah approached her, checking all the straps as he glanced up at her, speaking so only she could hear.

"What you saw was not as it seemed. I was waiting for you when she came..."

"Did you wait an entire moment before you offered to entertain her?" Lily said, her tone sharp.

"It was not like that. I was pushing her away. Please allow me to speak with you when you return."

"I need not do anything you ask Mr. Reeves, good day." She kicked her horse into a cantor, her companion quickly moving alongside her. There was nothing for Noah to do but watch them disappear into the morning mist as it crawled over the fields. He felt his father's hand on his shoulder as he gave it a squeeze.

"She is a lady now, son. That father of hers expects of her a great deal. Do not think too harshly of her."

"I could never do that, she is too good for me." His gaze returned to the field where she had disappeared from view. "Too good for His Grace as well, though I doubt he realizes that." With a heaviness in his chest, he walked back into the stable and returned to his chores. Knowing would leave in a fortnight. He did not know if there would be enough time to make amends or if she would even stay after her father's guests left. He knew the season was fast approaching and with it the end of any chance he had of winning Lily's heart before the earl married her off to the highest bidder.

When the pair returned, Noah was exercising the few horses that had remained in the stable. He had expected them to return much sooner so that the duke could join the others as they walked the fields, thrashing out grouse and pheasant. Instead, they had been absent for hours. He was becoming anxious, debating the merits of setting out to look for them when he saw Lily dashing over the knoll at the edge of the woods, her companion in pursuit as she laughed.

Leading the string of horses, he worked back toward the stable. He could see her cheeks were flushed as she smiled back over her shoulder at Hawthorne. "You, my lady, are a superior horsewoman. It has been some time since anyone has bested me." He swung down from his saddle, approaching her with hands raised to assist Lily from her saddle. Noah's jaw tightened as he watched her body slide against the man slowly before touching the ground. She remained in his arms for a moment, looking up at him until Noah came forward to gather the reins.

"Lady Martin is even faster when riding astride, Your Grace," Noah said, keeping his eyes on Lily. He thought he saw her cheeks redden a bit more at his comment, but she turned her attention back to the tall gentleman as his expression became questioning.

"Pay no mind to Mr. Reeves, he speaks of when I was a child," she elaborated as she took his arm, leading him back toward the house. "His father has been with us all of my life. I am afraid the long acquaintance causes him to forget himself."

"Fine thing to have that continuity for the horses," the duke stated tightly as Noah watched them walk away. If the man could feel his gaze, it would have burned holes in his fine riding coat.

The gentlemen had spent the next two days in the fields, Hawthorne included. However, in the evenings he would walk the garden with Lily as Noah watched from the stable. Lily seemed to avoid him during the day, keeping to the house, and he worried he would not have the opportunity to speak to her again. Two mornings later, he found Sally in the kitchen garden and inquired as to Lily's whereabouts. The older cook had been with the household all his life and always seemed fond of him, saving a few cookies for him or a warm biscuit. She gave him a welcoming smile as he approached, setting down her basket of vegetables and wiping her hands on her starched apron.

"Tis a fine thing to have you home, Noah. I know your dear mother will be sad to see ye leave."

63

She placed a warm, chapped hand to his cheek as she looked up at him.

"It has been a joy to be home, indeed. Have you seen Lily about this morning?" Sally gave him a knowing smile.

"Saw her in the library not long ago. Perhaps you could bring her this." Walking to the edge of the garden, she plucked an ivory rose that climbed the trellis along the stone wall. "She is quite fond of them." She gave him a wink, and he leaned in, kissing her wrinkled cheek before moving to the back door. He kicked the mud from his boots before walking inside, where he saw Violet scurrying by with a basket of linens. She smiled brightly at him, but he paid her only a passing glance. He would not be drawn into conversation with the girl again. He had a mission and would allow no one to distract him.

He came to the open door of the small library, the smell of paper and ink mixing with the faint smell of the earl's favorite tobacco. He turned to his right quietly, knowing he would find her in the window seat with her nose in a book, as she had all her life. When he caught sight of her, the sun warming the soft caramel highlights that ran through her darker tresses, making his heart feel light. Then he saw the glint of tears on her cheeks. Without thinking, he rushed to her side, startling her.

Her hands came up quickly, dashing the evidence of her sadness away as she turned her face from him. "What are you doing in here? You should not be wandering about the house." Her tone was fierce, yet thick with the tears he had seen her shed.

"What is it Lily? Has he hurt you?" He took her chin in his hand, turning her to face him.

"Of course not, father isn't even here." She attempted to pull from his grasp, but he held her, locking eyes with her.

"That bastard Hawthorne. Has he done something to you?" At that, she stood, stepping away from him, her head held high.

"The only man to hurt me of late is you, not that you truly could. I would have to have feelings for you to be hurt. You need to leave this instant before the hunting party returns." She swept past him, her skirts brushing his arm. He moved swiftly, grasping her arm and pulling her back.

"I am sorry, Lily. Not that there is anything to apologize for. I was telling Violet that I have no interest in her when you arrived. I was waiting for you." He lifted the rose to her, gently brushing the petals against her cheek. "There is no one else for me. You are my match. We belong together, Lily."

She lifted her chin, not taking the flower he held out to her. "As if I would marry you, a soldier. What can you offer, a tiny cottage somewhere to keep tidy while you are away for months? Children grasping at my skirts while I toil away at your hearth. You'll travel the world in search of glory or a light skirt to warm the frosty nights while I hold vigil in our empty bed?" Her pale blue eyes pierced him like her words.

"It would not be so, I promise you. In a year, I can resign and make a life for us. I have money set aside and I would take care of you; I love you Lily." His heart was pounding as she stood before him, not speaking. He could see something in her eyes, emotions swirling, but he could not fathom what she was thinking. He held his breath, willing himself not to drop to his knees and beg her to accept him. Then his heart shattered as she laughed. It was not a joyous sound; it was laced with malice, something he had never heard from her.

"You have nothing to offer me. You speak of love as though that will keep a roof over my head or clothes on my back. I have seen what love purchases. It brought my mother misery and an untimely death and I will not have it." He could only stare at her. The suddenly hard lines of her jaw as she ran him through with her words. No hint of the sweet girl he had loved appeared in her gaze at that moment. Noah realized in that moment, he was too late; her father had broken her. Without another word, he turned and walked away, dropping the rose at her feet.

Lillian stood rigidly, chin held high as she listened to Noah's boots thudding down the hallway. She had lashed him with the very words her own father had spoken when she spoke of her deep regard for Noah. Her heart was beating so hard she was certain it would burst from her chest and fly to him. She had wanted those words from him for so long, wanted nothing more than to allow him to take her in his arms, to carry her away from here, but his words had come too late.

The deal was struck. Her father had sold her to Hawthorne, for the cost of his debts and an agreement to place his support behind the duke in any undertaking in the House of Lords. The man had no money, yet he still held much sway among his peers. Her father reminded her she would be a duchess, married to a handsome, wealthy man that seemed to enjoy her company. Surely they would grow to love one another in time. It was all for the best; she told herself as the tears threatened once more. Hawthorne had left that morning as soon as her father had informed her of the arrangement.

She was to return to London tomorrow, where she would live with her aunt and uncle until the wedding at the end of August. It would be a lavish reception attended by all of high society. No one would look down on her again, no one would dare. Her children would not know the shame of a father buried beneath bad debts hidden by a good name. They would be true nobility and she would not allow any daughter of hers to be sold away as she had been. She knew this was the correct decision even as she ran to her room and threw herself on her bed, finally allowing her tears to flow once more, the last tears she would ever shed for Noah Reeves.

Chapter eight

Lillian sat with Mary Bingham in the salon of Lady Windham, sipping tea from delicate floral tea cups as other young ladies and their mothers twittered on about the latest en dite of the season. Of course, her own betrothal to the Duke of Hawthorne had been the talk of the season when announced in early June. She was well aware of the words spoken behind her back, the knowing glances of those that were aware of her situation and marveling that she had somehow garnered the most sought after a gentleman in London.

She simply held her head high as though it were all beneath her. Those were her aunt's instructions before the first event of the season. "Rise above it all dear, you will be a duchess. These same hens will emulate you before long, begging for any scraps you deign to toss them." Lillian did as instructed with everyone. All save Mary. No unkind word ever passed her friend's lips. She was the one lady Lillian knew she could count on to see her through the trials at each ball or musicale they attended.

"Have you seen your dress as yet?" Mary asked, her hazel eyes sparkling with excitement.

"I am to have a fitting at the end of the week. Would you care to join me? You will be my maid of honor after all."

"I should love nothing more, as long as it is not Thursday as I am unavailable." Lillian gave her a questioning look, but Mary continued to smile at her, not divulging anything further. She had been absent from most events held on Thursdays, speaking of an obligation at an establishment that assisted the poor in London. Lillian had visited with her on one of these occasions before the announcement, but had not returned since.

68

She marveled as her petite friend had moved without concern through a room filled with rather rough-looking men and downtrodden ladies, their thin, dirty children clinging to their skirts. Mary would smile as she carried a basket handing out bread or fruit. She even gave small gifts to the children, such as a sweet from her pocket or a rag doll she had made with her own hands. Lillian could not say why her friend felt the need to do such things. She could certainly make a donation to such places without coming here herself.

There had been a young man that would walk beside her as she saw to the needs of the poor souls and Lillian noted how his eyes would follow her, seeming to take her in anew each time their eyes met. Poor man had to know he would never truly catch her eye. She was a lady of the peerage expected to make an advantageous match. Her thoughts had turned for a moment to Noah standing in the library, the petals of that rose touching her cheek like a lover's caress.

Shaking off those unpleasant memories, she turned her attention back to the ladies milling around them. A few had stopped to congratulate her on her good fortune or to ask where the wedding trip would be. Hawthorne had spoken of spending time at his ducal seat so that she might become better acquainted with the staff and her duties there. "We may travel to the coast next summer for a month," she told Lady Marlow. Daphne Marlow had been fluttering her lashes at the duke from the moment he entered the first ball, unaware the ink had already dried on the betrothal contracts. It had displeased her, to say the very least, when they made the announcement, and Lillian knew of the venomous comments she had made behind her gloved hands.

Still, she recalled her aunt's words again and smiled, her chin held high. "I do not know how you spoke to her so cordially with the things she has said," Mary huffed. It warmed Lillian's heart to have such a dear friend. Something she thought never to have growing up. Reaching out, she patted Mary's hand. "Thank you for your concern. I am glad of your friendship each day." Mary looked down at their hands, an odd look crossing her face for a moment, then disappearing. "Are you unwell? Should I find your mother?" she asked with concern.

"No, no, I am well. I was only thinking about how I will miss you," she said with a sad smile.

"Don't be silly. We will see one another often. We will visit often and once you marry, our children will surely play together. You will see." Mary smiled but Lillian could see that it did not reach her eyes as it usually did, but Mary would not admit to anything being amiss and so she stopped bothering her with questions. Instead, they turned their attention to their surroundings and indulged in a bit of gossip themselves.

Two nights later, Lillian stood by her aunt and uncle, fanning herself after sharing a dance with Viscount Farthinghill. He was lively for a man nearing seventy and often asked several young ladies for a dance at each ball he attended. She enjoyed his wit and compliments as they circled the floor anytime she joined him. Her betrothed was currently dancing with Mary, for whom she remained concerned. Her friend had been rather sullen of late, not at all like herself. There was something bothering her, but she would not share it despite their friendship. Even now, as she moved through the steps of their dance, she barely looked at Hawthorne, moving without her usual grace and joy.

Lillian's attention was drawn by Hugh McDrummond as he told her uncle of his recent hunt at his keep in the highlands of Scotland. "Never have ye seen such a sight as that buck, antlers as wide across as the distance between you and me. Took 'im with one shot." The man had such a boisterous way of telling a story one could not help but listen. Though he was a Scot, he held a title from an old family and the *ton* seemed to embrace him.

When she turned her attention back to the dance floor, people were lining up for the next set. However, Mary and Hawthorne had not returned. She looked about and thought she caught sight of them moving through the door to the balcony. Perhaps Mary needed air. She had not looked well while they were dancing. Concern for her friend pulling her forward, she made her way to the large French doors and stepped out into the night.

The air was cool, and she drew in a deep breath, or as much as her stays would allow, and waited for her eyes to adjust to the low light. The pair were nowhere to be seen. She continued to search, becoming even more concerned. Harsh whispers echoed to her right, and she noted the balcony wrapped around the side of the manor. She was certain she recognized Mary's voice, the sound thick with tears. Hurrying now, she stopped in the shadows, stunned by the sight that greeted her.

Mary was in a man's arms, her hands against his chest. It was Hawthorne, pleading with her, "Please my darling, you must know how I desire you." His face was close to Mary's as she shook her head.

"Do not do this. What of your betrothal to my dearest friend? Why do you pursue me so? I have told you before that I do not want your attention." She continued to struggle as Lillian remained frozen to the spot.

"Damn the betrothal, I will break the engagement...you are the lady I wish to marry. Simply say the word and I will make you my duchess. I…" His head turned, following Mary's now shocked gaze. Her voice distraught, she called out as Lillian turned in a daze and walked back toward the ballroom. "Lillian, I am sorry. I didn't know how to tell you he had been making advances. I wanted to…" Lillian spun around, her face in a mask of anger.

"Will you lower your voice? Do you wish to ruin me?" Mary stepped back, seeming unsure what Lillian was saying. Turning her back again, she lifted her chin and walked away without a glance back at her friend or her betrothed, who was now in pursuit. She felt Hawthorne's hand on her shoulder and she slowed, sliding her arm in his as he walked stiffly beside her. Both of them kept their eyes forward, nodding to acquaintances as they passed. Mary vanished from the ballroom as Hawthorne's bright blue eyes finally slid to the side,Th waiting for her to make some sort of scene in the middle of the ballroom.

"Lillian?"

"Not here," she snapped at him.

"I... will you be speaking to your father about... this?" he stammered out, making her laugh, which only seemed to disconcert him further.

"Do you think my father would care? As long as you pay his debts and take me from his house, he will gladly keep your bargain." Her voice was steady and cold as she turned to him. "Now smile as though you are pleased to be in my company. We wed in a fortnight. Seeing as the woman you love has rejected you, I see no reason to endure the scandal of a broken betrothal. We will not speak of this again."

The Duke of Hawthorne stood before her, seeming at a loss for words as she curtsied low. He bowed out of habit, years of training keeping him from faltering as she turned from him and went to her aunt, feigning a headache. They left the ball, and she sat silently in the squabs as the last hopes of a happy life died within her heart. She was alone, unable to trust anyone. Even her dearest friend had betrayed her. She appeared to be spurning his advances, but how could she be certain? Perhaps she only wished to be pursued longer? Had he given Mary gifts, stolen a kiss, though he had yet to give her one? She felt a fool, but she would not allow herself to wallow in such feelings. Instead, she allowed them to harden, building a shield around her heart that she would never allow to drop again.

Lillian stood beside Hawthorne in ivory lace encrusted with tiny pearls, looking every bit the duchess she now was. Mary had left London behind as well as her family, leaving a brief note stating that she must follow her heart, whatever that meant. Lillian did not care to know.

All the ladies that had attempted to belittle her now simpered before her as she accepted their congratulations. She smiled as each one dipped low, bowing their heads as they addressed her as Your Grace. She nodded regally, her arm tightly in Hawthorne's. The wedding breakfast was a lavish affair attended by over 200 guests, all paid for by her husband, of course. Though looking at her father holding court, one would think he had provided the funds.

The money he received had paid his creditors and anything he had left, he would squander at his club before the ink was dry on the marriage certificate. She would not see him again. At last, she was out of his reach. Any money her husband wished to waste on the man from now on was his own affair. She watched as her husband tossed back another glass of whiskey. It seemed she would have at least one night's reprieve before she had to attend to her wifely duties. The man would likely pass out before the sun set.

She enjoyed another glass of champagne as her young lady's maid brushed out her hair. The girl was likely only sixteen herself, with brown hair pulled back tightly from her face, her lips pursed as she attempted to remove the small tangle left by her intricate wedding style.

"Ouch, be careful," Lillian snapped. She missed Rosie, who had been with her mother for so long and then with Lillian, but her father would not allow her to come to London. A last cruelty on his part.

"Sorry Your Grace," the girl sniveled.

"That will be all."

Bobbing a curtsy, she asked, "Shall I let His Grace know you are ready?"

"There will be no need," Lillian scoffed. He was likely sound asleep, or at least so far in his cups, he would not emerge before the morning. The girl scurried from the room. Lillian shook her head as the door closed. She had never been harsh with staff before, but she did not know these people. Certain their allegiance lay with

74

Hawthorne, she was truly alone here. Her heart ached for home, for the people that cared for her. For Noah... No, she would not allow him to invade her thoughts. There was no place for him in her life any longer. Best forget him and get on with her life.

She heard something thump against the door that adjoined Hawthorne's chamber. Banging followed by slurred words had her creeping toward it, uncertain what to do when she heard him again.

"Damn it, you will not lock this door!" he yelled. Taking a deep breath and letting it out slowly, Lillian turned the knob.

"It was unlocked, Your Grace." He leaned in, his breath foul with drink and his shirt open. He wore no coat and his hair looked as though he had been running his hands through as she noted he did when frustrated. Stumbling in, he grasped Lillian's shoulders to steady himself and she found herself overwhelmed by his weight as she struggled to keep him on his feet.

Landing on the bed, he rolled on top of her. "Suppose we it is not official until we get this done," he mumbled into her neck, his hands grasping her nightgown. She pushed against his chest, but he was too heavy. She could not move him. His hand was pulling up her hem as she struggled.

"You're drunk, go to bed Joseph."

"So you do know my name...you'll know whose name to call out then." She did not know what he was speaking of, only that he had her nightgown around her waist as he pulled at the placket of his trousers no. Her struggles became more frantic now as he pinned her arms over her head. Then she felt a burning pain between her legs as he thrust into her without warning. She cried out, begged him to stop, but he payed no heed as she felt bile rise in her throat.

Thankfully, he did not last long. In moments, she felt him stiffen as he groaned a name… "Mary." He lay there, smothering her for a moment as he gasped for breath, then his weight lifted away. She lay there as he stumbled back through the door, slamming it behind himself.

Lillian remained on the bed, frozen to the spot for what seemed like hours. Finally she rose, looking back at the bed, the blood of her innocence staining the white linen. Crossing to the washstand, she cleaned herself before turning back and stripping everything from the bed. She curled in on herself on the bare mattress, her dressing gown pulled over her as she cursed her father and Hawthorne for what they had done to her. No man would have power over her again. She would be in control of her own destiny.

Chapter nine

Mercifully, Lillian found herself with child after two months. Hawthorne had come to her, smelling of whiskey, leaving as soon as he finished. He never undressed or even attempted to woo her. He would likely treat a whore with more tenderness, she thought bitterly as she lay alone in her bed after the last time. She no longer needed to wonder if he would enter her room at night. Instead, he spent his nights elsewhere, seeking his own pleasure as she carried his child.

On those rare occasions they were in public, he would make a show of escorting her and ensuring she was comfortable before engaging the other gentlemen in conversation. A few others were expecting their first child, and they stood about, chests puffed up like proud roosters as though they were solely responsible for the grand feet.

Lillian spent much of her time at Hawthorne Manor, his ducal seat, where she saw to the redecoration of several of the rooms including the nursery. Since this would be her prison, she would make it to her liking. Aunt Rowena visited and remained for nearly a month fussing and cooing over her and she felt cherished for a time. She only wished her mother were alive to share this time with her. Lillian wanted nothing more than to rescue her from her circumstances and bring her to a fine home such as this, where she would be comfortable and cared for.

As she watched her aunt's carriage depart, she wanted nothing more than to break down and weep from loneliness. She did not know the enormous staff and even on the rare occasions that Hawthorne came, he would spend only a day or two. His only interest in her was that she remained healthy to deliver him a fine son. He would inquire as to her welfare, seeing to the estates books with his man-of-business, then be on his way.

Admittedly, she took some comfort in her husband's misery at the news of the scandal surrounding Mary Bingham. She had run off to Gretna Green and married a merchant, causing her family to cut her off completely. She thought it must gall him to know that she preferred a commoner to his company and Lillian had not bothered to hide her smile as she delivered this news.

When she reached the end of her confinement, her aunt thankfully returned a week before her pains began. She woke to soaked linens followed by a deep ache in her back. Her maid had moved swiftly, changing the bed and laying down several old quilts as Aunt Rowena walked her around the large room. After hours of worsening pain, the physician arrived and ordered her back to the bed. Sweat beaded on her forehead, making her hair cling to her face as her aunt and her maid, Kitty, each held one of her hands. She cursed Hawthorne through the pain as she pushed the tiny life into existence.

After two hours of agony, her son was born. Cleaned and swaddled, they handed him to her and she marveled at what she had done. He had wisps of downy hair that drifted over his wrinkled face, still red from the ordeal of his birth, and she was certain she had seen nothing so beautiful in all her life. She kissed his head as he clutched her finger in his tiny hand and tears spilled onto her cheeks. This little boy was truly hers.

With a bit of assistance from one of the older maids, Lillian could feed him for a few moments before mother and son fell asleep. When she woke, it was with a start. She looked around for her son, who had been in her arms. Had it been a dream? Fear filled her heart until she saw the cradle at her bedside, her baby sleeping peacefully. When he stirred, she took him to her breast again, cradling his tiny head and smiling down at him.

The door flew open, announcing her wayward husband, who had ridden from London when he received the news of her labor beginning. He knelt beside the bed with a tender expression she had never seen, his eyes like the ocean, now damp with tears. The boy was sleeping, having had his fill, and Lillian reluctantly handed the bundle to her husband. She watched him gingerly position their son in the crook of his arm and stood, bringing him to the window for a better look.

"You have done well Lillian. You have given me a son. I will be forever grateful." He gave her a soft smile that made her heart flutter. Even before the ugliness, he had not looked at her in such a way. There was a small glimmer of hope that perhaps this child would soften the edges of their sharp relations. She returned his smile.

"What shall we name him?" she asked softly.

"Jonathan, after my father. Jonathan Martin Joseph Stanhope." He continued to stare down at his son as Lillian looked on, feeling oddly pleased that he should include her family name. At least she need not name him Edmund. No child of hers would bear her father's name.

Soft grunts followed by a rather shrill cry brought a panicked look to the duke's face and he called out, "Send Eloise in immediately." He held their crying son away from himself, unsure what to make of this change in the child's countenance.

"Joseph, give him to me. He may be hungry again." Her husband gave her an appalled look.

"I realize, raised in the country as you were, that women may have nursed their children, but surely you must know a duchess does not do such things. That is why I brought a wet nurse from London for you." Lillian stared at him for a moment.

"I would prefer to care for him and myself. There is no need…"

"Lillian, do not challenge me on this. You have a household to attend to. I can;t have you entertaining guests with a baby at your breast. My God, woman." Tears were stinging her eyes as the nurse came in, taking her son away. Turning, she pushed her still tired limbs out of the bed and stood for a moment as dizziness swamped her. She staggered slightly, then smoothed her nightgown and reached for her night rail. She moved slowly, still weak and sore from the birth, but determined to follow her son.

Joseph grasped her by the shoulders and turned her back toward the bed. "You mustn't exert yourself. Now get back into bed and rest. The boy is in excellent hands." Touching her cheek tenderly, he left her speechless. He had never been this way before. He brought the covers up over her and smoothed a loose strand of hair behind her ear. "Sleep now my dear, I will make certain no one disturbs you." He turned and left the room, closing the door quietly behind him.

For the next several months, Joseph was home more often. He would visit the nursery and bring her gifts or flowers from the garden, and Lillian basked in the glow of his attention. She spent time in the nursery as well, sitting with little Jonathan in her arms as she gazed at his sweet face. He cooed and gurgled as she tickled him or told him silly stories. She remained unhappy with the use of a wet nurse. Though it seemed a small price to pay for his increased attention.

They entertained, having various guests from London and the surrounding estates who wished to see the heir to Hawthorne. The christening party was a lavish affair, and she marveled at the ivory silk gown that Joseph's mother brought for the occasion.

"It is an heirloom. All the first-born sons have worn it." She sipped her tea as Lillian continued to examine the garment, feeling a sense of pride at having given her husband an heir. The line was assured, and he was such a lovely boy, soft brown curls and large blue eyes that were currently attempting to focus on the small silver rattle his grandmother had brought for him.

Now that the physician had deemed it safe, Joseph began visiting her bed chamber at least once a week. At first she was apprehensive, certain there would be more pain since giving birth. However, her husband was gentler than before without the scent of whiskey on his breath. He treated her kindly, though he remained rather businesslike about it. He remained in his nightshirt, only lifting her hem for their coupling, leaving when he reached completion. At least he would leave her with a sweet kiss on her forehead.

Perhaps he had let go of his old desire for Mary Bingham and their own marriage could flourish, she thought with a light heart. It had surprised her when, only six months after Jonathan's birth, she felt ill and tired. When another month passed without her courses, the physician confirmed she was again with child.

Six months later, Little Andrew was born. Another son, a spare, as many were fond of saying to her. Their second child was born with a full head of dark hair, much like his father's, where Jonathan favored Lillian with his soft features and lighter hair and eyes. Andrew was a quiet child while Jonathan ran about, knocking things over and yelling at the top of his lungs.

As the boys grew, Lillian was often looking in on Jonathan, seeing to his education and assuring herself that his manner befit his impending title. Andrew sat with the governess, reading so quietly that at times, Lillian forgot he was in the room. As the boys grew, Joseph's visits again became less frequent. He would spend a few days each month in residence at the manor, where he would review accounts and ensure that his sons were being properly educated.

Lillian found herself lonely once again and so she threw herself into Jonathan's life, certain that he was the key to making Joseph happy. With only a monthly visit to her chamber by her husband, she was shocked to find herself with child again. It had been eight years since she had given birth to Andrew and Lillian worried that there would be difficulties as she was older.

"You are still well within your child-bearing years, Your Grace. There is nothing to fear," Dr. Morgan assured her as he pushed his wire-rimmed spectacles higher on the bridge of his bulbous nose. "Just do as you have in the past and you will likely have another fine son." Joseph entered the chamber shortly after the old physician's exit, his brow furrowed. He had been away in London for several weeks and had returned while she met with Dr. Morgan.

"Are you unwell, my dear?" he asked as he sat beside her. "Why was the doctor here?" Lillian remained silent a moment, unsure how she felt about having another child. She would have been better off having only Jonathan. Her husband had been attentive after their first child. She had hoped that their relationship would grow closer, yet when Andrew was born, he seemed to pull away again. Now, with another child, she wondered what his response would be.

"It seems I am to have another child," she finally blurted out. Joseph's eyes widened, then his smile grew as he took her hands in his own.

"This is wonderful news. What a surprise you have turned out to be." Lillian wonder at his odd comment. "My mother was certain it would be difficult for you, given that your mother only had the two children. With the passing years, I thought she must be correct, yet here you are giving me another child." Lillian stood and walked about the room, her fingers lightly tracing objects on the dressing table before turning to her husband.

"Does this mean you will be at home more often?"

"Are you unhappy with my absence? I would have thought you preferred it."

"What would give you such an idea?" The duke appeared perplexed by her reaction and stood, walking toward her.

"I thought you understood your role here."

"What does that mean exactly?" She narrowed her eyes at her husband, waiting for his reply.

"You have provided me with two heirs, likely now three. I have provided you with all the comforts you desire. Beyond that, what more do you expect. Your father has served me well in the House of Lords. Because of that, I am more prosperous than ever, which will serve our children well."

"You wish nothing more from this marriage, nothing more from me?" she asked as her chest tightened. Then he did something unexpected. He laughed. It froze Lillian to the spot as cold swept through her body, encasing her heart.

"Lillian, this is how things are done. Have I not given you everything you could wish for?" Her mind raced with thoughts of the gowns, jewels, and gifts he had given her over the years. She had thought they were tokens of his growing affection for her. Instead, they were just what he believed she expected. "Of course, Your Grace. I only wished to be certain I had done all you expected of me, though I wonder if you would have expected more of Mary?" His jaw tightened as his blue eyes turned to ice.

"I will be away for the next two months. I have business at my other estates, some troubles have arisen that I must see to personally. I am assured that the staff will care for you in my absence as always."

"Of course," she replied, giving him a smile that, had he been paying her any mind, would likely have chilled him to the bone. So he still pined for Mary Bingham, or Parsons, she should say. Perhaps knowing that he still suffered would be enough. She would no longer pine for his return. He had made it brutally clear that she was simply a brood mare to him.

The dowager-duchess pulled her aside two days later for a chat in her private parlor. The woman lorded over the place, regardless of Lillian being the current Duchess of Hawthorne. She always felt overshadowed in this room with its heavy draperies and imposing paintings of the previous dukes and their duchesses. Elizabeth Stanhope had been a great beauty in her youth. Even now she was a handsome woman, regal in her deep blue gown and fine lace shawl.

She asked Lillian to pour the tea when the tray arrived as she sat back on the velvet settee.

"You must spend more time in London, my dear. It is important that they see you entertaining, furthering my son's position in society." She took a sip of her tea, looking over the delicate rim with her sharp blue eyes.

"Your son has not expressed a desire for me to attend to him in London. I believe he has... other interests when he is in town." Lillian looked down into her tea as she stirred in a bit of sugar. "Besides, I have the boys and another on the way..."

"Don't be ridiculous. This is how things are done. You have a nurse and a governess. Once this child is born, make a place for yourself." Lillian remained silent, unable to look at her mother-in-law as she lay a hand on her growing belly. "It is our lot, you know," Elizabeth said as she moved closer, placing a hand over hers. "The sooner you embrace your role here, the happier you will be. Men have their vices, drink, gambling, a mistress. We must make our own lives, it is the way of things."

Elizabeth stood, leaving Lillian to think about what she said. The clock in the hall chimed four times, reminding her it was time to look in on Jonathan and hear the report from his tutor. As she made her way down the hallway, Andrew ran from the nursery. "Momma, Momma." His hands reached for her and she looked down into the bright blue eyes as he smiled. "Will you come see what I've made?" The nurse came out after him.

"My apologies, Your Grace. He wished to show you his drawing." His expression was pleading, his desire for her approval clear. Yet all she could see were his father's eyes and her heart hardened. He

85

was a child, but her anger at her husband was too close to the surface.

"Carolyn, you must watch him more closely." She bent down as she removed his hand from her arm. "Young gentlemen, do not shout or run around the house. You must remember your place in this world and play your part," she scolded. He dropped his gaze to the floor as his fingers twisted together in front of him. "Now, go with Carolyn and finish your lessons. I have things to attend to."

Chapter ten
1817

Lillian watched Andrew as he chased little Rachel around the edge of the pond that bordered the fanciful garden that he had created for her. She shrieked with laughter as he snatched her, swinging the girl up over his head.

She wondered how he had become such a good man. It had nothing to do with her or his father. He adored his children and the light she saw in his eyes when Laura entered a room was something she had never experienced herself with Joseph. She watched as Andrew assisted his wife from her chair, placing his hand on her rounded belly, as he often did. He knelt down and Laura laughed as he spoke to their child as though it was in her arms already.

Lillian shook her head at the silly display as sadness filled her. She had been alone in her confinements, Joseph always away tending to his estates or his mistresses rather than his wife and children. She had always comforted herself with her mother-in-law's words, thinking all men behaved as her husband did. Yet watching the man's own son dote on his wife and play with his children told a different story.

Henderson cleared his throat behind her, pulling her from her self pity. "The guests are arriving. Would you prefer your own tea here in the parlor or will you be joining the party in the garden, Your Grace?" She looked out the window again and longed to stand in the sun even if it meant dealing with Minerva Edwards and her brood of orphans. Perhaps for a short time.

"I shall take my tea with the family Henderson, thank you." She ignored the butler's surprised expression, making her way toward the garden door. She could hear the children as their shoes slapped along on the marble floors. Minerva and her maid scolded them to mind their manners as they followed behind at a more dignified pace.

"Good day, Your Grace. I am glad you could return before the baby made his appearance." Minerva gave her a reserved smile, likely still wary after the reservations Lillian had expressed at the idea of her son marrying a commoner.

"I arrived yesterday, though I was afraid I would arrive too late. Poor girl looks dreadfully uncomfortable." Minerva and Ginny both gazed at Laura with sympathy in their eyes. Of course, neither had ever carried a child. They could not understand the discomfort at the end. Laura made no complaints, however, as she happily greeted her company. The women embraced her and admired her girth with bright smiles.

"I thought we were to meet your nephew," Laura said, looking past the group as the children ran about them like a pack of frolicking puppies.

"He rode separately, wanting to take in the scenery from his horse. He should be along shortly. The man is always moving. With his time in the military and the travel involved in his business dealings, he has never been one to sit idle."

"Fascinating man," Andrew commented as he set a squealing Rachel back on her feet. "We spoke about his dealings in India and I believe he may be an excellent contact for Robert and me to expand our venture there." Laura came forward, taking his arm with a soft laugh.

"At least I know he will entertain you this afternoon while the ladies visit." Andrew touched her cheek, lowering his head to look into her eyes.

"You're not too tired, darling? I do not wish you to overexert yourself." She gave him a quick kiss on the cheek before reassuring him she was fine, then strolled back to Minerva and Ginny. The sound of hoofbeats coming around the back of the manor had them all looking up. A gentleman rode up, Minerva's nephew, Lillian assumed as she turned back to her tea.

Andrew immediately walked to the stable to greet the man, both giving cordial bows. As they approached, Lillian could see her son gesturing, likely pointing out the finer points of the estate he had molded to his family's purposes. She continued to watch them, her eyes traveling over the tall frame of the older man at Andrew's side. Something in his demeanor struck her, the tilt of his head as he listened and the curve of his mouth as he smiled. Removing his hat, revealing a head of dark blonde waves with a bit of silver at the temples, he turned to greet the ladies and Lillian, the ever regal Dowager Duchess of Hawthorne, dropped her teacup. The warm liquid spilled down the front of her blue gown, the cup breaking into several pieces as it struck the tray.

Leaping from her chair, her head bowed as she dabbed at her skirt before her eyes rose to connect with his again. Those striking grey eyes still danced as they took her in. She straightened her shoulders, ready to greet the newcomer. Yet when he smiled, all reason escaped her, and she turned on her heel without a word, walking back to the house as all eyes followed her.

Noah rode down the tree-lined lane that led to the vine covered manor of Andrew Stanhope. It had surprised him on his arrival at his aunts to find the young man in his shirtsleeves stacking freshly split firewood by the kitchen door. The surname struck him immediately, but it couldn't be *that* Stanhope, not working as a laborer for his elderly aunt. Then Minerva came out to greet him. "I see you have met the duke."

Dumbfounded, he watched as the young man shook his head at her. "Really Minerva, is it necessary to be so formal?" He turned to Noah, "Andrew is sufficient." Taking a drink from the cup his aunt provided, he turned back to his work. "Please, go in and visit. I'm nearly done."

"Please come in when you finish, Your Grace. How it is you come to be here assisting my aunt."

Sitting in the kitchen, Noah noted the young duke appeared quite at home as he casually made conversation while sipping a glass of lemonade. Taking him in, it was obvious who his father was. Lord knew he was the image of Hawthorne when he had courted Lily. He was finding it difficult to concentrate as memories of the woman he had spent his life attempting to forget came rushing back. It embarrassed him when Andrew had to repeat his invitation because of his wandering thoughts.

"Of course. I would enjoy that very much," he blurted at his the invitation to visit the day after tomorrow. Now here he stood in a magnificent garden, looking into her eyes. There was silver threaded through her chestnut locks. Tiny lines crinkled around her soft blue eyes, but it was still his Lily. She hadn't known, being as surprised to see him as he was. With her dress stained, she only stammered, then turned and ran away, leaving him thunderstruck.

"I apologize Mr. Ambrose, I don't know what is the matter with my mother-in-law," Andrew's lovely wife said as her eyes followed Lily's retreating form. Turning to her, he could only smile.

"I am afraid I have startled her. It has been sometime since we have seen one another." At the surprised look he was receiving, he could only shrug. "Excuse me a moment, please." He bowed, then moved toward the house. When he inquired as to her whereabouts, the maid led him to a comfortable parlor and asked to wait there.

Wandering about the room, he took in the child's tea set and dolls. There was a chessboard that appeared to be left amid a game and a stack of well-worn books on a wooden table by the deep window seat. Struck by the feel of the space, it was unlike the parlors of other ladies he had met. He could feel the warmth of the family that spent time here, wondering if he had misjudged Hawthorne all those years ago. Perhaps he had made Lily happy if her son's home and life were any indication. The clearing of a feminine throat behind him pulled his attention, and he turned to find her in the doorway.

"I must apologize for my abrupt departure. You startled me and then..." her words dropped away as she motioned toward her fresh gown. He drank in the sight of her, taking a deep breath to steady his heart. It baffled him how she could still affect him in such a way after so many years. She stepped into the room, approaching him slowly as her gaze seemed to travel over him as well.

"You look as lovely as ever Lily, ur, um... Your Grace," he corrected himself. She looked away for a moment. Could she be as affected as him?

"You have done well for yourself if my son is to be believed. He has high praise for your business sense." The silence stretched out for a moment as Noah attempted to gather his thoughts, unsure of how to move past the awkwardness they were both feeling. An insane desire to kiss her entered his mind, but he quickly pushed it away.

"Andrew is a fine young man. You must be proud. Kind of him to assist Minerva as he does. You have done a fine job raising him." She turned, walking toward the window, keeping her back to him as she watched her son and his family with the others.

"You should not praise me, he became the man he is despite myself and his father I am afraid." Her head bowed. He wanted nothing more than to comfort her, hearing the sadness in her voice. So it had been as he feared.

"Was it so awful for you?" he asked, already knowing the answer that was never spoken. He watched as her shoulders straightened. Turning to him, he saw the tears she fought shining in her eyes.

"I... I should allow you to return to the garden. It was good to see you, Noah." She moved toward the door, but he took hold of her arm.

"Lily, please, I... Won't you join us?" Shaking her head, she pulled from his grasp and left the room. He remained there for several moments, unsure of what to do. Every fiber of his being wished to go after her, yet he knew if he pushed, she would only shut him out. She was a proud and stubborn woman, that much he remembered. Best to allow her some time. Finally, he returned to the garden, knowing there would be questions to answer.

Chapter eleven

Andrew sought his mother out once their guests had departed, finding her in the sitting room upstairs with a book in her lap. She stared out the window into the garden, not noticing as he entered. Unsure how to begin, he sat in the wing back chair across from her and waited. When she finally looked at him, her expression was unreadable. He had never seen her flustered in the way he had today, and he found it unnerving.

"Reeves said the two of you knew one another in your youth. I gather there is a story there," he said with a wry smile. Her eyes shuttered in that way of hers. He had seen it often as a boy when he attempted to engage her, wanting desperately to have her attention the way she was with Jonathan.

"It is the past and nothing you need concern yourself with." Picking up her book, she silently announced the subject was not up for discussion. Andrew was having none of it.

"Seeing as I plan to do business with this man, I would prefer to know if there will be some difficulty. Who is he to you, Mother?" Lillian set her book aside as an annoyed expression crossed her face.

"His father worked for my father and we grew up together until he went off to the army. It simply surprised me to see him after all of this time. Now if you will excuse me, I would like to freshen up before dinner." She rose, leaving him with a head full of questions. There was something in her eyes he had never seen before... fear.

Andrew entered their bedchamber and found his wife napping peacefully on the bed. Quietly, he stepped toward her and placed a blanket over her. He fought the desire to kiss her, not wanting to disturb her rest. She had been uncomfortable, sleep eluding her much of the night as she attempted to find a comfortable position. Many nights he woke to find her gone, usually curled up in the window seat where she had retreated, not wishing to disturb him.

He closed the door softly behind him and went to his study to begin work on the proposal he wished to present to Noah Reeves. His brother-in-law would arrive tomorrow and he was excited to speak to him about his ideas to work with Reeves on expansion into India. He heard Charlotte and Rachel running through the hallway, their footsteps echoing as they squealed and argued.

"Both of you come in here," he called. The pair came in slowly, noting his tone. "Stay down here for a bit, please. Your mamma is sleeping and I don't want her disturbed." Little eyes looked up at him, concerned.

"Is she alright Pappa?" Charlotte asked. He could see the memory of her mother's death four years ago weighing on her as she spoke, and he knelt down to reassure his daughters.

"She is tired. It has been difficult for her to sleep, but it will all be worth it when the baby arrives. Nothing to worry yourselves over."

"Could we visit her later? I made a picture for her." Rachel chimed in. Laura was the only mother she really knew. Patricia had been absent most of their lives. She had not been interested in being a mother; a role Laura cherished. The girls and any others that came along would never know the loneliness that he and his siblings suffered at his parents' indifference.

"She would love nothing more. Go on and play in the garden. I will be with you soon." He tapped his cheek and each taking the hint, gave him a quick peck before running off.

He thought of his mother again and her odd behavior this morning. Their interactions remained strained, but thanks to his wife, there was at least a dialogue between them. He marveled every day at Laura's ability to forgive the woman and that had treated her with such disrespect, even offering her money as though she were a common light skirt in search of a wealthy patron. Her refusal of the offer and her temerity in the face of her thieving uncle's treatment of her had swayed his stoic mother. The revelation that she knew Mary Parsons, Laura's mother, passed with no further comment. She had passed her coveted signet ring on to his wife as a sign of good faith that she would not stand in the way of his happiness.

He found himself curious about his mother's past with her ties to Laura's family and now this man he wished to approach about joining in his next shipping venture. His Aunt Thea had once said that his mother had her reasons for her icy demeanor; something about her father selling her off and his father's poor treatment of her. Lord knew Joseph Stanhope had been no saint, spending his time in London with various mistresses. He could not fathom doing such a thing to his wife. Unfortunately, it was far too common in London society. The very reason he avoided it as much as possible.

The sound of rapid footsteps approaching his office had him looking up from his work. "Your Grace," Claudia said frantically. "You must come quick, sir." She ran for the steps without another word. He knew the girl was not one to fuss unnecessarily and quickly followed, calling out to her retreating form.

"What is it, is it Laura?" She turned when she reached the top of the steps as a cry from the direction of their chamber echoed off the white paneled walls. He was running now, passing the small maid.

96

Laura doubled over, rocking as she held her belly. There was blood pooling on the carpet beneath her feet as she cried, strands of her auburn hair sticking to her damp cheeks.

She looked up, reaching out a hand, "Andrew, something's wrong, aargh." She crumpled toward the floor and he reached her in time to stop her head from striking the floor.

"I've sent for the doctor, Your Grace," Ian said as he entered the room and assisted him in placing Laura back on the bed. She was so pale, just like Patricia when she... No. He shook the memory away. He would not lose her. This was different. Patricia had been attempting to rid herself of another man's bastard when she died. She had been as weak in body as was in her morals. Laura was a strong woman, stronger than any he had ever known.

Word spread quickly in the house, and the staff was bustling about doing what they could to assist. They all adored Laura and many worried faces passed by the door, hoping for word. Moira and Maggie had arrived quickly from the kitchen with linens, hot water and broth. His wife had brought Moira to his household before they wed, wishing to assist her friend who was being beaten by the so-called gentleman that had been keeping her. They had remained close, sitting at the table in the kitchen along with Maggie, who had already worked for him.

He thought of the day he realized Laura had been working in his kitchen rather than asking for funds to assist Minerva and the orphans they cared for. Damn stubborn woman, Be stubborn for me now and fight. It felt as though days had passed until Dr Shaw and Grace arrived from the village. The pair ordered everyone from the room, including himself, though he refused; that was, until Grace forced him out physically. "Out wit ye. Or must ye be tossed out by a woman?" He raised his hands in surrender, taking one last look over the formidable woman's shoulder at his wife. Grace's eyes softened slightly when she saw his concern. "Go on, we 'ave 'er. Give Bram a moment te see what's what then ye may return."

She placed a hand on his arm and gently but firmly pulled him through the door before returning to assist her husband. He paced the hall, his hands running through his hair as he waited for news. His mother approached along with his sister, clasping hands, worry etched on their faces. "The girls?" he asked, looking at Julia.

"I took them to the nursery. Miss Evans is keeping them distracted, so they are unaware. How is she?" Julia and Laura were like sisters now, and he knew this was difficult for all of them.

"The doctor is here. That's all I know." His mother remained quiet, taking a seat that Ian, his footman, had brought for them. She reached out and took his hand, brushing her thumb over his knuckles in an uncommon gesture of support. He had little time to think on the odd sensation of his mother's touch as the door opened and Dr. Shaw emerged, glasses in hand as he absently cleaned them with the tail of his waistcoat. Looking into the many anxious faces, he maneuvered Andrew to one of the wooden chairs. He heard it creak under his weight as he slumped, preparing for terrible news. "Is she…"

Shaw knelt down, placing a hand on his shoulder. "She lives, but there is a great deal of blood. I fear the placenta has detached. I will not know the damage until I deliver the baby." Andrew's head dropped into his hands for a moment. Pushing back his hair, he looked at the man before him.

98

"You need to save her. Whatever you need, tell me, please."

"Laura wishes to speak to you," he said, motioning for Andrew to follow. He felt eyes on him as he rose slowly, then a hand grasped his arm. His mother held a handkerchief up, dabbing at his face, then combing his hair down with her fingers.

"Hold yourself together. Be strong for the both of you...it is all you can do." She gave him a weak smile of encouragement, then pushed him toward the door that now stood ajar.

Grace was wiping Laura's brow with a damp cloth as she fought not to cry out at the pain he knew she was experiencing. Taking her hand, he sat beside her on the bed and pulled her close. She was shivering and her gown was damp as he cradled her, looking into those warm green eyes, the gold less visible as her vision seemed to cloud.

"I'm sorry, Andrew," she said weakly.

"Shhh, my darling, there is nothing to be sorry for. Only a little trouble that we will overcome together; though I am afraid you will bear the greater burden for now." He kissed her damp brow, brushing the hair back and over her shoulder. Dr. Shaw and Grace stepped away, allowing them a moment to speak in private. She clutched his hand as her eyes closed with the next pain.

When it subsided, she reached up and caressed his cheek, but her hand dropped away, too weak from loss of blood to even hold her head up from the pillows stacked behind her.

"You must let Shaw take the baby if it is to survive. It is what I wish," she whispered. His mind raced in confusion at her words.

"What do you mean, I don't understand?" Laura looked to the corner where Dr. Shaw stood conferring with his wife. Stepping toward them, he looked gravely at Laura and then at Andrew.

"If I make an incision, I can remove the baby, but I must do it now. If the placenta has ruptured, the child is dying. But I have explained to Laura that it is very possible she will not survive, given the blood loss she has suffered. She has allowed this for the sake of your child." He placed a hand on Andrew's shoulder, but he pushed it away, turning his gaze to his wife.

"No, I will not allow you to decide this. You cannot leave me, I forbid it." Tears obscured his vision as he pleaded with her, but she would not change her mind.

"You will lose them both if I do not act now Andrew, it is time." Strong hands pulled him back, Ian and Henderson fighting to drag him from the room as he watched Shaw lay out the instruments he needed.

"No." With all his strength, he pulled from their hold and knelt by his wife, holding her face, kissing her. "I will not leave you, we will do this together." He grasped her small hand in his. "Feel this, my strength is yours, take it all." She gave him a weak smile, then nodded to the doctor.

There was a rustling on the other side of the bed, but he would not look away from Laura's beautiful face. A hand placed a thick strip of leather in her mouth and she bit down, preparing herself for what was to come. Someone pulled her other hand from his and he looked up to protest, seeing his mother grasping it to her chest.

"Mary would want you to fight, my dear. She is here with you. Can you feel her?" Laura closed her eyes, taking a deep breath as her

100

body seemed to relax for the first time in hours. Looking at his mother, she nodded weakly.

"I feel her."

Chapter twelve

Lillian sat beside her son as tears stained his cheeks. He held his son close, rocking slowly as the room remained eerily quiet despite the many people that sat around them. Minerva and Ginny had arrived, brought by Noah, who now stood behind his weeping aunt with his hand on her shoulder. She could feel his gaze light upon her from time to time, but she had no time to think about his presence now. Her son needed her.

Laura had been brave, barely crying out as Dr. Shaw made the cut needed to save this precious little boy. She had not lied to the girl. She could feel Mary's powerful presence in the room as her daughter willingly sacrificed herself to save Andrew's child. Maids and footmen moved silently through the room, their own grief clear as they brought tea. Julia moved forward, offering to take the baby from her brother, but he held the boy tighter as though he was life itself. Lillian gave her daughter a reassuring nod. "Why don't you fix him some tea, plenty of sugar…"

"I want nothing. Why can't you let me be as you always have before?" he snapped. Lillian saw Noah step toward them, but she waved him away. Harsh words would not deter her. Life had made her impervious.

"You need your strength if you intend to keep holding your son, and what of your daughters? They all need you more than ever. You would not abandon them now, would you?" She saw more tears as he shook his head.

"I am s-sorry, both of you, I…" Julia wrapped an arm around her brother, devastation in her eyes. Lillian knew he had been a source of strength for her youngest child, always there for the girl as she had not been. It was likely why he was the father he was, so she supposed oddly she could take some credit there, though it gave her no sense of pride. She felt Andrew shift, suddenly coming to his feet, and looked up to find Dr. Shaw in the parlor's doorway. Everyone stood, eager to hear any news, yet dreading what might come. The man's greying hair stood on end, his bloodied shirt untucked as he came to Andrew.

"I have done all I can. It is in God's hands now. She is not conscious, which is likely a blessing with all she has endured. If you wish to see her, that is fine, but I will not have her disturbed. Only Andrew for now," he said to the others in the room. He led her son upstairs, the baby still in his arms. Julia leaned into her as tears flowed freely for both of them. She rubbed her daughter's back slowly, attempting in her clumsy way to offer comfort.

"She is alive. Now we must do all we can to see that she remains so." She pulled back and looked into Julia's eyes, so like her own. "We must be strong for all of them. Where are the girls?"

"Still in the nursery but they know something is wrong with all these people arriving."

"Then we must go reassure them." Taking her daughter's hand, they moved toward the stairs before she stopped and addressed the others. Please have some tea. I believe I may speak for His Grace in saying that you are more than welcome to remain here as you are her family. Noah was at her side without a word, placing a hand on her arm with a gentle squeeze. She nodded, acknowledging his presence, then went to see her granddaughters.

103

The two of them sat on the rug in front of the fireplace, Charlotte holding her little sister. "Is Momma going to heaven like our mother?" Rachel asked, her voice from the tears that threatened.

"All will be well, you'll see," Charlotte said in a reassuring voice that belied her nine years. Lillian was struck by the poise she saw in one so young. Of course, she had always cared for her sister. Julia sat beside them, pulling their small bodies into a fierce hug as Lillian took the chair beside them. Their eyes took her in, looking for any sign of what was happening in the house, so she wasted no time speaking.

"You have a brother." Those eyes now lit with joy as they both jumped up, ready to run down the hall looking for their father. Julia took them by the shoulders, sitting them back down so Lillian could continue. Taking a deep breath, she went on, "Laura had some difficulty and will need time to heal, so you must do your best to be quiet and respectful."

"May we see her?" Charlotte asked, her blue eyes seeming to read the concern in her own.

"She is sleeping and your father is with her now. I am certain he will come for you when it is time to see her." Someone cleared their throat in the doorway and they all turned to find Minerva and Noah.

"I think we should pick a nice bouquet for her. Will you assist me?" Minerva said, holding out her hands to them. The girls ran to her without hesitation. Lillian knew they saw the woman as a grandmother and were always comfortable in Minerva's presence, whereas they remained wary of her. The years of absence from their lives and her own harsh criticism of their father over the years stood between them.

104

"Would you care to join us for some air, ladies?" Noah asked, offering his arm to her and then Julia, who gladly took it.

"You were very kind to bring your aunt and Ginny here so quickly," Julia said as they walked into the waning sunlight.

"I couldn't have them driving themselves, upset as they were. Besides, even in our brief acquaintance, I think the world of your brother and his wife. Rare people." Julia nodded in agreement.

"I fear Andrew will be lost if Laura…" Julia could not finish the thought as she brushed a tear away. Noah stopped, taking her hand, "Now, now. Only good thoughts. She seems a strong young lady, and the love is clear between them. That will hold her here. A love such as that is rare indeed." He glanced at Lillian and she felt an odd thrill wash down her spine at those grey eyes that were once so familiar. She found an odd comfort in his presence despite the many years apart. He had been her friend, and those had been in short supply over the years since they parted. Julia walked closer to the girls, leaving them alone for the first time since their conversation in the parlor. Somehow that seemed like days ago, though it had only been one.

Lillian stepped away, unable to look directly into his eyes. She realized he must have mistaken this as discomfort when he spoke, "I understand if you wish me to go, I can return tomorrow for my aunt if my presence is difficult for you."

"No, please," she paused, attempting to gather herself. "I am glad to have you here. It is a fine thing to have a friend, if you are willing."

"I never stopped being your friend Lily." She smiled at the name, one only he called her. "I suppose I should not be so familiar, Your Grace…"

"No please, we need not be so formal." She sighed heavily, and he tilted his head to look at her.

"Are you unwell? I realize this has been a terrible day. Perhaps you would rather rest?" She shook her head, taking his arm and leading them toward the three girls gathering peonies for Laura.

"Those are her favorite. I have seen Andrew bring her a bouquet on many occasions." Noah led her to a stone bench and sat beside her, keeping her arm in his, and she welcomed the warmth of his presence. As he watched the girls, she took a moment to look at him. His features were sharper than she remembered, no longer any boyish softness. Silver graced his temples, though his hair was still mostly the same dark blonde as it had been. He moved with purpose without the loose jointed gait of youth, but it had been his eyes that seemed to have changed the most.

His grey eyes, always so full of joy and mischief, were now hardened with a hint of sadness. She recalled his telling her about his time in India and the difficulties in Scotland and she wondered what other sorrows he had witnessed in the passing years.

"How long did you remain in the army?" she finally asked. He turned back to her, his eyes seeming to take her in for the first time.

"I have been a civilian for a year now, since we finally put an end to Napoleon's advances at Waterloo." Lillian drew in a breath. She had heard stories of the horrors that were witnessed there, and it pained her to think of him there.

"I am happy to see you remain in one piece then."

"Despite the best efforts of several Frenchmen, yes, I am. Though they got a few licks in." At her pained expression, he patted her hand. "A few stitches here and there is all." They sat in silence for several moments, neither certain how to reach across the chasm of time that spread out between them. Rachel ran up to them, pulling herself up to sit beside Noah, who smiled down at her. "What do you have there?" he asked as she held the large pink bloom to his face.

"Aren't they pretty? My Mama likes them the best.

"I can see why, they are lovely." He took the blossom and tucked it behind her ear. "There now, it is even prettier. Rachel giggled at his light touch and gave him a broad smile.

"I like you. Will you stay with Granny Minerva forever?" Noah laughed and Lillian could not help but smile.

"I shall stay until she is tired of me if it is your wish." The child nodded, then looked at Lillian as she noted her arm in his.

"Do you know my grandmother?"

"I knew her when she was a little girl like you." Rachel seemed stunned by this revelation.

"You were little?" she asked, her hazel eyes the size of saucers.

"We all were children once, even your father." This brought about several questions, which Lillian answered patiently as Noah chuckled beside her. Lillian realized she had never done this with her own children, sat and spoke to them of the past, or anything else and a sense of loss spread over her. She had not only deprived them, but herself. Glancing at the man beside her, she wondered if things would have been different, if she would have been different, if she had followed her heart as Mary had.

107

Her mind filled with questions as she wondered about the life Noah had led. Had he married, had children? There had been no mention of a family, but perhaps he did not feel comfortable speaking of them with her. Though he had told Rachel he would stay... of course, those were kind words spoken to a child. She could read nothing into them.

The flowers gathered, they all returned to the house, Julia and the girls chatting as Lillian and Noah walked behind them in companionable silence. When they entered the parlor, they found Minerva and her maid, Ginny, speaking to Dr. Shaw's wife Grace. The nurse gave Lillian a sour look that she quickly returned to the woman. The two had taken an instant dislike to one another when Lillian had sought Laura at the infirmary. Granted, she had been attempting to intimidate the girl away from her son, but tossing a slop bucket on her and ruining her gown and slippers was uncalled for.

Putting her feelings aside for a moment, she addressed the woman with as much respect as she could muster. "I wish to thank you and your husband for coming to our aid so quickly. Has there been any change?" Grace stood, dropping a small curtsey, though Lillian could see it nearly killed the woman to do so.

"We'd do anythin' fer Miss Laura, being such a fine lady and friend as she is." Lillian flinched slightly at the veiled barb, knowing full well Grace did not think *her* much of a lady. "She's sleepin', been tryin' te rouse her, make 'er drink some beef tea but she ain't stirred a hair."

"Is my son still with her?" she asked, wondering if he still clung to his child as well. They would need to find a wet nurse for him, as his mother would need all of her strength to heal.

Before Grace could answer, Andrew appeared in the doorway, still holding his son.

"Give us the lad now, take some tea while I see te this angel. Ian arrived with a nurse just now. Child needs te eat as does 'is father." Lillian breathed a sigh of relief as Andrew finally released his child and sat heavily in one of the larger chairs that accommodated his frame. His eyes were red, his lids drooping, though he continued to fight the sleep he desperately needed. His hair fell in heavy waves over his forehead as he rubbed a hand over his face.

She watched him, unsure what to do, then saw Noah hand him a glass, the amber liquid most likely scotch. He sat beside her son, sipping his own drink in silence, and she noted Andrew's eyes closing as his body relaxed. Julia placed a blanket over him, not wishing to wake him despite being in a chair. Henderson came in and bent to Lillian's ear. "A coach is approaching, likely Mr. Parsons."

She jumped up and went to the foyer, closing the doors softly behind her, wishing her son to continue sleeping. They had forgotten Laura's brother was to arrive today with all the commotion. She hurried outside with Henderson, Julia coming out a moment later, realizing what was happening. Good, Lillian thought. Julia would be better able to keep him calm. Robert Parsons emerged from his fine carriage with a broad smile. "Quite the welcome. Has my sister delivered then?" His smile faltered as he took in the expressions that greeted him. "Dear God," he said in a strained tone. He took off

109

toward the door, but Henderson stopped him, pleading with him to wait as he told Parsons that his sister lived. With a relieved sigh, he stopped and looked at Julia, who had her arms wrapped around her chest. "There is still something wrong, isn't there? Tell me, please." Julia touched his arm, gently pulling him into an embrace.

"It was a difficult birth. Dr. Shaw had to remove the baby by, by…" Lillian stepped forward.

"Dr, Shaw had to cut her to remove the baby. She is weak but alive." She could see the anger burning in his eyes.

"Of course you people allowed him to butcher my sister for your precious heir," he spat out as he pushed toward the door again. Julia reached him first.

"It was not as you say. My brother fought the idea, but Laura insisted. Dr. Shaw assured us we would have lost them both had he not taken those steps." Parsons seemed to stagger as Julia stumbled, attempting to keep him upright. "Laura and the baby are alive. We must pray for them now and for my brother." At the mention of Andrew, Parsons pulled himself up.

"Where is he?"

"Blessedly, he has succumbed to sleep. He stayed with her through all of it, then held their son, unwilling to rest or eat until he knew Laura was alive. Poor dear fell asleep in the parlor and we do not wish to wake him." Parsons nodded, then embraced Julia again.

"I know this is difficult for you as well. We both love them very much," he said as he continued to hold her. Lillian finally cleared her throat, not at all comfortable with the sight of her daughter in the young man's arms.

"Perhaps we should all go inside and allow Mr. Parsons to see his sister." After Henderson took his coat, Lillian led Robert upstairs. Candles burned in the lamps now that the sun had set and the house felt cold and empty without the laughter of Charlotte and Rachel preparing for bed. Andrew would usually chase them up the stairs, growling like a vicious beast as they squealed. Instead, he slept fitfully in a chair as the woman he loved fought for her life. It all seemed so unfair. She had been blessed with three children so easily, though there was nothing but coldness between them. Her son did not deserve the sadness that permeated his home now.

She heard a soft cry from down the hall as the nurse saw to her grandson. Robert Parsons turned to the sound, standing still for a moment. "You have a nephew," Lillian said, placing a hand on his arm. "Dr. Shaw assures us he suffered no ill effects from the birth. He is strong like your sister." Parsons gave her an odd look. She knew he was aware of the difficulties she had caused, but she hoped she could make amends. "I am certain your mother and father were at her side through it." The young man nodded with a lift of the corner of his mouth.

"Yes, they will always be with us."

She opened the door for him, seeing Grace seated by the bed, holding her hand. At sight of Robert, the woman stood, allowing him to sit with her in private. The two women now stood in the hallway silently. Grace had her arms crossed over her chest, giving Lillian a hard stare before she spoke. "Ye and I have no love betwixt us and ye were mistaken in yer harsh treatment of that dear girl. All that said, ye stood by 'er and yer son when many a lady would 'ave fainted dead away. I kin respect that." Lillian nodded.

"I respect your strong affection for Laura and I can only hope that I might earn her forgiveness in time." Grace gave her a nod of approval.

"Isn't in the girl te hold harsh feelings. I'll be wantin' some tea, might I get some for ye?" Lillian shook her head, but thanked the woman for her kindness. It was a start, she thought wryly as Grace walked away down the stairs.

Chapter thirteen

Noah sat quietly in the parlor, the scotch in his hand barely touched as he watched over Lily's son. His aunt sat vigil with Laura now that her brother had emerged from her chamber. The doctor and his wife had gone back to town to rest and see to their other patients at the village infirmary. Minerva told him earlier of the courtship between her friend and the young duke and the attempts made by Lily to come between them.

It was difficult to reconcile the girl he knew with the woman she had become. The trappings of nobility had meant little to her during their time together, but he would have to admit to seeing the change beginning when the Duke of Hawthorne had entered her life. Learning of their betrothal had torn out his heart, and he had buried himself in his life as a soldier. He volunteered for dangerous postings in the ensuing years of the war with Napoleon's forces, even infiltrating the enemy camps to gather intelligence.

Andrew moaned beside him, the sound agonizing like those he had heard on battlefields after the cannons were silent. The man was fighting his own war now, attempting to hold body and soul together while the woman he loved suffered. To stay in the room as the doctor cut her open was likely worse than seeing his comrades felled in battle. He could see the deep affection these people held for the duke and duchess, and he wondered what it would have been like to have Andrew as his own son.

There had been no children for him, only Claudia. Her sweet smile had calmed the screams of battle that still haunted his dreams. She would hold him until his heartbeat slowed, and the nightmares faded enough to allow sleep to take him again. Now faced with Lily, the woman he had loved all his life, he felt a pang of guilt. He had never given Claudia his whole heart, as part of it would always belong to Lily.

He was to return to London tomorrow but sent word to her he would be detained on business for his aunt for at least another sennight. The lie made him ashamed as he called to mind her honey blond curls and warm brown eyes, the way she smiled when he was with her. He reminded himself that Lily was a dear friend in need of his support in a difficult time, nothing more. Yet his heart knew it for the lie that it was when she entered the room to check on her son.

He watched as she approached, eyes on his sleeping form filled with concern, but there was a hesitancy about her he had never seen in his own mother when he was ill or in pain. Lily seemed unsure and Noah could see how it pained her. It made him want to take her in his arms and kiss away her tears and promise her all would be well, that he would see to it, but it was not his place. She was not his, and another woman waited for him in London.

Lily turned her gaze to him, an eyebrow raised in question. "Has he woken at all?" she asked.

"No, though he has been fitful. Poor lad is done in." She gave a light chuckle.

"You sound like your father." Her face shadowed slightly. "I was sorry to hear of his passing and that of your mother. They were good people." She took a seat beside him after adjusting the blanket over Andrew's sleeping form.

"Thank you, I know they thought the world of you." She seemed about to comment, but closed her lips firmly. She was still beautiful beneath the stoic demeanor she seemed to wear like a cloak of protection. When he looked, he could still see that light in her lovely blue eyes, though dimmed by the weight of the life she had lived.

"It pains me to think yours was an unhappy life, Lily. You deserved better."

"Did I? I made choices and I must live with them." She looked at her son again. "I was a terrible mother, especially to Andrew. He tried so desperately to please me, but my entire focus was on Jonathan." Noah tilted his head, uncertain who she was speaking of. Had she taken a lover that kept her away from home? The pang of jealousy took him by surprise, and he pulled back from her. Seeing his confusion, she went on, "He was my eldest son. Such a beautiful boy, hair like mine, with soft features. I was certain he was the one man that would love me unconditionally and when he was born, Joseph was more attentive. Selfishly I clung to him, neglecting my responsibility to Andrew and then Julia as their father became distant again."

Her gaze clouded as though lost in the memory and he watched her, placing his hand over hers gently, glorying in the contact. Her skin was soft and warm beneath his touch, and he stroked the back of her hand in slow circles. He could see her chest rise and fall more rapidly as she seemed to respond to his touch. Then sadness filled her eyes, and she pulled away, standing and walking across the room to pour herself a sherry. She drank it in one go, and he almost laughed at her unladylike behavior.

"What happened to Jonathan?" he finally asked. She filled her glass again before returning, this time sitting in a chair across from him. The distance bothered him, but he dared not move as she spoke.

"It was such a waste. He died from a gunshot he suffered in a duel. I had chosen a lovely girl for him to marry, but he was far more like his father than I cared to admit. He continued to pursue a married woman. Her husband called him out and Andrew stood as his second." She took another deep drink of her sherry. "I blamed him for not stopping his brother. Of course, the lord himself would not have stopped him, but I was so angry. I had placed all my hopes in Jonathan, groomed him to be a better man than his father, all the while dismissing Andrew as just a spare as his father called him."

"It is not ours to dictate who our children become, Lily. They must follow their own path." She searched his face now, and he knew her question before she could ask.

"No, I have no children." He could not bring himself to speak of Claudia at this moment, though he knew he should. Instead, he lifted her hand, kissing it lightly as their eyes met and held for a long moment. He felt the familiar pull toward her as he leaned in, then Andrew woke with a start. Lillian quickly went to her son, smoothing the hair back from his brow.

"How long...is Laura still...I must see her." Lily placed her hands on his shoulders, pressing him back into his seat.

"She is asleep. Minerva and Ginny are sitting with her. Her brother arrived a few hours ago."

"I didn't wish to sleep. I should be with her. Oh God, the girls, I haven't spoken to them." His eyes were wild and Noah could feel his pain from across the room.

"Julia and I have spoken to the girls, and they have eaten and we tucked them into bed. Now that you have had some sleep, we should find you some dinner." He tried to argue, but she leveled a stern look at him. "You will be no good to anyone if you do not care for yourself. Everyone is where they need to be. Now sit while I speak to the cook. Mr. Reeves, please see that my son remains in this room." He nodded with a smile as she left the room, her son now staring at him.

"I am afraid events have kept us from becoming better acquainted with Mr. Reeve. I apologize for my behavior." Noah raised a hand, stopping him.

"There is no need and please call me Noah, may I have leave to continue using your christian name as well?"

"Of course. As you are a relation of Minerva's that makes us family." Noah could see the stress in the way Andrew held his shoulders and the set of his jaw and was well aware there was only one thing to be done.

"Why don't you look in on your daughters and then sit with your wife. I will see that they send your dinner upstairs and then see if I can persuade your mother to retire." Andrew ran his hand through his disheveled hair, then gave Noah a nod.

"I hope my mother does not give you a scolding."

"Not to worry, I have had experience in dealing with her when she is in a mood." This caused Andrew to tilt his head at him, but he made no further comment, likely eager to see his wife and daughters.

Several more minutes passed before Lily returned with a tray. Noticing her son's absence, she turned on Noah. "I thought I told you to keep him here." Her eyes blazed, and he stood, taking the tray away from her before she used it as a weapon.

"He needed to see his children and look in on his wife. I said I would have his meal sent to their chamber." Before she could retort, he took her hands in his with a gentle squeeze. "One look at him and I could see he would not have eaten a bite until he knew his family was safe. You must trust me in this." Grudgingly, she nodded as her shoulders slumped and fatigue settled on her features. "Now it is time to see you settled in your bed."

Her head immediately lifted, and he smirked at her appalled expression. "For heaven's sake, Lily. I am not making advances. I simply mean you need to take your own rest. Everyone has been seen to, as you yourself said. Take this opportunity to rest. Your son will need you tomorrow." He lifted the tray and motioned toward the stairs following in her wake. When they reached her door, he paused, setting the tray down and turning to her.

"You say that you have regrets about your children. There is still time to repair that. As long as you have breath in your body, there is time. I am sorry about the loss of your eldest son, but there is nothing to be done for that. Sleep tonight and in the morning continue to assist Andrew. He sees your effort, and it is making a difference. I can see it." It surprised him when she rose on her toes and kissed his cheek lightly.

"Thank you Noah. Henderson will show you to a room when you are ready."

"Good night, my little Lily," he said with a mischievous smile. She entered the room and turned to close the door, but before it closed fully, he heard her give a little huff and the door clicked shut.

Lillian sat on the edge of the bed and waited for the maid to finish fussing about the room. Once the girl left, she let out the breath she felt as if she had held the entire day. It would be a lie to say she was not glad of Noah's presence. It was odd that he still calmed her spirit after all these years, yet one look and one touch and she was young again with her future laid out before her. Except it was a lie. She looked in the mirror by the window and saw an old woman staring back at her. There were silver strands woven through the chestnut locks that were neatly plaited for the night. The braid was still thick as it hung over her shoulder against the white of her nightgown. She ran her hands over her body, still lean even after three children, although the skin had stretched, leaving the scars of motherhood.

She knew he had scars too, but would he find her repulsive? She shook away the ridiculous thought. They were friends, no more. He said he had no children. Perhaps he still had feelings for her. She was certain he was about to kiss her before Andrew woke. That thought sobered her muddled mind. As a mother, she had no right to be thinking of such things while her child was suffering. She was being ridiculous. She was no longer some chit looking for a husband.

Her life was as it should be. She had the wealth and respect that befit her station. A place in society she had fought hard for. She had paid a heavy price, but there was no turning back the clock. With that thought, she finally climbed into bed, exhaustion overtaking her. Dreams quickly came, images of Noah with a small boy on his knee. The child laughed as his father bounced him. Lillian, with the soft bloom of youth in her cheeks and holding another child, leaned over and kissed Noah's soft lips and her heart seemed to take flight.

The scene changed to one of darkness except for the light of a single candle as Noah rose over her in their bed, his caress intoxicating as he loved her. "My sweet Lily," he whispered in her ear as her hands moved over his muscled back. A sigh of pleasure escaped her lips as he kissed her deeply. Then light invaded the room. She fought to hold on to the dream, but the sound of china rattling pulled her the rest of the way to wakefulness. She quelled the desire to snap at the girl that had disturbed her, sitting up as the maid arranged pillows behind her back.

"Is my son awake?" she asked as the events of yesterday re-entered her mind.

"Yes Your Grace, he is taking breakfast with the young ladies in the nursery." She was pleased to hear this. The girls were a much needed anchor for him.

"I would like to dress now. It will be a busy day, I am certain, and it is best I get started." The maid, what was her name? Ruth, that was it. She knew she must acquaint herself with the staff if she was to remain. When she was ready, she thanked the girl as Laura always did, garnering a surprised look from the girl. Ignoring this, she went to the nursery where she found Charlotte and Rachel chatting away as they admired their new brother sleeping in Andrew's arms.

Lillian was pleased to note the plate before him was nearly empty. "I see you have met your brother. Does he pass inspection?" The little family turned to her and her son gave her a weak smile. He still looked drawn, but he was trying for the children.

"Would you like to hold him, Mother?" He asked, rising to hand her the small bundle. She marveled at the tiny face, so peaceful. He had a dusting of reddish dark hair and she wondered if he would look like Andrew as he grew.

"Isn't he sweet, Grandmother?" Charlotte asked as Rachel moved closer to gaze at the baby.

"Charlotte says I can't be a baby anymore. It's not fair. I still feel like a baby." Andrew scooped her up, kissing her freckled nose.

"You will always be my baby, as will you," he said, snatching Charlotte up with his other arm. The three of them looked down at the recent addition, his sisters' eyes filled with wonder.

"What is his name?" Lillian asked. "We can not go on calling him the baby forever." Andrew set the girls down and let out a breath.

"I will wait for Laura to decide." Lillian's heart lurched as she held back the words that she might not wake. It was a possibility, but she did not wish to frighten the girls. The nurse came forward as the boy squirmed and fuss.

"Time for his breakfast," the woman said with a nurturing smile. Andrew's own face fell, no doubt saddened that his wife could not take their son to her breast. He bent down, giving each child a kiss on the forehead, then reaching for the vase filled with the peonies they had picked yesterday.

"I will place these right beside Momma's bed so that she can smell them."

"Can't we please see her?" Charlotte begged.

"Maybe later when she wakes up, she needs to sleep right now." Lower lips pouting, the pair followed their governess to their classroom as Andrew watched them go. He turned to his mother with a quick nod, then he was off down the hall.

Ruth had informed her that Julia was taking breakfast with the rest of their company in the dining room, and so she ventured downstairs to join them. When she saw Noah seated beside her daughter, her dream came back in a rush, nearly making her gasp. He looked up at her, concern flooding his features. "Has something happened? Is Laura worse?" he asked.

"No, all is the same, I... I did not expect to see everyone so early," she lied. Taking a seat that Noah pulled out for her, Maggie set a plate with coddled eggs and toast in front of her. She had not realized how hungry she was until she saw the delicious food and quickly took up her fork. Conversation resumed around her as Minerva spoke of their plans to return home. Lillian schooled her features, not wishing anyone to see the sadness she felt at the thought of Noah not being close at hand.

"I am certain Lizzie has done a fine job with the little ones, but it is a great deal to ask that she continue by herself." Minerva said as she dabbed at the corner of her mouth with her napkin.

"Please come whenever you can, all of you," Julia chimed in, placing a hand on Noah's arm. Lillian smiled at the thought of her daughter feeling so comfortable with her friend and she spoke up as well.

"Yes, we would be pleased to have your company. Perhaps the children would visit Charlotte and Rachel to keep their spirits up." Julia coughed at her mother's words, then looked up, startled, but said nothing.

"Thank you, Your Grace. I am certain they would love to come." The ladies stood, as did Noah, who took his aunt's arm, stopping in front of Lillian.

"We shall return tomorrow if that is agreeable. May we pay our respects to your son and his wife before we go?," Minerva asked. Lillian gave them a nod, motioning them forward as she, too, rose. She escorted them upstairs and knocked on the door before entering.

Andrew sat on the bed, cradling Laura, who remained still and pale in his arms.

"Our guests are leaving and hoped to say goodbye." He reluctantly left his wife's side and came to the door, ushering the ladies in while Noah remained just in the doorway, speaking to Andrew quietly. Lillian stood back, allowing them all some privacy as she took in her daughter-in-laws sickly form. If she did not recover, what would it mean for her son, for the children? She had seen him after Patricia's death when he retreated into his family, his daughters' wellbeing, all that mattered, but he had not loved her.

"Laura, Laura dear, can you hear me?" Minerva's frantic voice drew her attention to the bed again. "Andrew, she is waking," the old woman called out as she motioned for him to return. Pushing past Lillian, he was at his wife's side in a heartbeat, holding her hand to his lips.

"Laura darling, open your eyes, come back to me," he pleaded as a soft groan came from her dry, cracked lips. Lillian came forward with Noah close behind as Laura attempted to move, then cried out in pain. "You have a wound. Try not to move too much... bring me some water," Andrew called out and Ginny quickly responded, pressing the glass to Laura's lips as Andrew supported her head. "Just a little more please, sweetheart," he coaxed, as fatigue overtook her. He eased her head back onto the pillow, then leaned down to touch his lips to hers.

Lillian felt tears threaten as her son tenderly looked at his wife, smoothing strands of her auburn hair behind her ear with the smile she feared never to see again. "The baby?" Laura whispered.

"We have a son, strong and beautiful like his mother." She gave him a weak smile as her eyes shifted around the room. Lillian knew what she was searching for and hastened to the nursery in search of the nurse, returning a moment later with the baby. She passed the sleeping child to Andrew so he could show him to Laura. She kissed his head, taking in his tiny features as everyone moved away, giving the couple a moment with their child.

Noah assisted his aunt and her maid into the cart, then turned to Lillian, taking her hand. "I will bring Minerva back tomorrow unless you send word that we should wait." She squeezed his hand, fighting the feeling of emptiness at his departure and unsure what to say.

"It was good to see you again, Noah," she whispered. He gave her a bright smile, gently lifting her chin with a touch of his finger.

"I will return tomorrow, I promise." His touch lingered a moment longer as warmth spread through her body. Watching as the old cart trundled down the tree-lined lane, she did not move until it was well out of sight. She drew in a shaky breath as she attempted to slow her heart and quell the desire to beg him to stay with her. She would not lower herself in such a way, no matter how desperately she wanted to.

Chapter fourteen

Noah spent the afternoon splitting firewood, making certain there was enough for several days. He knew he and his aunt would return to Merveille tomorrow and he did not want to worry about Ginny and the children being cold or unable to cook. The maid had her hands full enough without the help of Minerva. He marveled as he watched his elderly aunt with the youngest two of her brood, patiently teaching them the proper way to milk a goat.

The creatures were loudly bleating as, one by one, the children coaxed the goats to the milking stool. He was taking a break, leaning against the fence, watching the proceedings as the sun soothed his sore muscles. It had been over a year since he had put in a day of hard labor and he enjoyed the warm strain of it in his body. The life of a gentleman could make one soft quickly. Not that he was idle. He had been working as a proctor, using his contacts from his military service to negotiate deals for the purchase and transport of goods.

Hawthorne had spoken to him about working with himself and his brother-in-law in their shipping venture, which was already quite successful. Those negotiations would have to wait until the duchess was well again. It pleased him that the young man's wife had survived her ordeal and hoped to become better acquainted with the family in time. Of course, being in Lily's company again made this even more desirable.

He had come perilously close to kissing her the other night and should not tempt fate by spending more time with her, but he could not stay away. He wished to learn more about the woman she had become, perhaps even help her heal the divide between herself and her children that she had spoken of. What would their children have been like, he wondered, as he watched the young boy named John take his turn on the milking stool.

He looked down when a grey nanny goat nudged his hand, calling out loudly for a snack. He ruffled the tuft of hair atop her head before peeling a few leaves from the head of cabbage in the basket by his feet. She butted his hip again, and he held out another leaf. "Aren't you a greedy girl?" he chuckled as she continued to nudge at him. He brushed her away when she began nibbling at his waistcoat.

He returned to stacking, the pile filling in the space by the kitchen door nicely. He waited by the door when he saw his aunt toddling toward him from the barn, holding the smallest child's hand. She wore a bright smile as she looked down at the chattering girl, eyes alight with love. These children were fortunate to have her as a patron. The thought of Uncle Thomas' absence saddened him. He had been a jolly man, and he had adored his wife. That they never had children only seemed to strengthen the bond between them as they began taking in these little lost souls.

"My, you have been hard at work today, my dear," his aunt said as she took in the large stack of wood. "Come in and have a drink, you have certainly earned it." Noah followed her and the children and enjoyed a lunch of bread, cheese and apples with a glass of cider while the children continued an animated discussion about how best to entice a goat to your side.

Listening to them, he again thought about what life would have been, had he married Lily. Knowing he would likely have difficulty keeping his hands from her, they would have many children. The thought made him laugh softly to himself. Perhaps he could entice her to take a ride with him tomorrow if all remained well with her daughter-in-law. It was always a joy to see her on horseback, her hair flying and cheeks flushed with excitement as they ran.

"Letter for you Mithter Noah," Jane said as she handed him the wax sealed note. The girl still had a bit of a lisp, though Laura had apparently been assisting her with her speech. He smiled at the pretty blond girl and he saw her cheeks pink before she dropped her gaze and scurried away. He glanced up at Ginny who was chuckling as she shook her head. "Poor little thing is besotted with you," she said as she wiped her wet hands on her apron. He glanced after the girl with a wistful look that had his aunt questioning him.

"What is in that head of yours, Noah? She is far too old for you." She swatted him with a dish towel, pulling him back from the memory of Lily at the tender age of fourteen to marry her.

"You would be correct, and far too good for the likes of an old soldier like myself." Minerva patted his shoulder as she passed his chair, then leaned down to kiss his forehead.

"A letter from London?" she asked, noting the missive in his hand. He quickly stashed it in his pocket as he commented on it being about business.

"I will be back down after I change my shirt." Retreating to his room, he opened the letter from Claudia.

My Dearest Noah,

It saddened me to receive the news that you would be detained, but I understand your need to look after your aunt. You have such a kind heart. I am keeping myself busy with the household in your absence and have made a few improvements that I hope you will approve of. This house has needed a woman's touch. I anxiously await your return, my darling. Please do not tarry too long.

127

All my love -

Claudia

Guilt weighed heavily on him as he folded the letter and tucked it into his valise. She cared deeply for him and yet he was staying away, not for his aunt, but so he could be with Lily. Claudia trusted him and wanted nothing more than to please him, yet he kept his distance. Even before he had seen Lily again, her memory caused all others to pale in his mind. He couldn't leave her, not yet. He needed more time. Perhaps his memory had made her more than she truly was, and once he saw that, he could move on. At least that was what he would tell himself.

The following afternoon, he sat beside his aunt as they made the turn to Merveille. The place was a wonder, tucked away in the trees and surrounded by lush gardens, and he felt a sense of peace wash over him just as he had the first time he rode up. There was a thrill in his belly this time that was not there before. This time, he knew Lily was here.

He looked to his side and found Minerva scrutinizing him with her pale blue eyes surrounded by a web of wrinkles. "The dowager-duchess seems to think highly of you," she said lightly as she continued to watch him. "Can't say I have ever seen the woman smile until she was in your presence."

"As I said, we got on well when we were both at Martin's Nest." He attempted to keep his voice steady, not wishing her to hear his anticipation. She narrowed her eyes further, remaining silent for a few moments as they approached the circular drive.

"It is difficult to imagine her as the carefree girl my sister spoke of all those years ago, but I suppose we all change. Some of us more than others." Noah wanted to speak to her last words, however they had arrived and the stable hand was reaching up to assist her from the cart. Once his feet were on the ground, they could hear Charlotte and Rachel as they ran forward.

The girls hugged his aunt, and it pleased him when little Rachel wrapped her arms around his leg as well. Unable to resist her sweet smile, he lifted her up with a gentle squeeze. "I have never felt so welcome as I do at this moment. Thank you, my dear," he said, giving one of her curls a little tug. "How is your mother today?" Her face fell at his question, and he felt her tense in his arms.

"We visited her last night, and she liked my picture, but she got really tired. Papa said we couldn't see her now because she is sick." He looked at his aunt, sharing a look of concern as they moved to the door, where Julia stood to greet them.

"What's happened, Julia?" Minerva asked, her voice weak.

"The fever has started. Dr. Shaw warned us it was a possibility before he left yesterday, but she seemed better when she saw the girls. We thought she would be alright." Tears shone in Julia's eyes, and Minerva embraced her tightly.

"You must not lose hope. Laura is a strong woman." She cupped a hand to the girl's cheek, smoothing away a tear with her thumb. "Perhaps Rachel and Charlotte can introduce my nephew to the swans." Quickly taking her cue, Noah reached for the girls' hands.

"That sounds like a wonderful idea." Little hands settled in his, and the three of them walked toward the pond as his aunt went to see her friend.

Lillian sat in the chair that was set outside the chamber Andrew shared with his wife. She found it odd that Laura had chosen not to have her own room, but the two of them seemed pleased with the arrangement. Even with a shared chamber, she had stumbled upon them embracing in Andrew's study, or the parlor and several times in the garden. What must it be like to enjoy the company of your spouse that much? She wondered.

As had been happening frequently of late, her thoughts turned to Noah. He said he would return today, and she was eager to see him. With Laura taking a bad turn this morning, it was becoming increasingly difficult to maintain a brave face. She noted the shadows on her son's face after an arduous night, and it pained her to see him so distraught. Though she had suggested he take one of the guest rooms, he had insisted on sleeping beside his wife. Between taking care not to jostle her and the fever during the night, she doubted he had slept at all. When she had last looked in, Andrew sat in a chair beside the bed, bathing her face with a damp cloth, attempting to cool her scalding brow.

Dr. Shaw planned to return later today, yet there was little he could do that was not already being done.

Julia came up the stairs, followed by Minerva Edwards, both looking somber. "Is Andrew with her, Mother?" Lillian nodded.

"He is worn out, but there is no reasoning with him. Perhaps you might do better." She looked to Minerva, whom her son respected, and giving a nod, the old woman knocked, then entered the room without awaiting a response. As the door opened, she could see Andrew mopping Laura's brow, speaking so softly she could only see his lips moving. Minerva lay her hands on his shoulders and his body slumped as though they held the weight of the world. Lillian could not bear to watch him break down again and so she left Julia there to sit in her chair while she went in search of Noah.

She stood in the shadow of the roses, watching as he held Rachel's hand while the two of them listened to Charlotte. Her hands moved fluidly as she told some story or other and Noah smiled down at her as Rachel clung close to his side. She hated to disrupt the scene but found herself drawn forward, calling out to the children. Rachel held out her other hand so that Lillian could walk with them and she felt at peace for the first time in the past two days.

"How is the baby doing?" Noah asked when there was a break in conversation.

"Little Jonathan is thriving, eating well and sleeping several hours at a time. The nurse is pleased."

"So he has a name now." Lillian smiled wistfully.

"When Laura was awake, they decided to name him after Andrew's brother. Jonathan Robert Stanhope."

"A fine name indeed," Noah remarked. As they moved around the edge of the pond, Lillian caught sight of a figure seated silently within the floral arch covered in pale purple wisteria. Robert Parsons' head was down, his eyes covered with one hand as his shoulders shook. He and his sister were close, and she knew this was difficult for him. Andrew would hardly allow anyone else to sit with his wife, and it was taking a toll on everyone, including her son. She would speak to him again, remind him that there were others that needed time with her.

Bending down, she pointed him out to the girls, who rushed to him. He embraced them, wiping his eyes with the back of his hand surreptitiously. The pair climbed up on the bench with him, each with an arm about his waist, and she hoped their company would soothe him. She and Noah continued on in silence until she gathered the courage to speak. "You have a way with the children. Why did you have none of your own?" He paused and she held her breath, awaiting his answer.

"I suppose, as you yourself pointed out years ago; the life of a soldier." He shrugged, turning his face away to look back at the swan as it glided across the mirrored surface of the pond.

"I feel I owe you an apology for my harsh words that day when you... spoke your heart. I was cruel to you and it was, well, I was not truthful." Noah turned to her, but said nothing, waiting for her to explain.

"I have thought of it many times since that day, how life might have changed if I..." She closed her eyes, fighting to control her turbulent emotions until he lifted her chin to look at him.

"Why did you do it Lily? Had I hurt you so terribly?" She turned away, unsure how to continue feeling ashamed of her weakness in the face of her father's insistence.

"You mustn't think that, yes I was angry at you, but that wasn't it. Look at me." She motioned to her fine gown, the pearls at her throat. "No one dares to disrespect me as they once did. I need not worry where the money will come from for the estate or the people that work there. I refused to be weak as my mother was and yet here I am, just as she was."

"I doubt anyone would mistake you for your mother," he said with a chuckle. Lillian's eyes flashed at his words.

"Of course, what man wants a woman that can think for herself. No, I was never soft and sweet, a woman that was loved for herself." She looked around her, searching for what she did not know. "I should see to things in the house. I am certain you can entertain yourself. Perhaps there is an obliging chamber maid about." She stormed off toward the house, leaving Noah staring after her.

She slammed the door of her son's study, knowing he would not need it at present. Her heart slammed in her chest as she poured a glass of scotch. Not accustomed to the harsh spirit she coughed as it burned down her throat. She swallowed the rest as her eyes watered, then spun and smashed the glass against the marble fireplace, not feeling the shard that sliced into her palm as she sunk onto the sofa.

She did not know what had come over her? One moment she was apologizing, the next she was seething. The soft look in his grey eyes had unnerved her. He could so easily take her in again and then break her heart. He had done it before, as had Joseph when Jonathan was born. Noah was wrong. She was like her mother, the desire to be loved making her weak. She must never forget that. Best to keep her distance from him from now on.

Chapter fifteen

Noah sat on the bench beside the water, uncertain of what had happened. He swore he had seen the look in her eyes, that same sweet look when she was young that said he was everything to her, then in an instant, she was pushing him away with her harsh words. He wanted to go after her, shake some sense into her, but damned if he didn't want to kiss her senseless in that moment as well.

"Mr. Reeves?" the young man asked, standing behind him. He turned to find Robert Parsons bowing to him.

"Yes, good day. I am sorry for your troubles," he said, motioning to the bench. "Please join me." Parsons sat down heavily, and Noah could see the shadows beneath his hazel eyes. He favored his sister, though he had dark hair and his eyes were more brown than green.

"My brother-in-law wrote to me about his desire to bring you on as a partner in our business. I am sorry that circumstances have impeded our discussions." He looked down at his hands, fingers locked together, likely in worry.

"There is no need to be concerned. Such things can wait until the duchess is well again." Parsons nodded, his dark brows knitted. Noah placed a hand on his shoulder, giving it a light squeeze. "You must believe she will be well. It is all any of us can do."

"We lost our mother in childbirth. Laura was only ten. After that, she cared for me and our father, cooking and cleaning. She even assisted with the business, such a head for figures. She is a marvel." A single tear slid down the young man's face and he dashed it away quickly.

"Why don't we see if we can coax Andrew to eat a bit. It sounds as though he has been sitting vigil for some time." Parsons nodded, and the pair walked back to the house. It surprised them to find Andrew descending the stairs when they came to the foyer. His clothes wrinkled and his hair in disarray, but he gave the men a nod and adjourned to his study for a drink.

"Henderson, will you have lunch brought to us? Whatever cook has prepared is fine." The butler bowed and turned toward the kitchen, pleased his master planned to eat. Entering the study, they found the maid cleaning up shards of glass by the fireplace. She held a cloth that appeared to be stained with blood.

"What on earth happened here?" the duke asked.

"Beg yer pardon, Yer Grace, a bit of an accident. Nothin' to worry o'er." She picked up the dustpan and scurried from the room as the men glanced around, but there was no sign of what had occurred. A kitchen maid entered a short time later with sandwiches, cakes, and tea, so the men ate in companionable silence. Neither Noah nor Parsons asked about the duchess, wanting Andrew to continue eating. When the dishes were cleared, Robert asked about Noah's time in the army and his connection to India.

"I am acquainted with several merchants and the harbor master, so I believe I could be of assistance to you both. As I said earlier, there is no rush. I have a few things to tie up in London before I take on another venture." He took a sip of his drink, savoring the warmth as it soothed his mood from his earlier encounter with Lily. Rising to his feet, Parsons bowed and excused himself. Noah thought he was likely taking the opportunity to sit with his sister while Andrew was being looked after. He topped off the duke's glass and sat across from him. Both men were tall and their legs stretched out before them. Noah appreciated the larger furniture the man seemed to favor.

135

They decorated the entire house with comfort in mind rather than being a display of wealth. He was certain Hawthorne Manor was a different story altogether, so he could see why the man preferred to reside here.

"I only met your father briefly, though in that time I could say you are quite a different man. I hope that does not offend you?" Andrew gave a quiet laugh.

"I take that as the greatest of compliments, I assure you." Noah looked at him over the rim of his glass.

"Were your parents happy?" Seeing Andrew raise an eyebrow as he lifted his own glass, Noah thought better of his inquiry. "Nevermind, I apologize for my rude question." Andrew continued to study him as he drank deep, then set down his glass.

"As I can see that there is some history between you and my mother, I will say this. They made each other miserable. I hardly saw them together, which was a blessing. When they were in the same residence, it was tense." He leaned forward, resting his elbows on his knees. "Would you tell me who you are to my mother?" It was Noah's turn to study the man before him.

"We were close once, friends since we were children."

"Somehow I think there was more to it than that." Noah smiled as he set aside his empty glass.

"I had hopes, but your mother's path was chosen for her." He allowed that comment to stand for a bit. "Her father was a... difficult man to go against."

"My Aunt Thea said that Martin sold her." Noah sat back in his chair and blew out a breath.

"I have no doubt. The man squandered every penny he had and expected Lily, ur, your mother, to save him from his creditors." Andrew sat for a moment longer before rising and walking to the door. Before he left, he turned to Noah, "I don't know you well, but I believe I would have rather had you as a father." As the door clicked shut, Noah thought that he would have liked to have had him as a son as well.

Andrew climbed the stairs slowly, unsure how much longer he could bear watching his beautiful wife, the light of his life, being consumed by the fever. He stopped in the nursery first and found the girls sitting by the cradle, looking down at their little brother. They giggled and fussed as he made soft cooing sounds and Andrew felt a bit of the weight lift from his soul. That was when he decided.

He carried Jonathan as Charlotte opened the door to their chamber. Rachel carried a pitcher filled with a variety of blooms from the garden, setting in on the table by Laura's head. Minerva gave Andrew a light kiss on the cheek before leaving the family alone, closing the door behind her. The dear old woman had assisted Maggie in washing Laura's hair and changing her gown. He thought hearing her family around her could help, but he did not want the girls to be frightened. They had seen their mother on her deathbed, and he had no intention of reminding them of that.

Charlotte and Rachel took turns reading from their favorite book as Andre sat beside Laura, holding their son close to her. Her chest rose and fell slowly as sweat continued to bead on her brow. Charlotte dabbed a cool cloth over Laura's face while her sister took over the reading. When his mother arrived with a tray of tea and cakes, she joined them as they ate and talked as though it were any other tea time in the family parlor.

When Jonathan fussed, his mother offered to take him to the nurse for his feeding and, to his surprise, she bent and kissed him on the head, something she had not even done when he was a boy. "I am proud of you, Andrew," she whispered. As she moved away, he reached for her arm.

"Mother... If you could go back and change things, do you think you would?" She did not pretend ignorance of his reference. She just smiled at him.

"Who is to say if I would have had you or Jonathan or Julia. That I can never regret, though you deserved a far better mother than myself." He gave her arm a squeeze.

"I think we do the best we can and sometimes we learn from our past. Sometimes our past can help us find a happy future." He gave her a knowing smile, hoping she understood the blessing within his words. When she left the room, he sat back, leaning in to kiss Laura's damp hair. He lingered a moment, then grasped her hand. It was cooler, he was certain. He let out a breath it seemed he had been holding for days... the fever had broken.

***

Despite the grey skies and torrential rain that had erupted an hour ago, the mood in the house was light and joyful. A maid was humming to herself as she picked up various items left behind by family members. Henderson, the elderly butler, smiled as he passed in the hall. Noah even heard the girls giggling down the hall. The duchess's fever had broken that afternoon and it seemed she would recover from her ordeal.

Looking out at the ever darkening sky, he knew that he and his aunt would spend the night at the manor. It would be far too treacherous to attempt the roads at this late hour, with the rain showing no sign of stopping. Noah had hoped to speak with Lily about this morning, but she had yet to appear since she ran from him in the garden. He was certain to see her at dinner, though he wished for a moment in private.

It had been an odd day for him. Lily's outburst being followed by the comments from her son. If things had been as terrible between them as Andrew insinuated, no wonder she was wary. He had meant no disrespect by his comments and so he hoped to clear up any misunderstanding.

His aunt entered the parlor with Charlotte and Rachel, their governess Miss Evans close behind. She was a quiet little thing with her simple dress and the severe way she wore her hair, but the children seemed to like her. Offering to pour the tea, she handed him a cup, barely touching his fingers. She pulled her hand back as though he had shocked her, and then he noted the blush come to her cheek. He mentally rolled his eyes, never understanding these young ladies and their desire for an older man, for that was surely what he was. He could easily be her father. She gave him a coy smile as she offered the plate of cakes, which he declined.

Minerva was smiling at him, seeming to enjoy his discomfort. Wishing to break the tension of the moment, he asked, "Has the duchess awakened?" Charlotte reached for a cake, her dark brown curls dropping over her shoulder, replied that she had taken some broth and was currently with her brother.

"Papa said he needed to wash and dress before he came down." Indeed, Noah thought. Poor man had been in the same clothes for days with a rather impressive beard taking shape at his jaw.

When Andrew finally entered the parlor, he looked much improved, even smiling at his children as they came to greet him.

"Have my little monsters been behaving?" he asked as he embraced them and Rachel gave a rather kittenish growl in reply. It relieved Noah to see him return to his happy temperament, and he noted the same change in his aunt as well. She appeared years younger as she chatted with Charlotte over her cup of tea. Now if only Lily would appear.

As though conjuring her with the thought, she entered the room in a fresh gown and went to the tea tray. When she reached out, he noticed something wrapped around her hand and without thought reached to touch it. "Whatever happened?" he asked. She quickly withdrew her hand with an airy explanation of a minor accident in the study. So that explained the glass. She was cordial but would barely meet his eye as conversation lingered around them. He watched her as he sipped his tea, eager for a time he could have her alone.

She pushed back a strand of her chestnut hair that had come loose from its knot and he longed to run a hand through it as he had when they were young. The desire to touch her grew with every moment in her presence, though thoughts of Claudia made his heart heavy. His soul cried out for the woman seated across the room, regardless of what his conscience said.

Dinner was a celebration with a variety of items laid out and the house-staff invited to eat and drink along with the family. They brought little Jonathan downstairs for everyone to have a look. Noah could see the rigid set of Lily's shoulders at sight of maids and footmen milling about the dining room. He found it odd, since she had not been above sitting with the small staff at Martin's Nest. They had been her family, though he doubted she was allowed to behave in such a relaxed manner in her husband's home.

Moving to her side as the festivities continued, he asked if he could have a moment. With a look of trepidation, she led him to the conservatory, closing the tall white doors behind her. The windows were dark as the rain continued to patter against the glass. There was a low fire burning in the hearth with several candles burning in sconces along the walls, casting a warm glow about the space. He stepped closer to her; her back nearly touching the door as she moved back a pace.

"I fear you misunderstood earlier today. I did not mean to say anything to upset you." She looked toward the windows, avoiding his gaze.

"It was nothing, I assure you, just the stress of the past few days. There is no need to be concerned." She turned back to the door, "If that was all, I should return…" He placed a hand on the door, effectively stopping her departure.

"I thought highly of your mother, as I know you did. When I said no one would mistake you, it had nothing to do with her finer qualities." He caressed her cheek softly and he could feel her expel a shaky breath. It delighted him he affected her as she did him. "You are beautiful just as she was, but you are much stronger in the face of adversity."

"You shouldn't tell me lies Noah, not you."

"I wouldn't dream of it. You are strong Lily, look at you and all you have endured." She was shaking her head, fighting back the tears that shone in her blue eyes. He tucked that still errant curl behind her ear, bringing his face closer.

"If I had been strong, I wouldn't have allowed my father to sell me off like all of his other possessions." One tear escaped, sliding down her rounded cheek, and he swept it away with the pad of his thumb.

"My mother told me what you did for them when your father died, how you ensured they could remain at the manor."

"Joseph planned to sell it, but I couldn't allow them to be evicted. We... struck a compromise. One of many in our marriage." She could not hide the bitterness in her voice. "He could be so vile when he had been drinking. I should not have spoken of it while he was in his cups, but I knew he was more likely to agree just to have me leave him alone. He felt the property was worthless just as I was." Her voice was trembling now and his fist clenched at his side as he kept the other soft on her cheek. If the man were not already dead, he would have gladly killed him himself.

"You did what was necessary to survive and care for the people of the estate, and they are all grateful. You are far from worthless, my dear Lily." Her eyes locked with his, then dropped to his mouth as her breath came quicker. There was no turning back for him and he closed the distance, taking her mouth with his. It was not gentle. He devoured her as the years of longing ended. His hands were in her hair and he deepened the kiss, tasting her sweet lips then teasing his tongue inside her mouth, wanting all of her.

She melted against him, hands gripping his arm as she sighed against his lips. He pressed her against the door, unable to stop. This was what his body craved, to be pressed against her, to make her his own.

"Grandmother, are you in there?" Charlotte called as she tapped on the door. Lily pushed him away, gasping for breath. "I will be out in a moment, dear," she said through the door in a remarkably calm voice. They could hear the child's footsteps retreat and Noah drew her to him again, but she held up her hands against his chest.

"We should get back." Noah dropped his forehead to hers as he caught his breath, desperate to kiss her again. He touched his lips to hers, soft this time.

"As you wish, but we shall continue this later," he said with a wolfish grin before releasing her. There was no stopping him now. He would seek her out wherever she was.

Chapter sixteen

Lillian strolled back to the dining room, hoping Noah would have the good sense to allow a few moments before he emerged. What was she doing, behaving like a lovesick girl? Her lips burned with the memory of his kiss and she wanted nothing more than to run back into Noah's arms. He said they would continue later, and she found herself giddy with anticipation of being in his arms again. She had never felt this way, even when he had kissed her as a girl. Something was different, perhaps the knowledge she had as a woman of what she had survived without all those years in her husband's cold shadow. He had taken his delights where he wished, leaving her alone and unloved. Noah had reawakened a passion in her and now that it had ignited, she wanted nothing more than to fan the flames.

She saw him enter the dining room from the other door, engaging Robert Parsons in conversation. Andrew was absent, likely having returned to his wife's side. Was this how it was between them? They were rarely apart, and they always seemed to touch. Did she dare to hope that she could have love such as they did at this time in her life?

The thought of her age brought an additional worry. Wouldn't Noah want a young wife, someone that could give him children? He had said he never married because of his life in the army. Perhaps now he intended to have a family. It filled her mind with doubts until she looked up to find him watching her, his eyes sweeping over her as he moved closer. Before he could reach her, her granddaughters grabbed his hands, tugging him toward the table laden with tarts, cakes and other sweets.

Rachel pointed to a cream cake and Noah set it on a plate, handing it down to her with a sweet smile. Charlotte was telling him about each item on display. "Miss greyson makes the best blackberry tarts," she said, suggesting he try one. Taking a large bite, leaving a bit of cream on his nose and pretending he did not know, he had the girls squealing with laughter.

"What is so funny? Your Grace, do you have any idea what these two find so hilarious?" She stifled a laugh as he crossed his eyes at her.

"Oh, I see. There is a little something on your face," she said, attempting to keep a straight face as he purposely wiped at the wrong spot. The girls continued to giggle until he finally allowed Rachel to clean his face.

"Thank you, my lady, you have saved me some embarrassment," he expounded as he bowed elegantly and kissed her hand. He gave her a wink as the girls drug him back to the desserts, making her heart flutter. She needed to collect herself. This behavior was unseemly for a duchess. The question was, did she care anymore what society thought of her?

While the food was cleared, and conversation waned, Lillian looked in on Laura. She knocked lightly on the door, but there was no answer. She opened the door quietly and paused, her breath catching as she watched her son kiss his wife. Laura remained propped against the pillows, still pale and weak, but she giggled softly as he moved from her lips to her cheek, then her ear, his hand caressing her hair. Andrew smiled, his face lit from within. He was in love. Closing the door, not wishing to disturb them, she wondered at how lonely he must have been until he met his wife. She had done him a great disservice, forcing him to marry Patricia, then attempting to come between him and the woman he loved. She had been no better than her father.

Andrew had cautiously allowed her back into his life in the last year, but realizing what she had done to him beyond even how she neglected him as a child, she wondered if he could ever truly forgive her. Could she forgive herself? She suddenly felt unworthy of love herself, having brought so much misery to her family. Of course, it had not only been her, Joseph and her father shared some of the blame, but she was responsible for her own actions in the end.

She walked along the hallway, her footsteps muffled by the thick blue patterned runner, as quiet descended over the manor. Candles flickered in their sconces, elongating her shadow as her thoughts wandered through the many mistakes she had made in her life. She found herself in the guest wing without conscious decision, raising her hand to knock on Noah's door. Candle light spilled from the open door as he stood in his breeches and shirt, a smile lighting his face at sight of her. Pulling her in and closing the door, he kissed her softly. "I had hoped you would come to me," he said, leaning in to touch her lips again. She stopped him with a hand on his chest, causing him to raise his brows.

"I am sorry for all the pain I may have caused you," she whispered. "I have been so careless with the feelings of others, my children, Laura's mother, you. There is too much for anyone to forgive." Her head bowed, she turned away, but he took her hands, leading her to sit on the bed.

"You believe you are the only one to make mistakes? What I did to you, the way I behaved that first time you told me you loved me; I

146

regret my behavior that night. Yes, it was not the right time, but I did not consider your feelings. There are many people I have disappointed in my life." A shadow seemed to take over his features for a moment, then disappeared just as quickly. "Can we not forgive one another here and now?"

Lillian touched his cheek, feeling the day's growth of beard prickle her palm. The hair was darker than that on his head; she noted as she took in his lovely face. Her fingers traced his lower lip, slightly plumper than the upper one, and he kissed her fingers teasingly. His arms came around her, pulling her close. "Allow yourself to be loved, allow me to love you, Lily." He kissed her deeply and this time she responded, bringing her hand to his cheek. She lost herself in the feel of him.

His hands moved over her back up into her hair, where he pulled it free from the pins so that it tumbled down her back. He ran his fingers through the soft strands with a murmur of approval. His tongue teased the seam of her mouth, begging for entry, and she sighed as he tasted her mouth. She felt as though she were drunk as his hands continued to explore, one coming around to cup her breast. Shocked by the sensation, she pulled back, but he quickly drew her back in as he gently squeezed the soft flesh. She moaned as his fingers teased her nipple through the fabric of her gown and she arched into his touch.

No man had ever touched her like this. Her encounters with Joseph had been quick and purposeful, not intimate like this. Noah pulled down the shoulder of her gown as his lips burned a path down her throat. She fisted her hands in his hair as he kissed lower to the curve of her breast, all the while his fingers were working the

147

buttons down her back. Her bodice slid toward her waist and she scrambled to cover herself, uncertain of what was happening. One would think her a virgin for her behavior, but she had never been naked before her husband.

"I want to see you, Lily. Don't hide yourself, you are so beautiful." She saw only sincerity in his grey eyes, but she felt self-conscious of her inexperience. "What is it? Have I done something wrong?" he asked, holding her arms.

"No, I... It's just that I never, I mean..."

"Lily, you have three children. You can't tell me you have never been with a man before." His voice was teasing, and she felt the heat rise up her neck into her cheeks. "Lily, what is it? Tell me."

"Joseph, he never wished to disrobe. It was always brief. There was no... the way you are touching me, he never did that." She could see something in his eyes. Was it anger?

"I'm sorry, I understand if you don't want this." She was pulling at her bodice, attempting to stand, but he pulled her back down. Taking her face in his hands, he kissed her forehead, her nose, then her lips before sitting back slightly with a gentle smile.

"I am at a loss how the man could resist you? If you were my wife, I would have bedded you at every opportunity. Pardon my saying so, but your husband must have been daft." Lillian could not help herself and burst out laughing, quickly joined by Noah. Finally, bringing himself under control, he looked at her seriously.

"It seems educating you in the art of lovemaking has fallen to me," he said, his face brightening quickly as his lips took hers again. He laid her back on the bed, pulling back a moment to remove his shirt. Her eyes grew wide as she ran her hand over his chest. Despite his age, he was broad and strong, likely the army did not allow soldiers to become soft. There was a dusting of dark blonde hair beneath her fingers and she leaned forward, wanting to know how it would feel against her lips.

He groaned as his hand moved down over her hip, cupping her bottom, and she could feel his arousal. Finally divested of her gown and stays he gazed at her hungrily. She squirmed, feeling exposed, but he continued to whisper endearments close to her ear as his body covered her. When she felt his hand move between her legs, she thought he would take her, but instead his fingers teased along her opening, creating a sensation like nothing she had ever felt. His eyes held hers as he continued to stroke her, heat building as something unfurled in her belly. Her hips moved on their own, wanting more of him as the speed increased.

Fear shot through her as her legs stiffened. She didn't know what was happening to her, and she pulled away, but Noah continued. "Let it happen, my love. It will be wonderful, I promise." She kept her eyes on his face as the sensation continued to build until she was spiraling with pleasure. He kissed her, swallowing her cries, then held her as her heart raced.

"What was that?" she asked breathlessly.

"That, my darling Lily, is how it should to be between a man and a woman."

"But you didn't... we weren't intimate." Her face was flaming again as he looked down at her, a look of pure joy on his face.

"There are many ways to give pleasure and that was only one. Shall I show you another?" She nodded enthusiastically, eager to learn all of what she had been missing. He stood and removed his breeks, and she could see what she had only ever felt. Her eyes widened as he moved over her and joined with her, slowly allowing her to become accustomed to him. She thought she would lose her mind when he finally began to move. The feel of his skin, his warm masculine scent, overwhelmed her as she felt the pleasure building again. He kissed her tenderly then buried his face in her neck as he moaned her name. His thrusts growing deeper and faster, she pressed into him, her hand gripping his shoulders.

"Noah, it's... Oh my."

"That's it Lily, I'm with you. Let go." His words were the end of her and she shattered again as he thrust deep and then stilled at his completion. He rolled to his side, bringing her with him, cradling her in the crook of his arm. They lay there for several minutes in silence, and he kissed the top of her head.

"So that is the way of it when you are with a woman?" she asked tentatively. He looked into her eyes, then kissed her lips.

"No," he whispered and her gaze dropped, certain she had been a disappointment to him. He lifted her chin to look at him. "I have never felt with any other woman what I feel with you." He kissed her again, deeply. "You have made me a happy man." She snuggled into his side contentedly.

"I had no idea I could feel like this," she said as she ran her hand over his chest. She could not stop touching him. She felt a rumble beneath her fingers as he chuckled.

"If I were a younger man, I would continue your education, but for now I am afraid I require a brief rest." He gave her a squeeze and the two of them dozed off in each other's arms.

As the sun came through the window, he watched her sleep, taking in how she had changed and how she was the same. It struck him how young she looked at this moment, a sweet satisfied smile on her lips as her lashes fanned over the curve of her cheek. They had woken to make love again in the hours before dawn before drifting back to sleep and his body was pleasantly sore from the exertion.

Lily had been a quick study, and her ardor awakened new sensations within him. He loved her. Still, there was doubt in his mind, yet neither of them had expressed the sentiment. Their bodies had spoken for them and he spooned around her, wanting nothing more than to stay in this bed all day with her. Unfortunately, there were things to be dealt with in the light of day. He knew he should wake her, as she likely wished to return to her room before the house awakened. She was a widow, yet she would not want the staff to gossip.

He nuzzled her neck, nipping lightly until she stirred with a girlish giggle that sent his heart soaring. Then the sight of the sun had her sitting up in a panic. He placed a reassuring hand on her shoulder, "It is early yet." She nodded but shimmied to the edge of the bed, reaching for her gown and pulling it over her head. Grabbing her stays and her shoes, she moved toward the door. Leaping from the bed like a man half his age, he gathered her to him. "Not without a kiss, my little Lily." She smiled at him, raising up on her toes to brush a kiss over his lips, then quietly exited the room.

Noah returned to the bed, breathing in her scent now mingled with his own with a contented sigh. Should he ask Andrew for her hand he wondered as he stretched? He was unsure how one went about claiming a mature woman. Claudia had no family, so there had been no need… His heart sank. What had he done? He was a scoundrel, plain and simple. Bedding Lily had been impulsive. It was a disgrace that he had so easily forgotten the young woman that awaited him in London. He had made her a promise only to toss it away when he held the woman he truly loved. He should leave now for London. It was time to face the music.

Chapter seventeen

Lillian could not keep the smile from her face. She had returned to her room without incident that morning and greeted the little maid happily when she entered an hour later to assist her in dressing for the day. Making her way to the nursery, she looked in on her grandson, who she found gurgling in his father's arms.

"Good morning mother," Andrew greeted her. His blue eyes were bright and his posture had returned to that of the strong young man he was, the weight of grief no longer pressing down on him. She came to his side, taking in the sweet child in his arms, and ran a finger down his chubby cheek.

"It was kind of Laura to name him after your brother." Andrew continued to smile down at his son.

"I was about to bring him to see his mother if you care to join me?" Lillian was stunned by his invitation. Mayhap the stress of the past week had opened his heart further. Though she appreciated his invitation, she declined.

"You should have time alone as a family now. I shall have a visit a bit later." She looked down at the child again before cupping her son's cheek. "I am pleased for you, you deserve nothing but happiness, my son." It was Andrew's turn to be surprised.

"You seem in high spirits this morning," he said suspiciously. She smiled wryly at him with a little shake of her.

"There is much to celebrate, not the least being your little heir." She knew well that her son did not care if the child was a boy, only that the child and his wife were alive, yet the arrival of an heir was auspicious in Lillian's eyes.

Entering the dining room a few moments later. Lillian found her daughter happily chatting with Minerva Edwards. She saw no sign of Noah and found she was disappointed. She thought he would be up and about by now.

"She looks much stronger today thank the lord," Minerva said happily to Julia. "I am relieved that I am not leaving with Laura still in peril."

"You are leaving today?" Lillian asked, attempting to keep her voice light.

"Yes indeed, I have held my poor nephew hostage for far too long. He must return to London tomorrow and he had a few items he wished to take care of so that the duke may remain at home with our dear girl." Julia was smiling and promising to make a trip to the village to assist in any way she might. Lillian remained displeased that her children were spending their time in these pursuits. Andrew had estates to see to and Julia would have her first season in a month's time. They were already behind in preparations, and it was unlikely that Andrew would accompany them now that Laura was in a weakened state.

She wanted a good match for her daughter and would see her happily settled, not sold to the highest bidder. That said, she also hoped she would make an advantageous match worthy of the daughter of a duke. These thoughts filled her mind as she went in search of Noah. He had not said a word about returning to London.

She found him coming down the stairs and noted his expression seemed strained when he saw her, though a smile quickly returned. "Good morning, Your Grace."

"Good morning, Mr. Reeves," she said, returning his formal greeting. "Might I have a word?" She motioned toward the door of her son's study and Noah followed in her wake. Closing the door behind them, uncertain how to behave once they were alone. Noah answered that question, pulling her into an embrace, and kissed her gently.

"I hated watching you leave this morning," he said, his voice low and seductive. She blushed like a girl under his warm gaze. "I shall miss you." Lillian felt her heart sink at his words and fought to keep her tone even. "Your aunt mentioned you were off to London, on business, I assume?" She watched his features tighten slightly.

"Yes, I must complete a final negotiation before beginning work with your son and his brother-in-law. I have neglected things in London and must return tomorrow." Lillian stepped away, turning her back to him and walking toward the window, though she could see nothing, as tears blurred her vision. Breathing deeply, she willed them not to fall.

"Well, I wish you well. It has been lovely seeing you again," she said, barely looking back over her shoulder.

"Lily, last night was..." She turned, holding up a hand to stop him.

"I am a grown woman. There is no need to say anything further. We enjoyed each other's companionship and now it is time to return to our lives." She held her head up as she moved to the door, but before she could pass him, he grasped her arm.

"So that is all I was, Lily, companionship?" Anger flashed in his eyes as his fingers tightened. She tugged, but he would not release her teeth clenched. She would not allow him to see the pain she felt at his departure. Living by her own rules for years, she would not allow one night of passion to turn her into a weak minded, emotional fool.

"We shared a lovely night together, and now it is time to return to our chosen lives. It is as simple as that. Now if you will release me…" Noah stopped her words with a hungry kiss. She remained rigid in his arms and he angled his head, desperate for a response. Her resolve weakened as her arms came around his neck. "Open to me Lily," he whispered against her lips and she could not resist allowing his tongue to sweep between her lips, reveling in the taste of him as her blood heated.

When he finally pulled away, they were both breathless. He touched his forehead to hers, bringing his hands to her cheeks. "I want to know you again Lily, there are things that may come between us but know that I want you more than anything else in this world."

"How can you say that? We hardly know one another anymore," she said as she stepped away, attempting to regain her composure. "Go back to London, do what you must. Mayhap I will see you when I am in town." She saw the shadow again, that fleeting look that darkened his grey eyes and vanished. Minerva's voice echoed in the foyer as she called out, looking for Noah.

"I must go now," he said softly before brushing another soft kiss on her lips. She watched his retreating form as he left with his aunt. She squared her shoulders with a deep breath once the cart disappeared, turning for the staircase. In the nursery she sat alone, looking into the dark blue eyes of little Jonathan. She held him close in the quiet empty room as her tears finally fell, dropping onto the soft yellow blanket that swaddled him.

As Noah stepped from the carriage, narrowly missing the pile of horse dung beside it, reminding him of his dislike for London. The noise of the bustling crowds, the grey skies from the chimney smoke in the air, assaulted his senses. He wanted nothing more than to order the driver to return to the coach stop so that he could return to the country...to Lily.

He was a coward. He had faced down French troops in India and at the bloody battle of Waterloo, yet faced with a petite blonde lady who had done nothing but care for him, he wished to retreat. It was time to decide what he truly wanted. Drawing a steadying breath, he mounted the steps to his townhouse. The grey stone structure had never seemed so imposing in the nearly two years he had lived here. A large black door swung inward as Benning greeted him. The man had served him during Noah's last five years with his regiment, a luxury afforded to his rank once he became Major Reeves.

"Welcome home, Major," The lanky, brown-haired man. He was ten years Noah's junior, but the men had become friends over late evening chess games and cheap whiskey.

"No need for formality, Benning, we're not in the army any more. Come have a drink with me, help me slake the road dust from my throat." He glanced about, curious where Claudia was since she had not come to greet him. Benning, ever observant, leaned in. "At the modiste, sir. New dress for Wellington's reception on Friday." Noah nodded. With everything else, he had forgotten. Claudia had been bursting with excitement to attend her first London party. His chest tightened at the thought of her smiling face when they received the invitation. She had immediately made an appointment to have a new dress made, asking his opinion of color, fabric and adornments as if he had any idea what she was speaking of.

Benning handed him a glass and the two men sat in companionable silence for several moments as thoughts of Lily invaded Noah's mind. A slight shiver of pleasure ran down his spine as he recalled how her body had felt curled against his own after they made love.

"Will you be telling me what happened while you were away or shall I leave you to your thoughts?" Benning asked before taking a sip of his whiskey. "I can see the weight on your shoulders as sure as you were Atlas himself, holding up the world." Noah should have known he could hide nothing from the man.

"It is my trouble, I'll not burden you with it." Benning raised a thick brow at him, then took another drink.

"I was thinking of Reynolds the other day," his friend began. This was not a subject Noah enjoyed, but Benning continued. "Fine, young man, that one. Bit pig headed like some other men I know, couldn't stop him once his mind was set." This was not the first time they had had this conversation, and he knew it would not be the last. Benning was determined to assist, but Noah knew he was responsible for the young man's death.

"Noah, is that you, dear heart?" The melodic voice drifted through the door before the angelic blonde woman entered, her large brown eyes like those of a deer, shining as she ran to him. "Oh, how I've missed you." She held his hands as she raised up on tiptoe to kiss his cheek. Benning bowed quickly and left them alone.

"What kept you away so long? You said it would be but a fortnight and it has been near twice that." Her lower lip pouted, a sign of her youth, he supposed. Lily would never... He cut off the thought immediately. He could not think of her right now.

"I apologize my dear, as I said in my letter, a dear friend of my aunt was in a bad way and I wanted to lend her support and assist where I could while she visited." He placed his hands on her arms, giving them a light reassuring squeeze. This seemed to quell her pout as she asked about the circumstances.

"I suppose the elderly will become infirmed without warning. It was kind of you to stay." She moved to the settee and patted the gold damask surface for him to join her.

"Actually, the friend was the Duchess of Hawthorne, difficult birth of her son I fear. It was a near tragedy but all seems well now." Claudia's eyes lit as her pale brows rose in question.

"Did you meet her?" she asked, her tone rising to a higher pitch.

"Why yes, she and her husband were most hospitable. Merveille is a wonder, and I enjoyed entertaining their two daughters in the gardens while their father sat with his wife." She smiled brightly up at him, taking his hand.

"You will be such a wonderful father, I am certain of it," she said wistfully. Noah cleared his throat as his cravat seemed to tighten. Rising, he went to refill his glass, offering Claudia something as well, though she declined.

"Being as you were so kind, mayhap we will receive an invitation from them this season." Noah began coughing as he choked on his whiskey. "Goodness, darling, are you alright?"

Noah brought out his handkerchief, dabbing at his waistcoat to give himself a moment to collect himself. "I doubt they will attend the season; the birth was difficult for the duchess and she was nearly lost. I believe they will remain in the country for now." He took in the ladies' disappointed look.

"She must have been quite calculating to have captured the eye of the Duke of Hawthorne. I understand he was quite sought him after two seasons past. Not to mention she was a commoner and the cousin of the lady he was courting; it was quite the scandal." Claudia had a voracious appetite for the intrigues of the *ton* and ate up every scrap of gossip she could. He shook his head at her.

"You should not put stock in all the gossip. Laura is a lovely and kind woman. The duke's children adore her and you should have seen how the staff behaved. When they believed all was lost, they were all grief stricken. She and the duke are obviously in love. It was a privilege to be welcomed into their home." Claudia dropped her soft doe eyes, properly chastised.

"I should not have spoken so, forgive me, Noah." She stood and crossed the ornate carpet to his side. "I realize I am not a fine lady and I become caught up in all the goings on." Noah placed a finger beneath her chin, raising her face to look at her.

"You are a very fine lady, my dear. I am only saying that it is best not to spread idle gossip." He gave her a smile, which she quickly returned.

"Wait until you see my dress for the reception," she said, shifting the topic. "I so wish to do you proud. It is a pale rose with a lovely neckline of scalloped lace. I worry if I have anything appropriate with which to do it justice." Her sweeping lashes fluttered, and he grasped the *subtle hint* that she was hoping for new jewelry. One more task to see to in the morning after he met with Charles Bartlett.

The young man was Hawthorne's Man-of-Business, and they instructed him to meet with him to go over the proposal for joining in a venture with Parsons Shipping. As he gathered his thoughts, he realized Claudia was still tittering on about the upcoming party. Clearing his throat to gain her attention, he claimed fatigue from his journey and retired to his room for a rest. Claudia kissed him on the cheek, "Of course, my poor dear, you must be exhausted and here I am going on. Take your rest and I will see you at dinner." He gave her a nod and retreated to his chamber.

Noah stared at the ceiling, noting a small crack in the plaster. He had been inspecting the surface for about an hour, unable to will images of Lily from his mind. Whenever he closed his eyes, he could see her. Was it simply nostalgia for his youth that had driven him to her? Mayhap he was being foolish, thinking she would even want him seeing as she had walked away before. Yet when he recalled the look in her eyes when he was readying to leave, it told another story. She hid it with regal indifference, but he had seen the hurt in her eyes.

What was he to do now, he wondered, finally sitting up in frustration? Wishing he could speak to Benning, he knew he could not place his friend in such an uncomfortable position. He was a part of the household, after all. He would have to face Claudia every day.

Thinking of begging off dinner because of a migrem, he could not bring himself to do so when he had been absent for so long. With a brave face, freshly shaven and in clean clothes, he gathered himself and walked into the dining room.

Though it was not as large as that of the Duke of Hawthorne, Claudia had decorated it elegantly. She had added drapes that hung in elegant waves from the top of the casement in a rich blue that complimented the cream silk wall covering. Elaborate place settings decorated the table despite it only being the two of them, and he looked at Claudia in question. "Are we expecting guests?"

She swatted at his arm playfully. "No silly, I only wanted tonight to be special for your return." He pulled out her chair, and she sat daintily motioning for him to sit as well. "I had Matilda make all of your favorites," she said, reaching out to squeeze his hand. Matilda emerged from the kitchen with a rich soup filled with fresh vegetables and quail. Claudia continued to ask about the Duke and Duchess of Hawthorne, wishing to hear about the manor and the servants, the meals they served and the clothes they wore. Noah grew weary of her fascination and his own worry of revealing something he should not.

"What of the dowager-duchess?" she asked, causing him to fumble with his fork. He set the utensil down gently and reached for his wine. "Was she there for the birth? I have heard she is quite a formidable lady."

"She was there to support the family during all the difficulties." Claudia looked at him expectantly and he struggled at what to say. Benning entered and handed him a sealed note. He nodded at the man, relieved at the interruption.

162

"Something important darling?"

"Doctor Dresher was informing me he is in town for Wellington's reception." It had been at least a year since he had seen the man who had saved his life on at least two occasions. Unfortunately, he could not save Reynolds. Noah looked at Claudia, who was helping herself to more of the sponge cake and berries.

She had seemed so small when he had seen her after her husband's death. He had insisted on informing her himself when Ezra Reynolds died at Waterloo. It seemed only fitting that it should be him. When he found her in that tiny room over the neighborhood pub, he was appalled.

She had no family other than Reynolds and his mother, who had gone to live with her own sister earlier that year, and now she was alone in London. The drunken men moving about the alleyway made him afraid for her safety and after a sleepless night, he had arranged for this house and had her moved in even before he had returned permanently to town.

He looked at her now, pink cheeked, dressed in silk and could see no hint of the pale thin girl in the threadbare dress from that day. He owed that much to Reynolds, though he had not planned for what had happened in the months that followed that decision.

Chapter eighteen

Julia was sitting with Laura in the garden, Andrew having insisted on carrying her from their room so that she could enjoy the warm sunny day. Lillian watched the two young ladies as they laughed at the children running about with their father. She shook her head at her son, who was running about, growling like a beast as he scooped each girl off her feet and carried them off. He certainly did not look like a noble duke at the moment.

Laura took Julia's hands as Lillian drew near, "I am sorry that we will not be there to see you presented."

"You need to regain your strength and look after this little angle." Julia looked into the Moses basket that sat at Laura's feet. Jonathan slept soundly, his little hands fisted loosely above his head. Lillian sat beside her daughter-in-law and gazed at her grandson.

"Such a miracle," she said softly. Laura patted her hand with a smile that Lillian often felt she did not deserve. Mary should have been here at her daughter's side, and she felt she was a poor substitute.

"We are pleased you were here for his arrival. I hope you know you are welcome whenever you wish," she said kindly, almost seeming to read her thoughts. A stern voice interrupted the sweet moment as Grace, Laura's gruff friend from the infirmary, arrived.

"What are ye doin' outta bed, young lady?" she scolded. Andrew stepped forward, his expression contrite, with Rachel sitting proudly on his shoulders.

"I carried her down and will carry her back up when she tires. I thought the air would do her good."

"Such a good 'usband ye are. Tis a wonder," she commented, casting a look at Lillian. After casting a dark look in the woman's direction, Lillian leaned down and picked up her grandson, who had just begun fussing. She smiled at the little boy, then cuddled him on his shoulder in time for him to vomit down the back of her dress.

"Oh my, what a good lad," Grace chuckled as she retrieved the child, handing Lillian a rag. "Tis best ye have a clothe te guard yer fancy garments, Yer Grace." Julia took the proffered cloth and began assisting with the mess, though her mother caught the smile on her face at the damnable woman's words.

Lillian beckoned her daughter to follow once she finished. "There are still preparations to be made before our departure tomorrow. Best see to things with your maid." Julia frowned slightly as she looked back at Laura. The other young woman smiled back as Andrew approached. "You'll be fine, Julia. I know you have been looking forward to this," Laura soothed, grasping her hand. Julia returned the gentle squeeze.

"It's only that I thought you and my brother would be with me. This would be less daunting if I had some familiar faces near me." She breathed a deep sigh before turning to follow her mother. Lillian had watched the exchange with a tight feeling in her chest. Her relations with her daughter had improved as they had with Andrew however, they remained distant. She truly hoped the time in London would see them grow closer. Her first season was important, and she intended to be at her daughter's side, providing sound advice and support. She would admit to a growing excitement at possibly seeing Noah again. They had parted with no promises. However, he had seemed intent that they would see one another again. Despite her attempts to seem above it all, she very much wished to be with him again.

The two men bowed upon meeting as Charles Bartlett motioned him to a large leather chair in front of a simple but sturdy cherry wood desk. "Would you care for any refreshments, Mr. Reeves?" he asked politely. Noah shook his head and Bartlett dismissed the tall, spectacled clerk. "It is a pleasure to meet you, sir. The duke and Mr. Parsons seem eager to bring you into the fold." He reached for a stack of papers that had been set to his right by the junior clerk when they entered and laid them before Noah.

The duke's man-of-business dressed well without looking the dandy as some of the younger gentlemen of London society. This put Noah at ease, not being a slave to fashion himself. Bartlett's hazel eyes held a spark of intellect above an amiable smile, and he could see why Hawthorne liked the man. Quick to get to the point, he led Noah through the papers before him without flowery words or attempts to put on heirs. He was the duke's representative but did not behave as though he was anyone's better because of it.

Noah listened attentively, asking for clarification when needed. It sounded like an excellent opportunity that would be mutually beneficial to both parties. Once business was concluded and Noah had agreed to review the contract with his solicitor, the conversation turned into a social one.

"So all is well with Laura, er, Her Grace?" Noah's brow quirked at the slip, though he was not surprised. It had been obvious to him that Bartlett was a close friend of the duke and duchess and he doubted Laura stood on ceremony with the young man.

"When I left she was much improved, and the lad was doing well."

"That is a relief. I know it would have devastated Hawthorne had anything happened to her. She is strong enough to put up with His Grace so I should not have worried." He thumbed through a few pages, sitting on his blotter before inquiring further. "Did you happen to meet Lady Julia?" Noah smiled inwardly at the man's tone, knowing all too well what that look in his eyes was about.

"Yes, lovely young woman. Devoted to her family, especially the little ladies of the house." Bartlett's eyes brightened further at the mention of the children.

"Little Rachel will surely be the end of her father one day," he laughed as he glanced at something on the edge of his desk. Noah saw that there were several drawings obviously created by a child's hand at the corner of the desk. "The girls often send their works along. I find them stuck in between the pages of contracts from their father. I am uncertain if he adds them or they sneak them in," he laughed, noting Noah's attention to them.

"I had the pleasure of spending time with them in the garden during my visits. They could even melt this old soldier's heart." Noting the time, Noah stood. "I am afraid I have a few other things to attend to, but I will contact you once I have reviewed all of this," he said as he held up the documents and slid them into his case.

Making his way to Bond Street, Noah enjoyed the warmth of the day, though the scent of smoke and unwashed bodies permeated his nose. It would take another sennight before he accustomed himself to the crowds and smells again. Locating the jeweler, he entered and began looking about until the proprietor completed another patron's transaction.

"How may I assist you, sir?" the rather round gentleman asked as he approached.

"I am in need of a necklace and earrings. The lady is blonde and will wear a pale rose gown." Noah had no eye for these sorts of things, so he hoped the man could make some suggestions.

"Hmm, I believe I may have a few items to her liking." He ushered Noah forward and began laying out several pieces on the black velvet pillow on the counter. Having invested his earnings wisely over the years, price was not of great concern, though he did not wish to be a spendthrift. There was a rope of garnets set in gold with small diamonds between each red stone and matching earrings that would likely do. He looked at a few other pieces the man had just placed from another tray when he noticed the bracelet. It was exquisite even to him and he asked to inspect it. The opals were brilliant. The fiery veins within the translucent white surface shifted colors as he moved the piece in his fingers. They formed a lily with the body of the bracelet, a jade circlet. Tiny yellow diamonds peaked out of the flower representing the pestles. Without a moment's thought, he handed the piece to the man.

"I will take this." Looking down at the other items, the man seemed confused.

"You no longer desire the necklace?" Noah looked back at the set.

"All three please, though I wish the bracelet boxed separately." The shopkeeper gave him a knowing smile that had Noah shuffling his feet nervously. What was he doing? Taking another look at the bracelet, he could not help himself. He had to buy it for her. Though she likely had far more extravagant jewels, he wanted nothing more than to present this to his Lily the next time he saw her, whenever that might be.

Purchases in hand, he made his way back home.

Later that evening, he sat in the parlor with Hugh Dresher enjoying an after dinner brandy. Benning had joined them and the three men spoke of mundane things, skirting any mention of the atrocities they had seen on the field of battle or the aftermath. It seemed an unspoken code between members of the military. The horrors that had bound them need not be spoken of, though they never forgot.

Noah found himself on the ground after being thrown from his mount in the onslaught. Finding his sword at his feet, he grasped the cold metal as he found his footing. Mud flew up as a cannonball landed several feet away; the screams of men rang in his ears. He hollered orders, attempting to keep his men together. Lieutenant Reynolds was at his side reporting troop positions and orders being passed among the ranks. Noah looked at him, about to order him to rally at the flank, but the man was shouting something over the din, his hoarse voice not penetrating as he pushed Noah backward, causing him to fall on his back. Stunned, he looked up at Ezra Reynolds as his eyes went wide. The man coughed as blood came from his mouth. Then he fell forward, his body blanketing Noah's, and he thrashed to move out from beneath him as he shouted for assistance.

He could hear his name, feel hands on him as he struggled to break free, needing to save Reynolds. "Noah, wake up. It's only a dream, please wake up." Her soft features, her sweet voice, her scent. He wrapped his arms around Lily, allowing her warmth to soothe him as she rocked him. He took her mouth, then realized something was wrong.

"Noah, I knew you wanted me, I'm here." He was being pushed back to the pillow by a petite body as blonde hair spilled around him. Grasping her shoulders, he pushed Claudia back, taking in her puzzled expression.

"Forgive me. I should not have done that. I was not fully awake and…" Noah was fumbling, as his mind reeled. He had nearly taken her while thinking she was...Dear lord.

"Noah, allow me to stay with you. I only want to take away the pain as I did before," Claudia said sweetly as she caressed his cheek. Leaning in, she brushed her lips over his as her soft fingers toyed with the hair of his bare chest. He grabbed her hand, rougher than he intended, bringing it to his lips briefly in apology.

"Thank you, my dear, for your concern. I am alright now, you should return to your own bed."

"I want to be here with you. I'm not a virgin, as you well know. What does it matter if we share a bed before we marry? No one need know," she giggled.

"I would know; what happened that night should not have occurred. If I had not been in my cups…" He pushed away gently. "Please allow me to honor you by waiting." She gave him a petulant look, but finally acquiesced.

"Alright darling, if it's what you wish." She left the room, giving him one last smile before closing the door. He dropped back on the bed, feeling like a selfish bastard. He recalled that night, stumbling up the stairs after finishing the bottle of whiskey. It had been the only way to numb the pain. He would sleep without dreaming, escape the vision of Reynolds saving his life at the cost of his own.

Claudia had helped him to bed, lovely girl that she is and when he woke she was curled beside him. He had done the unthinkable. Of course, he had offered for her immediately. It was the right thing to do. She was young and vibrant; she wished to make a life with him and give him children, yet he lay in his bed longing for Lily. He wanted to wake beside her, sit with her in the evening and speak of their days, then take her to bed and make love to her as many times as his aging body would allow. He knew many would consider him daft for not wanting a sweet young wife, but despite his caring and concern for her, he did not love her.

Unable to return to sleep, Noah began pacing the room as he scrubbed a hand over his face. He knew this was madness. Would Lily even agree to be with him? After all, she was a duchess. Well, a dowager-duchess. She might spurn any further advances on his part. He was still a commoner, a soldier. Richer perhaps, but still...

The hazy light of dawn was brightening the windows when he finally dozed off, too exhausted to think anymore.

Chapter nineteen

Andrew Welesley, 1st Duke of Wellington, had made it clear he no longer wished to fight. His military career was giving way to one of politics. His men had respected him, and Noah was no exception. This reception would welcome many retired officers as well as members of the *ton*. Wellington's wife, Kitty, enjoyed her social pursuits, and it was certain to be a splendid evening. Claudia was shivering with nervous excitement as they climbed the steps of the duke's palatial London residence. "I hope I make a good impression," she whispered as they stood in the long receiving line awaiting their turn to be greeted by His Grace and the duchess.

"You are stunning, my dear. You need not worry," he soothed, watching her touch the necklace he had given her with delicate gloved fingers.

"Thank you for my lovely gift. The sentiment behind it will make it shine brighter than any of the finer jewels worn this evening, I am certain." She gave him a little smile before moving her hand back to take his arm. Noah furrowed his brow at her comment. Surely she realized he could not cover her in diamonds. She was simply lacking in some of the social graces given her upbringing.

He may have been a stable boy, but he had been raised in a fine home and his time as an officer had given him more polish, he reminded himself.

"Reeves, splendid to see you away from the ravages of war." Noah bowed to the handsome duke and his lady.

"May I present Mrs. Claudia Reynolds Your Graces." Claudia curtsied low, then raised her eyes to the splendid couple.

"You have a magnificent house. I am humbled to be here," she said, taking in the grand burgundy gown and the diamonds and rubies that adorned the duchess. Footmen in fine black livery ushered them forward, offering champagne. The large ballroom was brightly lit, with large crystal chandeliers overhead and urns spilling over with fresh blooms of white and pale pink.

Looking down at Claudia, he could see the wonder in her eyes as her delicate rosy lips formed an O. She sipped her champagne, giggling from the bubbles and the overwhelming scene laid out before her. "Have you ever seen anything so wonderful, Noah darling?" He did not reply as his attention turned to his friend Dr. Dresher, who was speaking to a lovely dark-haired girl in an emerald green gown. The girl laughed at something the older man said and Noah's heart skipped. Though her hair was much darker, Lady Julia's features were so like her mother's at that age.

Glancing around him, he could feel his chest growing tight. Then he saw her. Dressed in deep blue silk with pearls and diamonds at her throat, Lily stood regally as a greying gentleman in a black evening coat bowed over her hand. "Barrington," he heard her croon. "It has been some time. How is your son?" She gave the man a cordial smile as he answered.

"Lawrence is doing well, learning his way around the business of running the estates. He'll do me proud. You look more lovely than ever. It has been far too long since you were here. Your absence has made London a dreary place." Noah's hand fisted at his side as the man brought her hand to his lips, kissing her knuckles as his gaze swept over her.

"Noah, are you alright? You looked flushed." Claudia was tugging on his arm, looking up at him in concern. He waved his hand, dismissing her comment as he moved her to the other side of the room, avoiding the duchess but nearly running down her daughter.

"Mr. Reeves, is it truly you?" Julia beamed as she looked up at him. "I did not think we would see you again so soon, but glad I am that we did." She reached out her hand, encased in long gloves, and grasped his arm. Shifting her gaze, she asked. "Who is your lovely companion?"

Claudia's eyes narrowed as she took in the beautiful young lady, tightening her hold on his arm. "May I present Mrs. Claudia Reynolds, my lady."

"Soon to be Reeves," Claudia quickly added, giving Julia a pointed look. The lady's expression faltered slightly as Noah inwardly rolled his eyes heavenward. He doubted she was aware of what had transpired between himself and her mother, yet he did not wish for Lily to learn of his betrothal through her daughter.

"Congratulations to you both," she said, a perplexed look crossing her face that she quickly hid.

"Thank you," Claudia replied with a nod. "And who might you be?" Claudia looked at Noah, then turned back to the girl.

"Claudia, this is Lady Julia Stanhope, sister of the Duke of Hawthorne. We met at his estate while I was visiting." Claudia's demeanor changed slightly, though she continued to watch Julia as though she were attempting to snatch away her reticule. Wishing to ease the tension, he asked after the duchess.

"Laura is much improved. Andrew carries her down to the garden each day so that she can enjoy the sunshine and be a part of the girls'

174

games. Oh, and little Jonathan is just a darling child. It is good to see my brother so happy after all that occurred." Noah agreed with a nod. "Have you seen Mother? I am certain she will wish to greet you." Noah swallowed as Julia waved to someone over his shoulder. "Look who I have discovered, Mr. Reeves and his lovely fiance." Noah's gut clenched as he turned to look into surprised blue eyes. To her credit, there was no outburst, only a cordial, yet cool greeting.

"Lovely to see you again, Your Grace," Noah said as he bowed. "This is Mrs. Claudia Reeves, Claudia. May I present the Dowager-Duchess of Hawthorne." Claudia dipped a low curtsey.

"It is an honor, Your Grace."

"Yes." Was Lily's only reply. "Julia, Baron Rumsfeld was asking after you, we should say hello." She glanced back at Noah and his companion. "I hope you both enjoy your evening," she said with a nod. The ladies departed, Julia looking back at him apologetically as her mother led her forward without so much as a backward glance. He could not help but watch Lily as she moved about the room, seeming to keep a distance between them at all times. He stood with Dresher, who was chatting amiably with Claudia, allowing him the opportunity to think.

He had to find a way to have her alone, to explain. Not that he had any idea what to say. '*In a drunken stupor I bedded the widow of a dear friend and now I must marry her?*' That would go over swimmingly, he thought churlishly as he continued to chastise himself. He felt as though he was in a nightmare from which he desperately needed to wake, yet the firm grip of Claudia's hand on his arm assured him he was wide awake and in a great deal of trouble.

Damnable man never changes, Lillian thought as she avoided Noah's surreptitious glances. She had been right to be wary when he left for London. How many times had he tossed her aside for another pretty face? At least she had not been a virgin. Lord knew plenty of her widowed friends had taken lovers over the years. It had been as simple as that. She had taken her pleasure and now she could move on. Mayhap she would take a lover. Barrington had been hinting for the last year that he was quite interested. Looking about the room, she could see Noah and his little blonde chit by the refreshments and averted her gaze before he caught her looking. Spying Barrington, she walked toward the handsome marquess with a coy smile. She had never been one to flirt. She had not had the opportunity, having been sold off to Hawthorne before the season even began, yet she had watched and learned over the years. It was time to put those lessons to use.

"Have you any plans to ask me for a dance this evening?" she asked, as she leaned closer to the tall dark headed man. He was handsome, greying at the temples with a strong angular jaw and dark brown eyes that appeared almost black when he was attempting to seduce her. Those eyes now looked at her in surprise before crinkling slightly with his broad smile.

"I was only awaiting your word, Your Grace." He offered his arm, and the pair moved toward the dance floor. A waltz was beginning and Lillian happily moved into the man's arms as he twirled her around the floor.

"May I assume you are considering my suit?" he asked, dark brows raised as his eyes dropped to her mouth. She smiled, giving his shoulder a light squeeze.

"I am considering it." His gaze was dark with desire as he pulled her closer.

"After the festivities, might I join you for a drink?"

"I am here with my daughter, Barrington. It would not be seemly to have you accompany us home." She lowered her lashes as she had seen others do when being coy.

"Name the time and the place and I will be at your disposal my dear Lillian." She could swear she felt eyes on her back as the dance continued, making her skin prickle and she shivered. Barrington drew her scandalously close now as they danced, then she looked up to see Noah dancing with his fiance nearby. Of course, she was young and beautiful, able to give him children. He would be a wonderful father. She had seen him with her granddaughters and they adored his attention, as had she.

Chastising herself for her weakness, she returned her attention to the man who held her in his arms. When the music ended, Barrington suggested a stroll in the garden. She knew well it was more than a stroll he had in mind, and she gladly took his arm, allowing him to lead her toward the French doors that led to the veranda.

Before they could reach the door, Lillian felt a hand at her elbow. "Please forgive the intrusion," Noah said with a bow. "Might I have a word with Her Grace?" Barrington looked the man over with impatience. Noah wore his uniform this evening. The crimson coat, decorated with his rank and accomplishments. Lillian had to admit he was breathtaking, standing taller than the marquess with his silver grey eyes shining down at her. Even so, she needed to keep her wits about her. The feel of his hand on her bare arm sent a tingle through her she could not afford to acknowledge.

"Can this not wait sir, we were just about to take the air," Barrington said imperiously.

"I am afraid it is rather urgent." His eyes pleaded with her, and she finally agreed. Taking her arm from Noah's grasp, she lay a hand on Barrington's arm with a sweet smile.

"I will be but a moment." As the marquess harrumphed, Noah led her away. Once they exited the ballroom, he increased his pace as Lillian fought to stay on her feet. Locating a small empty salon, he pulled her in and closed the door, pressing her body against its dark wooden surface. His eyes turned stormy as his face descended toward hers. Easily reading his intent, she let her hand fly, striking him across the left cheek.

Noah grasped both hands, pulling them above her head as he pressed against her. She attempted to lift her knee toward his bollocks but he quickly blocked her by placing a leg between her thighs. Her breath was coming quickly as she seethed at him. The man infuriated her, dragging up her insecurities and her desires. She continued to glare at him, no longer able to feign indifference.

"Let me go, you bloody bastard, don't you have a pretty little chit to entertain?" She spat the words, wishing they were truly venom capable of scorching him.

"Yield woman," he said through clenched teeth as she continued to struggle. "Allow me to explain before you... aahhh" He stumbled back as she stomped the instep of his boot. "Bloody hell, Lily," he cursed as she attempted to open the door. He was too quick for her and had a hand on the door again, blocking her escape.

"Are you not betrothed? You had a bit of fun with me, then returned to London to the waiting arms of your pretty little piece. What further explanation do I require?" She felt her heart crack at her own words as she fought the tears she refused to shed in his presence. "I am certain your children will be lovely. Now if you will excuse me," she said, straightening her shoulders. "I have no more time for your lies." She turned her back to him, hand on the door, until he pulled her against his chest, his mouth beside her ear.

"Please Lily, I never wanted her. It was before I saw you again, you must know that." His breath caressed her neck, and she swallowed past the lump that grew in her throat.

"What does it matter? You should not have dallied with me when you knew there was someone else. You never change." She felt his grip loosen, but he did not release her, instead turning her to face him.

"It matters, Lily. And yes, I should not have kept this from you... seeing you again, speaking with you; it was as if no time had passed." She scoffed at his words as she recalled the beautiful face of the girl on his arm. How could he want her? She bore the lines and scars of a life lived. His eyes softened as he seemed to read her thoughts. "You are the most beautiful woman I have ever seen. The years make no difference to me. You will always be my little Lily."

He pressed his lips to her forehead, then her temple, and finally her lips. He lingered there a moment as his hand cupped her cheek. Pulling back to look at her, his eyes pleading. She could almost believe him. To her own vision he remained the handsome young man she rode through the fields with, the two of them speaking for hours about the future. She longed for their easy friendship and the warmth that it brought to her heart. Now that longing, coupled with the knowledge of how his body felt as it joined with her own. Yet what was to be done? He planned to join himself with another. It was as if their past was repeating only this time he was the one betrothed to another.

She pushed him away. His proximity was clouding her mind, she could not think. "Lily, please." She heard him call as she finally escaped the small room and ran for the security provided by the crowded ballroom. She did not see the lady who remained in the shadow of a marble bust on its pedestal to the left of the door.

Claudia remained in place for a moment after the dowager-duchess emerged from the salon door where she had been listening a moment before. Finally, straightening her skirts, she moved forward, a smile on her face. "There you are, darling. I was worried about you. Are you unwell?" she crooned as she placed a hand on his flushed cheek.

"Claudia, we need to speak, I..." She cut off his words as she fanned herself.

"Of course, I am just so fatigued. It is ever so warm in there, but we really must return. The Duke of Wellington was asking after you and you should not keep him waiting." She took his arm, tugging him along, not wishing to give him time to speak. She required time to think of what to do. The woman might be a duchess, but she was too old, at least fifty. He could not possibly want her. She could not even give him a child. She must make him realize she was the better choice.

It surprised her when he secreted the older woman from the ballroom. The woman's pretty daughter had been of greater concern

180

to her. She would have been a greater adversary, yet this aging duchess was no match for her. Standing close to Noah, she lay a possessive hand on his arm as he spoke with Wellington. She noted the dowager-duchess had just entered after being absent for some time. She moved toward her daughter and whispered in her ear. The girl had seemed concerned and the pair quickly left, stopping only a moment to speak to the handsome marquess they had been speaking to earlier.

Claudia felt her shoulders relax as she released the breath she felt she had been holding since seeing Noah with the blasted woman. Perhaps she could pay a call tomorrow. She had been introduced to Lady Julia after all; it would not be unheard of to pay her a visit. Seeing a footman pass with a tray, she asked him to bring a whiskey for Noah. He was more manageable when he was in his cups. Best get him started.

Chapter twenty

Noah had hardly slept, tossing about with thoughts of the two women in his life. Claudia had found him in the salon after Lily had fled, expressing her concern for his odd state. She thought he was ill, and his guilt consumed him as she fussed over him. Bringing him several glasses of whiskey, she likely hoped to calm what she assumed were nerves at being in the crush of society. She knew he was not one for such occasions. He had accepted them, though he knew drinking was not the answer to his troubles. He set them aside covertly after a sip or two, not wishing to seem ungrateful for her care.

When they had returned home, she had once again wished to share his bed, but he had reiterated his desire to wait out of respect for her. He had more regrets than she realized about that one drunken night. It would likely cost him the happiness of being with the woman he loved. Not that Claudia would not please him, he was certain she would be a wonderful wife and mother; it was just that she did not hold his heart the way that his Lily did. It would be a disservice to marry her when he could not give her all of himself.

Stumbling into the dining room in search of a fortifying cup of coffee, he found Claudia looking forlorn. Taking his steaming cup to the table, he asked, "What has you so pensive this morning?" Raising her soft brown eyes to meet his gaze, he could see the sheen of tears and automatically reached out a consoling hand. "What is wrong, my dear?" A single tear rolled down her rounded cheek.

"I was thinking of my poor dear Ezra. He thought so much of you, I only wish..." Tears began flowing freely as his gut clenched. It was his fault the man was dead, that she had been left alone in that squalid little flat. He squeezed her hand.

"I shall never forgive myself for being the one to survive rather than your husband." She bounded up from her seat, kneeling by his chair as she took his face in her hands.

"You must not say such a thing. He would be so happy to know that you live and that you are the one to care for me now. It means everything." She dropped her hands to his and brought his large, calloused hand to her lips and then cradled it against her cheek. "I never thought I would be so happy again as I am with you." He could only stare down at her as a lump formed in his throat, making it difficult to swallow.

Benning entered, stopping short at the scene before him, "I beg your pardon, but a' Mr. Bartlett has arrived for you sir." Noah was grateful for the intrusion, unable to muster the words he needed to utter to Claudia as she looked at him with adoring eyes. Withdrawing his hand, he stood and strode toward the study where Benning had placed the young man.

After the signing the contracts, the men chatted for a few minutes before Bennett excused himself as he had another appointment. After seeing him out, he asked after Claudia.

"I believe she went visiting," Benning said, not able to say where she had gone or when she would return. He had an idea, though he was uncertain if it was prudent. This could be an opportune time to call on Lily and her daughter at their home; he only hoped they would not turn him away. Benning cleared his throat behind him.

"Might I have a word?" the man asked, his tone strained. Noah ushered him toward one of the wingback chairs in his study.

183

"What is it, my friend?" Noah asked with concern. The man's demeanor was strangely uneasy, a state he rarely demonstrated. Benning took a moment, seeming to gather his thoughts before speaking.

"We have known each other for sometime now," he finally blurted and Noah raised a brow at his odd start. "That being said, you do not seem yourself. Ever since you returned from your aunt's, there has been a restlessness I have not seen in you since you were in battle. Even then I never knew you to be so ill at ease in your own skin."

Noah marveled at the man's perceptive words, but said nothing as he continued. "I am aware, of course, of the circumstances behind your engagement and I know it comes from a place of honor." He paused again as though to find the correct words. "Reynolds was a good man and your protection of his widow is to be commended, but she is a widow. She is not ruined by circumstance. I fear you are sacrificing your own happiness to pay a debt that is not owed."

Noah was taken aback by his words. "How can you say there is no debt? My lord, the man sacrificed himself." His voice was shaking and Benning stopped him by raising a hand.

"I am aware that you believe that, but it is not what Reynolds would have wanted. What he did was his choice and I am certain had the positions been reversed you would have done the same for him."

"Of course I would…"

"And would you have expected him to spend his life feeling guilty for it?" Benning asked.

"No I, that is not what I am doing. I am only…"

"What of your lady?" Noah's eyes went wide. How would Benning know about Lily? The man gave him a wry smile as he took in his expression.

"Dresher."

At the mention of the old doctor, understanding dawned. "What did the old busy body say to you?" Noah asked his friend.

"He came by early this morning looking for you, told him you were still a bed and so we visited for a moment. Did you think your attention to the dowager-duchess would go unnoticed by your friends?"

Noah's shoulders tensed. He had thought he was being discreet, but apparently not. Over the years, he had spoken of Lily to Benning and Dresher, usually when he was in his cups. Still, he had never revealed her current situation or title. Then he recalled Dresher speaking to Julia. Did the girl know of his feelings? Mayhap Lily had spoken fondly of him to her. His heart lightened at the thought before crashing down again. Claudia had made certain to reveal their betrothal there by turning Lily cold to him.

"Have you not suffered enough, my friend?" Benning posed. "You deserve some happiness. Claudia is young. She will marry again without difficulty, I am certain. She is a resourceful girl." Noah heard an odd insinuation in the man's words, but had no time to think on it. He needed to see Lily. Grabbing his hat, he was about to leave. Then he had a thought. Running up the stairs to his chamber, he dug the velvet box out of his drawer where he had stashed it the other day. His steps were purposeful as he turned in the direction of Hawthorne's townhouse. He would not leave until Lily accepted him. It was time for them to be together.

Jennings bowed as he entered the private sitting room where Lillian was reviewing invitations. "Pardon me, Your Grace, you have a visitor in the salon." Lillian looked down at the various items on her desk and sighed.

"Have tea brought in and have Julia join me." She descended to the second floor, smoothing her skirts before entering. She was pleased that Julia was already receiving callers, though after last night she was not in the mood for entertaining. Still, she would do what she must for her daughter. She heard Julia's cheery voice and forced a smile as she entered the elegantly appointed salon. Her cordial veneer faltered as she took in their visitor.

Julia was pouring a cup of tea for Noah's betrothed as the pretty little blonde smiled and commented on the general splendor of the decor.

"I have spent the past month choosing furnishings and wall coverings attempting to make our house a home. Noah is such a dear soul, allowing me a free hand. His greatest desire is my happiness." Lillian felt bile rising in her throat as Claudia continued to sing Noah's praises. Julia, to her credit, was a fine hostess, listening attentively and offering the tray of cakes as Lillian attempted not to scratch the girl's eyes out. Her heart screamed that Noah was hers, yet her mind reminded her she had once again been a fool.

Jennings appeared in the doorway to announce another visitor and Lillian happily stood, ready for a distraction. She met those piercing grey eyes as Noah strode into the salon, nearly running into her. He reached out, taking her hands, not seeing that she was not alone, and she quickly pulled back. "Mr. Reeves, what a surprise. You must be here to collect Mrs. Reynolds." She waved a hand toward the girl, who was rising to her feet with a perplexed look.

"Noah, how did you know where I was?" She moved toward him and he seemed frozen to the spot as he glanced between the two women. Breaking the tension, Julia rose and moved beside her mother.

"What a pleasure to see you again so soon," she said as she looked at her mother, who was attempting to school her expression. "Why, we were just speaking this morning about how lovely it was to have you at Merveille. You must come for a visit again. The girls would enjoy that very much." Noah gave her a nod and a smile as his eyes continued to dart between Lillian and Claudia.

"Noah, you have such a way with children. I know you will be a wonderful father," Claudia mused, brushing a hand over her stomach. Lillian noted the gesture with a sinking heart. Could she already be with child? Is that what he was attempting to impart at Wellington's? Noah coughed lightly and cleared his throat as he offered his elbow to the young lady.

"Yes, well, I suppose we should be off then." His eyes locked with Lillian's as Claudia and Julia said their farewells. He seemed to plead with her, but she had to turn away, unable to bear the myriad of emotions swirling within her. The couple left the room with Julia trailing behind to escort them to the door, then Lillian noticed a hat sitting on the chair closest to the door. She heard his voice growing louder as he approached the room again.

"I'll be just a moment. I've forgotten my hat." He moved inside quickly, grasping Lillian's arm to pull her further into the room.

"Lily, I must speak to you alone. May I please call on you this afternoon, three o'clock?" He held her hand as he spoke, and she felt the warmth spreading through her at his touch. It muddled her thoughts, and she nodded her ascent before she realized she had done it. His fingers squeezed hers lightly before he grabbed his hat and stepped from the room.

Lillian stood there, uncertain of what she had just done. She should ban him from her presence, not allowing him a private audience. He had always made her act foolish and now did not differ from when she was a girl. Julia returned, giving her an odd look.

"What is it, Mother? You seem upset." Lillian sat and lifted her teacup, taking a sip of the now cold liquid.

"Not at all, though I do not care for Mrs. Reynolds appearing at our door without an invitation to call."

"Mayhap she is not familiar with all the social graces. I suppose that is why Mr. Reeves seemed so concerned when he arrived and found her here." Lillian nodded absently as she warmed her tea from the pot. "It was a fine thing to find him here in London, such a kind gentleman. I hope he finds happiness with his new wife."

Lillian's jaw tightened. "What man of his years wouldn't delight in having such a lovely young wife?" she said acidly. Julia frowned at her mother's uncharitable words.

"I thought he was a childhood friend. Why would you not wish him well?" The girl questioned as she loudly tapped her spoon on the edge of the delicate china cup in her hand. "Is there a reason you do not wish to see him happily settled, Mother?" Lillian looked up from her tea, uncertain how to answer. Her daughter was more observant than she gave her credit for.

"Of course I wish him every happiness. I was only referring to men and their tendency to take such young girls under their protection." Julia smiled slyly over the rim of her cup, but said nothing further.

"You will see one day, my child, when the men of society barely glance at you because you no longer hold the blush of youth or ability to provide them an heir," she said acidly.

"I noticed the Marquess of Tremont was still paying you particular attention last night."

"Barrington is a rake. He likely gave his attention to many women during the reception." Lillian set aside her empty cup and swept from the room, leaving her daughter shaking her head with that damnable gleam in her eye. Moments like this, she looked a bit too much like her brother.

Lillian returned to her correspondence, locking herself away in her sitting room for several hours. When Jennings asked if she needed a tray for lunch, she waved him away. As the three o'clock hour approached, she found her stomach fluttering uncontrollably and had no appetite. She chastised herself for behaving as though she were some dewy eyed debutante awaiting a call from her desired suitor. She was certain he would make it known that Mrs. Reynolds was carrying his child, and he had an obligation to her and the child. What did any of it matter? She had wealth and privilege, as well as the freedoms afforded by her status as a widowed duchess.

When the clock read half-past two, she ceased the pacing she had been doing for the last half hour and donned her riding coat. She would be damned if she was going to sit about waiting for the man to tell her what she already knew. Calling for the footman, she instructed the lanky young man to have her horse saddled.

Chapter twenty-one

Forced to enlist a cab with Claudia, claiming fatigue after her visit with the Stanhope ladies. Blast it all. Why had she gone there? Walking into the salon with eyes only for Lily, he had come perilously close to blundering out his proposal in front of Claudia and Julia. He must put an end to this. He had never been one for intrigue. Lord Nevins, his commanding officer in his early days of service, had tapped him for a bit of espionage, infiltrating the camp of the Dutch in India. He had sported damp palms and nearly tossed his breakfast as he skulked behind tents, attempting to hear numbers in their ranks and locate the cannons.

He had told Nevins in no uncertain terms that he was not the man for the job in the future. Place an enemy before him and he would show no fear, but to lie and snake about left him a wreck. That was how he felt as he sat beside Claudia as she told him of how cordial Lady Julia had been. "Her mother, however, was not welcoming at all. She seemed to glare down her nose at me as though I were some guttersnipe dirtying her salon," she said in a huff. "I would have thought a woman of her station would have been a more gracious hostess."

Noah rolled his eyes as he let out an exasperated breath. "I do not recall them extending an invitation last evening. Was it Lady Julia that bid you to come?"

"We were introduced. I was not aware that one had to await a formal invitation, especially with how welcoming they were to you. At least the daughter was, as I recall, the dowager was rather rude to you as well." He looked down at Claudia, taking in her pinched expression.

191

"With the nobles, it is always best to await a formal invitation. You likely caught the dowager-duchess in the middle of some task or another. She is a busy woman, as this is her daughter's first season. She may have even received distressing news from the duke about her daughter-in- law or grandson..." He realized she was glaring at him and stopped speaking.

"Why are you making excuses for her? You should be angry at their treatment of me, being you claim them as close acquaintances."

Noah did not wish to have the needed conversation with Claudia while in a conveyance with a strange driver. He would not embarrass her in such a way, despite her current petulant behavior. He patted her hand, attempting to calm her temper. "We shall speak further when we return to the house," he said, nodding his head toward the driver, who appeared to be leaning toward them, taking in each word. Noah realized this was one of the ways that gossip spread about in London and he was not about to be fodder for the hackney drivers of town.

When they entered the house together, Benning gave him a questioning look, likely surprised to find them together. "Claudia, might we speak in my study?" He motioned toward the door of his small sanctuary to the left of the foyer.

"I am sorry, darling, but I am far too fatigued to speak of that vile woman at present. I have been feeling rather ill this morning as well." She folded her hands over her stomach with downcast eyes. "Mayhap after a rest I will be in better spirits." Before he could protest, she kissed his cheek, then disappeared up the stairs.

Taking out his watch, he noted he had a few hours until he was to meet Lily. He brushed the pocket of his coat that held the bracelet for her, absently. He would make all of this right. Turning toward his study, he told Benning that he would leave at half-past two and asked that his horse be ready. Sitting behind his desk, he retrieved a page and quill as he began formulating a plan. He would see that Claudia had a decent place to live and an allowance until such time as she remarried. Benning was correct. It would not take long with proper introductions for her to find a husband closer to her age. If she knew she would be cared for, he was certain he and Claudia would part amicably.

He had hoped to speak to her before he left, however Claudia had still not emerged from her room at two o'clock when he went upstairs to change into riding clothes. A bit of time on horseback would set him at ease. Lockney, his fine military mount, was waiting for him. His coat brushed so that his silky black coat shone in the sun and he saddled and ready for Noah right on time. Thanking Reggie, his young groom, he swung up into the polished saddle in anticipation of finally settling things with Lily.

He was a bit early as he approached the imposing townhouse of the Duke of Hawthorne. Good thing, for he turned the corner in time to see a familiar figure dash away on a chestnut bay. Noah cursed under his breath as he saw Lillian take flight, for he knew that was what she was doing. He eased Lockney into a cantor, gradually gaining speed as traffic on the street thinned. She was heading for the park and he gave chase.

It was exhilarating to feel the wind on his face again. It had been too long since he gave his horse a good run and Lily showed no sign of slowing as she entered the park. Two other riders came up short as she dashed through the gated entrance, their mounts prancing and whinnying at the sudden appearance of another horse in their path. When she was past them, she gained speed again. It surprised him to note she wore her hair in a simple braid under her hat and seeing it catch the wind behind her made him recall days chasing after her across the fields. His heart raced at the memory, fed by the current chase as he gained ground.

Likely hearing the rapid hoofbeats approaching from behind, he saw her glance over her shoulder. She frowned and turned the bay toward a stand of trees across a grassy knoll and gave the horse its head. He could not help but smile as he went in pursuit. It was a rare day when she had beaten him, and today would not be one of them. There was too much at stake, and he was tired of waiting for what he wanted. She passed through the tree line a moment before him, but he was quickly alongside her as she had slowed, unaccustomed to riding in the trees.

She showed no signs of stopping, however, so he reached out and grabbed her reins, earning a slap to his thigh from her braided riding crop. Despite the sting, he did not release her, pulling back until her mount slowed, then came to a stop.

"What do you think you are doing? Unhand my horse," she yelled indignantly. His smile widened. She was beautiful when her color was up and for a moment, he could still see that spirited girl he had fallen in love with.

"As I recall, you and I had an appointment, so it is I who should be put out. Where were you running to, my little Lily?" She struck out at him, but he quickly grabbed her wrist as she continued to struggle.

"I am not little and I most certainly am not yours. Remember, you are speaking to a duchess."

"More like an errant child, if you ask me," he retorted as she glared at him, chest heaving in outrage. He kept his hand on her horse's bridle, preventing her escape. Finally, she dismounted and stomped away from him as she cursed him under her breath. Tying the horses to a low branch, he went after her, chuckling despite himself. How he loved this woman, he thought. There was no one like his Lily, and she was his whether or not she would admit it.

His strides being longer, he caught her quickly. Grasping her arm, he pressed her against a large birch tree and leaned in, taking her mouth. Her taste was intoxicating, a vintage he would never tire of. He angled his head to deepen the kiss until he felt a burning in his lower lip. With a curse, he pulled back as he tasted the iron tang of blood on his tongue.

She spat in a very unladylike manner, then stared at him, her jaw clenched.

"How dare you? You have no right to…"

"Hold your tongue woman or I will hold it for you." Her eyebrows shot up at his insinuation, but she did not speak. "Now will you listen to me?" She nodded grudgingly, and he loosened his grip. When she could move, she bolted away from him but did not make it far as he took hold of both of her arms. "This would be much simpler if you would yield. You agreed to meet with me, so be the duchess that you claim you are and behave." Those blue eyes burned into him as he steered her to a fallen tree and sat her down, keeping hold of her hands.

Taking a deep breath, she lifted her chin, "I know what it is you wish to tell me so there really is no need for these theatrics."

"I am not the one being dramatic and how is it you would know my mind?" She looked around, seeming to fear someone would hear them or see them alone together. Seeing that they were alone, she turned back to him.

"You bound yourself to another and must be a gentleman and see it through. Does that sound like your situation?" He tilted his head, seeming almost amused. "Then I imagine you will say that even though you care deeply for me, she is carrying your child and you are honor bound to give her and the child your name." He swallowed audibly, still holding her hands as he looked into her eyes.

"You have woven quite a tale for me, I see. Now may I tell you what it is I wish to say?" Looking away as though she was disinterested, she nodded.

"I love you Lily." Her eyes snapped to his, likely not expecting such a declaration. "I have never loved another as I have you and I want only to spend the rest of my life with you." Drawing a steadying breath, he pressed on. "I did bed, Claudia, but before you get your petticoats in a knot, it was a drunken mistake, and before you and I encountered one another again. I had thought it right to offer for her as she was widowed... Her husband saved my life by sacrificing himself," he said, as his eyes clouded. "For that reason I owe her security, a home, funds to live on, but I realize now that this can occur without marriage."

Lily had not spoken, seeming dazed as he spoke his heart. Finally, when he paused, she asked. "What is it you are saying?"

196

"I am saying that you are the only woman I want. I am asking you to be my wife." She stood, and he watched her as she paced slowly. The leaves beneath her feet rustled, the only sound besides birds singing in the trees. He held his breath as she slowed and turned to him.

"You would marry me, give up any chance of having a child of your own, that's madness." She threw up her hands and stalked away from him. Giving chase, he stopped her before she could mount her horse. Anger flared within him as he looked down at her. "Who are you to decide I must have children? If I had married a woman that was barren, would you insist I leave her? If you do not wish to marry me, I suggest you find a better reason. My lack of title perhaps." She threw off his hand, dropping her horse's reins.

"You bastard. You believe that was why I married Hawthorne? As if I had any choice in the matter. I have had quite enough of men deciding what is best, as if I am too weak to think for myself. Nothing I've done has ever been enough," she grits out, her voice trembling with anger.

Noah stared at her, searching her eyes, but seeing only pain. "You have always been enough for me, Lily." He leaned in, kissing her brow, then descending toward her lips.

She was having none of it. She pushed at his chest with an angry laugh. "You say that, yet each time I opened my heart to you, you've run off to someone else. At least I knew what my father expected, and it wasn't long before I saw through Hawthorne as well, but you... You have always had the power to break me and by God, I won't allow you to do it again." Turning on her heel, she mounted skillfully and turned her horse for home, leaving Noah stunned as he watched her retreating form.

Lillian paced once more in her chamber, her hands clenching and releasing at her sides as she attempted to calm her racing heart. She had done what she must for him. As desperately as she wished to give herself over to him, she could not trust him or any other man; they all wanted something and in the end found her lacking.

Lydia, her lady's maid, arrived at her door an hour later to prepare her for the Atherton ball. Seated before the mirror, she allowed her mind to drift as the girl fused with her hair. This was her world, the one she had embraced rather than running off with Noah all those years ago. She thought of Mary Bingham, Laura's mother, and the life she had chosen. To hear her daughter speak of her family, Mary had been happy and in love.

Lillian's father had made the choice for her and it was likely the correct one. Noah would have left her in time. At least when Hawthorne turned his back on her, she was still a duchess.

Chapter twenty-two

Claudia found him in his study when she finally came downstairs. He sat in the darkened room, his shirtsleeves rolled to his elbows. She stood quietly in the doorway, taking in his slumped shoulders, his fingers steepled against his lips. He was a handsome man with broad shoulders, still strong and capable even in his fifties.

She recalled how Ezra had spoken of his commanding officer during their brief marriage, how he showed concern for his men no matter their station. She had thought marrying the young lieutenant would provide her with a secure future. He had been dashing in his uniform when she had served him and his comrades ale and meat pies at the pub where she worked long hours to support herself.

After her father's death, she had been alone. Though she did not miss the back of his hand, which struck her often when he had been drinking. Ezra had smiled and flirted with her, then asked if he might call on her before leaving for his next posting. The courtship had been short. She had allowed him to bed her on their second meeting to force his hand and they wed before he left with his regiment.

She had seen him several months later for a brief visit before he left to fight Napoleon's forces. He had returned in a pine box. She could not say his loss devastated her as much as the loss of his income. The situation forced her to return to serving in the pub where drunken sods pinched and groped her while out avoiding their wives.

Salvation had come, however, in the form of Major Noah Reeves standing in her doorway, hat in his hands as he apologised for her loss. Her husband had saved his life, he said, and he hoped he could assist her to repay that debt. Inspiration had ignited, and she made certain to present a pitiful face upon each of his visits. When he offered to take her into his home, she had put up a few polite protests, knowing the sort of man he was. He would never allow her to refuse. Once ensconced in his home, she set about seducing the older man, something she thought would be simple, yet he had shown tremendous restraint.

He was courteous and generous with her, never making advances, even though she left herself open to them. She resorted to filling his glass in the evenings when he was feeling the devastation of loss after years of war. She would speak of her poor lost Ezra, knowing this would play upon his guilt.

The night two months ago, when she had plied him with enough whisky that he could barely stand, she assisted him to his room. She had chosen that night, knowing the ever protective Benning would be visiting his sister. In his bedchamber, she sat him on the bed and removed his boots as he swayed. Standing between his thighs, she removed his waistcoat and untied his neck cloth before leaning in to kiss him.

It had surprised her to feel genuine longing when his warm mouth met hers. Maneuvering his hands to cup her breasts, she whispered, "Make love to me, Noah." To her surprise, her seductive words brought him to his senses, and he had set her away from him. He bid her to return to her own bed. There was no need to sacrifice herself to him for his assistance.

When he lay back in the bed, his snores coming immediately, she knew what must be done. Undressing his slumbering form, she disrobed, sliding in beside him. He had not awoken during her ministrations, nor during her attempts to kiss and stroke him.

Resigned, she nestled against his muscular chest, resting her hand there and drifting off to sleep.

The following morning he had woken beside her, certain that he had compromised her in his drunken state with no memory of what had truly occurred. To her delight, he had offered for her later that afternoon.

Looking at him now, he looked so like the devastated man he had been after Ezra's death, and she wondered what had made him so forlorn. Mayhap she could offer him a drink again. He had continued to keep her at arm's length despite believing he had already bedded her, and she was becoming frustrated. She knew if she were to have his child, she would bind him to her. Now that she was aware of his feelings for Lillian Stanhope, she was more desperate to make this happen.

She had planted the seed with the dowager- duchess and her daughter earlier in the day, wishing to deter the woman in any way possible. She already had money and security, Claudia would not allow the older woman to take what she had labored to secure. Noah was hers and she would not let him go.

She moved behind him, placing her hands on his shoulders and dropping a kiss on the top of his head. "I worry for you, my darling. What has you so pensive?" She rubbed her hands down over his chest, lightly embracing him. There was a glass of whiskey on the table beside him, and he glanced toward it.

"You should go to bed, I am not fit for company." He patted her hands, still clasped on his chest.

"Why don't you join me? I can make you forget whatever is bothering you." She leaned down and brushed her lips against his ear and felt him shiver. With a smile, she moved around to take a seat on his lap, nuzzling his neck. His arms snaked around her and pulled her closer and her lips found his. She nibbled at his lower lip, eliciting a moan from him, and she felt a sense of triumph as the kiss grew in intensity. His hands moved into her hair, freeing it from its bindings.

"I've longed for you to touch me again," she said, allowing her voice to convey her desire. At her words, he stood with her still in his arms and carried her effortlessly toward the stairs. She continued to tease his earlobe with her teeth and lips. He lay her back on the soft floral coverlet of her bed and she drew him down for another kiss and reveled in the feel of his body weight sheltering her. She could feel his arousal, knew he wanted her. He would finally be truly hers.

***

Noah sat behind his desk, looking down into the steaming cup in his hands. There was no headache or muddled mind this morning. He had poured himself a whiskey last night, but had not touched a drop before Claudia had come to him. His dear Lily had spurned him and rather than demonstrating his devotion, he had turned to another.

She had the right of it. The first time she professed her love, he could not run away fast enough, wishing only to be in Angelica's arms. The night he begged her to meet him, she had found him with another and though it had been a misunderstanding; he had handled it poorly. Now he had bedded her, all the while vomiting the truth of his circumstances. How could he expect her to trust him?

Claudia had been warm and welcoming, her body ready to yield to him, yet his eyes had only seen Lily before him. He had pushed away and run from the room, locking himself in his own chamber as he listened to Claudia crying just down the hall. It was time to end this. Even if he could not have Lily, it was time to release Claudia from their betrothal.

He found her in the dining room, sullenly pushing coddled eggs around her plate as he entered and sat beside her. When Eliza, his cook, entered to bring him a plate, he waved her away and waited until the door had closed behind her. Taking Claudia's hand, he brought it to his lips gently. Her eyes were glassy with unshed tears and it pained him to know that he was the cause.

"I am sorry for my behavior last night and for the past fortnight. I have not been myself but it is not your doing." She looked up at him with questioning eyes, squeezing his hand.

"It is alright my darling, I realize things have been difficult for you since we lost dear Ezra."

The sound of that name was like a knife to his heart, but he knew he must go on. "I realize now that I have done you a great disservice by offering for you. You are young and beautiful and could have many fine gentlemen vying for your favor." He released his hold from hers and smoothed his fingers over his trousers absently.

"Know that I shall provide for you until such time as you find a suitable situation and you may call on me at any time if you are in need of anything."

Tears spilled over onto her cheeks, and her hand came to her throat. "But you are what I need, my darling. You and no other; you cannot mean to cast me aside. Do you not love me as I love you?" She grasped his hands as she dropped to her knees before him.

203

"Have I displeased you? Do you not find me appealing anymore? Please, just tell me what I must do."

Taking one hand from her, he cupped her cheek. "You have done nothing wrong, but I am certain it is not love you feel toward me, it is merely gratitude for taking you in. There is no need for you to sacrifice your youth in payment. I only wish for your happiness."

"If my happiness is what you wish, then stay with me, marry me and give our child your name."

Noah's heart stuttered as he watched her lay a hand over her flat belly. His eyes grew wide as he shook his head. It couldn't be. They had lain together but once over two months ago. Of course, he realized it would take her that long to be certain. Why had she not said anything? She took his hands again and placed one on her stomach.

"I had it confirmed yesterday, and I had planned to tell you last night, but you were so out of sorts, I was certain how you would react. I hope you know I am overjoyed to be carrying your child. We only need you to be a family, but if you no longer want…" He stopped her by pulling her into his arms.

"This is wonderful news," he said, attempting to sound joyful through the tightness in his throat. At least she could not see his face, for he was certain his eyes would give him away. "I am so sorry, Lily," he thought. There was nothing more to be done. He would seek a special license and marry Claudia as soon as possible.

*** Lillian looked up as she heard a slight commotion in the foyer and was surprised when her son appeared in the doorway of the parlor. "Andrew, what are you doing here? Is Laura alright?"

He stepped into the room and moved toward the drink cart and poured himself a scotch. "All is well. Robert is with her. I have some business that could no longer wait and I wanted to meet with Reeves as well."

Lillian knew it had to be difficult for him to leave his wife and child right now, but there were things that required the duke's presence. "Will you be attending any events with us while you are in town?" She had wanted him to be present for the season to assist his sister's entrance into society.

"I will join you both for whatever events take place during the next several days until I return home." He took a sip of his drink and sprawled in the one large chair he had added to the parlor in the last year. His legs stretched out before him as he took a deep drink and dropped his head back. The fatigue washed over him, his hand loosening as his breathing slowed. Lillian took the glass from his hand, leaving him to rest in the chair.

Later that afternoon, Jennings informed Lillian that her son has received another caller, a business associate, in his study. She bid the young butler to have tea served to them and peeked in for a moment to welcome his guest since his duchess was not present in the house; it would be fitting for her to act as hostess. It was likely his friend Charles Bartlett.

Arriving in the oak paneled room, she found her daughter there with Bartlett and Andrew. Julia was laughing and Lillian could see the way the young man-of-business leaned in, grinning as her daughter lay a hand on his arm. She watched them a moment longer until Andrew came up behind her with the satchel he must have gone to retrieve.

"No encouraging him, Julia," Andrew said sternly, despite his grin. "I'll not have you telling all of my secrets Charles or I shall be forced to reveal all of yours." The two men continued to chide one another good naturedly as Julia poured tea, offering a cup to her mother, who had taken a chair by the window.

Watching the trio, she relaxed. Their youthful banter was soothing and she could see that her children were truly happy, although she would have to speak to Andrew about his friend. The man seemed quite taken with Julia of late. He would seek her out at the events they attended and would call at the house, the pair walking in the garden to take the air. It no longer seemed a matter of familiarity and Lillian wished to know Bartlett's intentions.

There was another knock at the door. It seemed the arrival of her son had brought visitors out of the woodwork. When Jennings announced the man, Lillian found herself trapped as Noah entered the room. The gentlemen exchanged bows and Andrew ushered him to take the other wingback chair by his desk.

Noah's eyes widened in surprise when he noted her presence in the corner, then she was certain she saw sadness darken his eyes. "Your Grace," he said softly as he gave her a bow. She nodded without a word, then stood to leave the room. Turning to her daughter, she added, "Julia, come along. We should leave the men to their business."

Lillian thought her heart would burst from her chest at seeing him. She knew she had done the right thing, however, that did nothing to lessen the pain. She did her best to go about her day. There were menus to finalize with the cook and a review of the week's invitations. When she heard deep male voices in the foyer, followed by the door closing, she breathed a sigh of relief.

She was not prepared to find Noah in the parlor when she entered. "What are you doing here?" she asked, her tone clipped and impatient. "I thought you had left."

"I needed to speak with you, Lil... Your Grace." She huffed out a breath.

"I thought we had said all that needed to be said. I have other matters to attend to and have no desire to continue the same conversation."

Taking her arm to stop her retreat, he blurted, "I am to be married." Lily felt as though he had just struck her. His eyes were searching her face, for what she did not know. Mayhap he wanted her to break down, to beg him not to do it. Instead, she lifted her chin, keeping her expression impassive.

"My congratulations to you and your betrothed," she said graciously. "Now if you'll excuse me." She fled the room before the tears that threatened could give her away. It was truly over now. Just as she had expected, he ran into the arms of another.

Chapter twenty-three

Claudia was giddily looking through the bolts of silk and lace, running her fingers over the soft fabrics as the modiste spoke with the two seamstresses. Noah had offered to elope to Gretna Green, but she had pouted, saying she did not wish to skulk off in shame. She wanted a wedding, the kind she had been cheated out of when she and Ezra had married before he left for his posting. She was going to be seen as a lady. There was no need to hide when she was marrying a man of honor and wealth.

One seamstress led her into the back to complete measurements and begin creating her wedding gown. When she emerged an hour later, she came face to face with Lillian Stanhope and her daughter. Julia was standing on a small riser while a girl pinned the hem of the artfully draped pale blue gown she was modeling.

Claudia looked toward the modiste without speaking to the other ladies. "I do hope you will complete the work before my wedding. I realize a fortnight is not much time but my dear Noah is quite eager to be wed." She then turned her gaze to Julia, "My, isn't that a lovely gown, Lady Julia; it is so good to see you again." The girl gave her a tight smile as she glanced at her mother. The dowager barely spared Claudia a glance from her seat to the left of the riser.

She ignored the older woman's sour look. She had won, so let the woman glare. The bell atop the shop door jingled, drawing her attention. When she turned, Claudia beheld one of the most beautiful men she had ever seen. She drew in a breath as she took in his tall, broad frame. His dark hair waved back from his sculpted face and when he smiled, she blushed, thinking his attention was on her. Then she heard Julia's delighted words.

"Andrew, I thought you would be detained all morning." The man walked up and tweaked Julia's nose.

"How could I resist joining you for your fitting?" he said in a teasing tone. "Actually, I finished early and hoped to enlist your help in ordering a few things for Laura. It would be nice for her to have something new now that the baby has been born." His eyes turned wistful as Claudia realized this was the Duke of Hawthorne. She stepped forward as she took him in, making a credible curtsy.

"Pardon me Your Grace, I have looked forward to making your acquaintance as you will be in business with my future husband." The duke looked down at her and his glorious blue eyes captivated her.

"To whom would you be referring, my lady?" he asked in his deep baritone, sending a shiver of pleasure down her spine.

"Major Noah Reeves, Your Grace." His eyes lit with recognition and he took her hand, giving her a low bow.

"Of course, he is a fine man." A look of puzzlement flitted across his face. "I suppose congratulations are in order. The major has not mentioned he was to be married." She felt a slight pang at this given Noah had met with the duke just yesterday. Regaining her composure, she gave the man a brilliant smile.

"I do hope you and the duchess will attend."

"I am afraid my wife is currently unable to travel and I will return to the country before week's end, but I thank you for the invitation. I am certain my mother and sister will be happy to attend, however." Claudia pressed her lips together as she glanced at the dowager-duchess who continued to frown at her.

"We will be certain to send the invitation," she said, giving a weak smile. "Might I extend an invitation to dinner tomorrow evening then. It would be lovely to become better acquainted." The duke looked over his shoulder at his mother, who appeared to be fussing with a nonexistent defect in her skirt. Claudia would be damned if she would invite that woman into her home and did not expand upon the invitation. Finally, the stunning gentleman accepted.

"Wonderful. Noah will be thrilled. I am afraid I must be off. It was lovely to meet you, Your Grace and I look forward to tomorrow evening." She curtsied again, giving the handsome duke a coquettish look before leaving the shop. Given what Noah had said about the difficult birth of their child, the duke would likely seek a lover before long. That was how things were done within the *ton,* despite what her rather naïve husband believed of the couple. Knowing they would be thrown together because of business dealings, Claudia would be happy to offer him comfort when he was in town.

She imagined he was quite generous with his lovers and she felt warmth pooling low at the idea of the man's delicious body pressed to her own. Shaking away her errant thoughts, she reminded herself there was work to be done for the dinner tomorrow. She would have tea at Lady Weatherly's later that afternoon. This was an invitation she had spent weeks attempting to obtain. She was a lady with connections and with her in Claudia's corner, she would gain entrance to the *ton.*

Noah had no desire to garner a place within London society, though he had not discouraged her attempts. It saddened her that the Duke and Duchess of Hawthorne would not be attending the wedding. That would have been a boon for her standing. Though she did not wish to have her there, the dowager-duchess would bring some prestige to the affair. The woman could do nothing to come between her and Noah now that he believed she would give him a child. She only needed to keep up the charade for a few weeks. Then, when her courses came, she would tell him she had lost the child.

***

Andrew stood beside his mother as they watched Julia and Charles Bartlett join the other dancers. "Have you spoken with your friend about his intentions toward your sister?" she asked. He gave her a wry smile as he shook his head.

"They have known each other for some time, they are only enjoying one another's company." Lillian rolled her eyes at her son. "You are blind if you do not see the way they look at each other. I am uncertain this is the best situation for your sister."

Laying a hand on her shoulder, he reminded her of the promise she made to allow Julia to choose for herself. "Charles is a good man and has done well for himself. I considered him a desirable choice as a husband." As she continued to glare at him, he chuckled. "I will speak with him before I leave, I promise you."

Out of the corner of his eye, he noted the Earl and Countess of Devon, who quickly moved away when he leveled an angry gaze at them. His wife's uncle had stolen her dowry and cast her out of his house when Andrew was courting their daughter. He had most definitely made the correct choice in pursuing Laura over her cousin. He could not imagine his life without her and his heart hurt for missing her over the past few days.

He noted his mother's look of distaste at the sight of the pair and had to smile to himself. She had championed their daughter, even accusing Laura of trapping him. He recalled the day he revealed the truth to her of the earl's betrayal, the way something had changed so suddenly in her eyes. He would admit he had been certain his mother would take their side in this, but she had quietly given her blessing to Laura, revealing her acquaintance with Mary Parsons in her youth.

Andrew knew very little of his mother's past, as she was not one to speak of it. He only knew what his aunt had revealed about her father selling her off to his father and that she resented it. Finally, he turned to her and asked the question that had been vexing him.

"What made you turn against the earl after championing his cause so tirelessly?"

Lillian appeared stunned for a moment and he had to admit his question came with no preamble.

"I-well, you proved the man to be a thief." Andrew continued to look at her with encouragement, wanting to know more. She shook her head and drew him away to a more secluded spot, though still keeping her gaze fixed on Julia and Charles as they danced. "Knowing he gambled away his own fortune and used an innocent girl to line his pockets was unforgivable. Bad enough he turned his back on his own sister all those years ago. I realized he withheld her dowry as well, so he frittered away a small fortune that did not belong to him then as well." Andrew placed a comforting arm about her shoulders, though she only allowed this for a moment before she waved him away.

"Now is not the time for such melancholy musings," she said as she straightened her shoulders and raised her chin to acknowledge

Lord and Lady Rutherton. Andrew respected her wishes, but vowed he would ask again once they were in private. Laura wanted the rift between them healed for the sake of the children and for himself. There was nothing he would deny his wife. That being said, he opened to the woman that bore him as he learned more about her. He supposed everyone had their own demons.

The following day, he sought his mother out in the parlor for a private chat. She set aside her book grudgingly, making a show of her annoyance, though he could see the apprehension in her eyes as he settled before her. Leaning in, he engulfed her small hands in his own.

"Laura and I wish for you to be a part of our children's lives, to find a way forward. To do this, I believe it would benefit us both if I knew more about your history. Aunt Thea once mentioned that it was a monetary arrangement between your father and mine for your hand. Is that why the two of you had such...difficulties?" Her sardonic laugh echoed in the room.

"That was a very diplomatic way to put it my dear." She shook her head, then released his hands to rise and pace the room. She ran her fingers over a small marble replica of Psyche revived by Cupid's Kiss. The Canova sculpture was a favorite of hers, the emotion behind it, one she had not experienced for herself. Lillian was finding it difficult to bare this part of herself to one of her children, yet her soul seemed to cry out to release it. Andrew had suffered from the hatred that grew between his parents, so perhaps he had a right to her pain.

She told him of her father's gambling and womanizing and of the death of her mother that left her at his mercy. Vaguely, she spoke of

213

her deep feelings for another and the heartbreak she had felt at being bartered like a mare to Joseph. "He was dashing and elegant and mayhap we could have found common ground in our marriage. I did my best to close off my feelings for the other man, certain nothing would have come of it in the end. Unfortunately, your father fancied himself in love with another and her refusal of him pierced his heart deeply."

She lifted her hands from the sculpture and moved to the small cart in the corner and poured herself a sherry. Taking a fortifying sip, she took in her son's rapt expression.

"I found them together one night and though I am able to look back with clearer vision now, I did not handle the situation well. I spurned a dear friend and went ahead with the marriage believing the title and wealth would console me."

Understanding seemed to flash in Andrew's eyes. "Laura's mother and my father…"

"She wanted nothing to do with him and I found him begging her one night, promising her he would break our engagement if she would accept him. Of course, you know she had other plans. I shunned Mary that night, then her family did when she ran away with Robert Parsons."

Andrew sat quietly for a moment, taking in what she had told him. "Was this why you were so opposed to Laura?"

"I suppose seeing her with you brought back old injuries, though none of it was Mary's doing. Laura is a great deal like her mother and I am pleased you did not allow my prejudices to sway you." He took her hands again.

"As am I." This made Lillian laugh, and he smiled at her. "I have one other question," he said as she wiped a tear away. "The man you cared for, was it Noah Reeves?"

Lillian's eyes dropped to her hands, still held in his. She could not speak as she thought of him married to another. Tears came unbidden, and Andrew offered her his handkerchief. She had never cried in his presence and he seemed at a loss as to how he should behave.

"I am sorry, Mother. It must be painful. I could see that there was something between you that day he arrived in the garden." Blowing her nose, she looked up into his eyes, the same vivid blue of his fathers, yet they held so much more life. This man before her was a loving father to his children and an adoring husband and she felt her heart bursting with pride, though the guilt of her absence in his life weighed heavily.

"My life is what I made it and now I must live with the consequences."

Lillian went to change for the evening's musicale. Andrew had a dinner invitation so would not be attending, however Julia had mentioned that Mr. Bartlett would be attending. She rolled her eyes skyward, praying for the strength not to interfere. She had hoped her daughter would marry a titled gentleman, though after revealing her past to her son she found herself open to allowing Julia to decide for herself.

Chapter twenty-four

Noah greeted the young duke, offering him a drink as Claudia was still dressing. It had not pleased him to hear of his betrothed's invitation, not because he did not like the man, but he did not wish for a reminder of Lillian at the moment. Still, the invitation was extended and accepted, so etiquette dictated that he must allow it.

The men enjoyed a sherry in the small parlor, exchanging pleasantries, and Andrew informed him of plans to go forward with the expansion into Indian markets. Noah introduced Benning, who they encouraged to join them for a drink. His old friend began expounding on tales of Noah's heroics in battle, causing him great embarrassment, but Claudia's appearance in the doorway saved him.

He did not recall ever seeing the pale pink gown she wore. It was similar to the one she wore to Wellington's, yet the bodice cut much lower, displaying a rather shocking expanse of milky skin. The necklace he had given her lay enticingly across the slight swell of the tops of her breasts, drawing the eye. She seemed to float into the room, immediately moving to greet The Duke of Hawthorne as she held out her hand to him.

The young man bowed low over her hand but refrained from kissing it as some might. "It is an honor to have you in our humble home," she crooned.

"It was kind of you to invite me," he answered, taking a small step back from her. Noah was not the only one watching the exchange. Benning was frowning at them and Noah cleared his throat, hoping to break the tension that seemed to descend on the room.

"Shall we move to the dining room?" Noah said, ushering the group forward. She had the table set with the finest china, silver and crystal, with a large arrangement of flowers and fresh fruit. Claudia had been eager to make a good impression, though he had attempted to allay her fears by describing the duke as not being a slave to appearances, preferring a more casual atmosphere in his own home. "It would offend him if we did not honor his station even in an intimate setting such as this." She had countered as she continued to fuss at his maid and footman.

Noah was still uncomfortable having many servants however, Claudia had insisted that these additions were a necessity to run a household. As he looked the table over, he noted there was not a place for Benning and he looked up in question. "We will require another setting," he called toward the kitchen, but Claudia held up a hand.

"I did not think Mr. Benning would wish to join us this evening."

"Please join us, Benning," the duke spoke up. "I should enjoy hearing more of your stories as I am certain Reeves will not share all the best details." He chuckled as he placed a hand on Benning's shoulder and Noah was relieved. Andrew Stanhope was truly one of the more welcoming men he had ever met. He felt a pang of regret as he had before. Would he have fathered such a man if it had been him who married Lily?

Claudia seemed a bit flustered but regained her composure, insisting that Hawthorne should sit at the head of the table, being of the highest station in the room. Andrew declined, stating he preferred not to stand on such ceremony among friends. "But Your Grace, it would only be fitting…" He held up a hand to stop her protests.

"I will not tell if you don't." He gave a wink as she smiled and took the seat to Noah's right, urging Benning to sit beside him. Claudia finally settled to Noah's left, and the meal went on without further difficulty.

In the end, Noah had to admit to enjoying the evening. Conversation was pleasant and flowed easily as wine and food were enjoyed. Claudia had four courses served as well as an elaborate dessert of fruit in delicate pastry with meringue and he felt he would burst should he eat another bite. Claudia had spent the evening engaging the duke in conversation about his business ventures, his estates and his pursuits when in town. He could tell the man would much rather speak of his family, but he good-naturedly answered her questions as she hung on every word.

Benning offered to show the duke a few of his own souvenirs of war and the men disappeared toward the study while Claudia arranged for port and Noah retrieved a fresh box of cigars he had bought earlier that day. When they gathered in the parlor again, Hawthorne invited them to join him at Merveille at the end of the week. When Noah attempted to decline, the man would not hear of it. "I am certain Laura would enjoy the company of someone other than myself and her brother and the girls have not stopped asking about you."

"Noah, it would be rude to decline such a kind offer and I would love to spend a few days in the country. I have heard marvelous things about your country home." The duke moved closer, taking Claudia's hand gently and raising it to his lips this time. "Then it is settled. I will expect you on Friday." His eyes met Claudia's for a moment as he smiled. Turning his attention back to Noah and

Benning, he added, "Robert will be pleased to have us all in one room to discuss our venture."

After Hawthorne left, Claudia immediately began making lists. "We only have two days to prepare. I will need to review my wardrobe and yours, of course. We must make a good impression. I will need to select a gift for the duchess, though I doubt we will see much of her given her frailty." Noah could not help but let out a laugh at this.

"Laura Stanhope may be many things, but frail is not one of them." Claudia turned to him, her lips pressed tightly. He placed a hand on her shoulder, seeing she was angry for reasons he could not fathom. "You should not concern yourself with appearances. Could you not see this evening that the duke is rather unconventional as is his wife? I promise you, we will receive a warm reception with no expectation. We will be certain to pay a visit to my aunt as well, since she is close by and a dear friend of the duke and duchess. It will be nice for you to visit with a new mother, someone that can give you advice."

"Yes, well, I suppose that will be fine... if she is feeling up to it." She turned back to her list, effectively ending the conversation. He kissed the top of her head before heading up to his chamber.

*** Lillian took a seat beside her daughter as Lady Elizabeth Fairchild, and her sister Margaret prepared to perform. Margaret was a wonder on the pianoforte and was a joy to listen to. Her sister, however, needed a bit more practice with her harp. For that reason, Lillian had allowed herself a second glass of sherry.

Bartlett, of course, took a seat beside Julia and she looked around her daughter at the young man. "Good evening Mr. Bartlett, mayhap

219

you would be more comfortable seated over here," she said as she indicated the chair beside her. Before he could reply, a deep voice rang out beside her.

"I believe this seat is already taken, young man." Barrington's darkly clad form moved beside her and he gave her a rakish smile. "I had hoped to see you this evening, Your Grace."

Lillian settled back into her chair as the first strains of the concerto floated into the room. Thankfully, the first piece was for the pianoforte alone and she enjoyed the lively piece. As the next piece began, Barrington shifted so that his arm was resting against hers. Each time he leaned in to comment on the performance, he seemed to press in closer and she was uncertain if the warmth she felt resulted from the crowd room or his masculine presence.

She had been alone since her husband's death seven years ago, though if she were being honest with herself, she had been alone all her life. The night she had spent in Noah's bed had awakened something in her, a feeling she had not known to miss. Now she craved the touch of a man, not just a man but Noah. Closing her eyes tightly and taking a deep breath, she pushed the thought away; he was out of her reach. Barrington continued to brush against her flirtatiously. He had made it clear he wanted her. Mayhap it was time to flirt back.

The next time he leaned in, she placed her hand on his arm as he commented on the pain being inflicted on his ears by the harp. She laughed softly. "I suppose no one would shed a tear if she were to break a string to end the performance." She looked up through her lashes at his pleased face. Placing a hand over hers on his arm, he gave it a light squeeze that she returned. As he seemed pleased by her touch, she allowed it to linger.

Barrington wore a touch of spicy cologne that tickled her nose pleasantly with his proximity, and she inhaled deeply. This could be just what she needed to push Noah from her mind once and for all. She glanced to her left, ensuring that Mr. Bartlett continued to behave respectfully toward her daughter. The two heads, one dark and one fair, tilted together in a whispered conversation, though there was no contact between them. Satisfied, she turned her attention back to the handsome gentleman on her right.

"Might you join me for a ride in the park on the morrow, Your Grace?" Barrington said, his voice warm and inviting.

"I should like that very much. At what time shall I meet you?" she asked, removing her hand from his arm but allowing it to brush the side of his leg enticingly before returning it to her own lap.

"Eleven o'clock by the gate?" She nodded her agreement as another off note pierced her ear.

After the music thankfully ended, Barrington escorted her as they followed Julia and Mr. Bartlett. "Looks as though your daughter has an admirer, though favoring you as she does there must be a line of callers daily." He looked into her eyes with an intensity that sent a shiver down her spine. "Until tomorrow," he whispered, kissing her hand before assisting her up into the black lacquered carriage that bore the Hawthorne ducal crest. She gave him a wave, feeling anticipation at his words.

The following morning, Lillian and Julia bid farewell to Andrew. He had completed his business in town and was eager to return to his wife and children. The season would end in a few weeks and for

221

Julia, it had been a success. Her dance card was always filled and, as Barrington had thought, she received many callers each day.

Despite her popularity, the girl showed no signs of making a commitment to anyone, which Lillian found comforting. The more she thought of her own marriage, the less she wished to see Julia rushed into a marriage. She was and always would be taken care of. Her brother had seen to that, so she was free to follow her heart. Lillian only hoped she would listen to her head a bit when deciding. Marry in haste repent at leisure, as the saying went.

The pair had decided they would spend the afternoon doing a bit of shopping. Lillian was enjoying the growing closeness between them. She had missed so much with her children, being too wrapped up in her own pain and ambitions to truly know them. She realized Mary's daughter had been the one to help her see that it was not too late to know her children. Laura was so like her and she realized that even though there was no way to mend what had happened with Mary, she could enjoy a relationship with her daughter.

Noting the time, she readied for her ride. An hour in the park, followed by lunch, would be just the thing before she joined her daughter for the remainder of the day. They had no engagements that evening, so they could enjoy the day without rushing.

Dressed in her midnight blue riding habit, she steered her horse toward Hyde Park. As she approached the gate, she could not stop the memory of her last ride here and how it had ended. She banished thoughts of Noah from her mind when she saw Samuel Barrington waiting by the gate. He was atop a fine black, sorrel, a perfect white star on its forehead. His burgundy riding coat was impeccably cut to show off his wide shoulders, and his face brightened when he caught sight of her.

"You look lovely, Your Grace," he said as his eyes roved over her and she blushed at his words. She urged her horse forward, and the two rode side by side along the path as other young couples promenaded in their finery. Lillian looked at them curiously, wondering if any of them were truly in love or destined for a marriage like her own.

Barrington was quiet, only speaking occasionally when he saw someone he knew or passing on bits of gossip about one of the couples that passed by. She asked about his plans for the week and he smiled slyly, "I hope you will fill my evenings." His meaning was clear. He wanted her as a lover. She held his gaze, "Behave yourself, my lord."

"You ask the impossible, Your Grace." He gave her a wink and guided her toward the trees. They dismounted and allowed their horses to take a drink while they sat on the bench by the water. Barrington took her hand in his. "I believe I have made my feelings plain, but you are still toying with me. Give me one night to show you how good we would be together."

Lillian leaned away, wishing for discretion when she heard a feminine laugh nearby. Glancing up, her stomach fell as she saw Noah and his betrothed walking in their direction. His gaze darkened as he saw her hand resting in Barrington's, causing heat to rise in her chest. What right did he have to be angry with her; She was not his. He had made his choice, and she was making hers.

Turning back to the man beside her, she nodded. "Shall we plan an evening, then?" The marquess leaned in, kissing her hands.

223

"I will count the hours, Your Grace."

Lillian looked into the man's warm brown eyes and smiled, fighting the desire to watch Noah as he passed by.

Chapter twenty-five

Andrew was exhausted, his muscles cramped after hours in the carriage, yet all of this disappeared as his daughters ran into his arm as his feet hit the ground. "There are my little monsters," he growled as he lifted them up in his arms. They giggled and squealed as they bombarded him with questions about his journey and wondering what he had brought them.

"Allow your poor father to catch his breath, for heaven's sake." Laura's laughing voice cut through the din and he set the girls down to embrace his wife gently, despite his desire to crush her to him. She looked well, but he worried for her after all she had been through. He took her face in his hands and kissed her. "I've missed you," she whispered against his lips.

With a mischievous smile, he scooped her off of her feet and carried her inside as Charlotte and Rachel ran behind him. "Shall we visit your brother?" He asked over his shoulder.

"He smiled at me this morning," Rachel declared with pride. Charlotte just shook her head.

"Eve said that was just gas after he ate."

Andrew saw a shadow cross his wife's face, but it disappeared in the blink of an eye. He furrowed his brow, but she reached up to cup his cheek. Once they were up the stairs and in the nursery, he set her on her feet.

"You know, I have managed to walk while you've been away," she said, teasing him.

"Precisely why I thought you could use a rest." He gave her a wink as she rolled her eyes at him. The nurse handed him his son, and he beamed down at him. His eyes had changed, taking on a green cast like his mother's, though the wisps of hair on his head were as dark as his own. Jonathan reached up a tiny hand and grasped Andrew's proffered finger. The nurse fussed about the room and told him how well the baby had been sleeping and eating.

He turned to comment to his wife, then realized she had left the room. Still holding his son, he told the girls to return to the classroom and finish their lessons, then went in search of Laura. He found her in their chamber curled up on the window seat, her knees drawn to her chest with her head turned toward the window.

"What is it? Are you unwell?"

"I'm fine, just tired. I believe I will take a rest now that you are home. Robbie is anxious to speak with you." She moved to her side, curling up with her back to him as she pulled her mother's quilt up over herself. He stood there for a moment, at a loss for words as his son slept in his arms. He had missed her desperately while he was away and she had said she missed him and yet she was withdrawing only an hour after his return.

She had been struggling before he left and he had hoped the bright greeting he had received meant that she was better. He could only stand here wondering as she remained turned away from him. Finally, he went in search of his brother-in-law, who currently sat behind the desk in Andrew's study. When he realized he was in the doorway, Robert stood and crossed the room to embrace him, careful not to crush the child between them.

"How was London? Were you able to meet with Reeves?"

"Yes, as a matter of fact, he will arrive tomorrow for a brief visit. I thought it was a fine idea to get the three of us in the same room again to make arrangements." He bounced his son a bit, walking

226

around the room as he fussed. This had always worked with Rachel, and the little boy quickly returned to his slumber.

"He is a fine lad. We can only hope he looks more like his uncle than his father," Robert teased. The two men took a seat in companionable silence for a bit until Andrew gathered his muddled thoughts.

"I am concerned for Laura. How was she during my absence?" Robert scrubbed a hand over his face with a sigh.

"I have worried for her as well. At times she seems like herself again, yet she falls into these dark moods that I cannot seem to free her from. I have an idea, however." Andrew leaned forward, eager for anything he could do for her. "I have noticed the look that overtakes her when the nurse is with little Jonathan. Our mother cared for us, fed us, and she often spoke of the joy it brought her. I fear it upset Laura that she could not do that for her child."

Andrew looked down at his sleeping child as he thought about this. She could not nurse him as she descended into her fever and Dr. Shaw had said she would be unable to if too much time passed. Most noble women preferred a wet nurse, yet he knew his wife was not like any of them. This made sense, unfortunately it was not something he could fix. He must make certain she had time with their child and not allow herself to wallow in this melancholy state.

That night, as he readied for bed, he watched Laura as she plaited her wild auburn curls. Moving behind her, he stopped her movements and ran his fingers through the long strands. He always marveled at her hair, the way it spread across the pillow as she slept, or curtained about him when they made love. He wanted desperately to lift her in his arms and carry her to their bed, make love to her

227

until the sun rose. Enough time had passed for her to heal, yet they still had not been intimate since Jonathan's birth.

He leaned down, moving her hair aside and kissed her shoulder. "You are so beautiful, my love," he whispered in her ear before gently nibbling on the lobe. He felt her shiver as he ran his fingers down her arms. Stepping around to face her, he drew her up and against him as he feathered kisses over her cheek and down her throat. Her hands came up to his chest, and he groaned softly at the contact. It had been too long.

"I want you, Laura," he said, his voice hoarse with desire. Her green eyes met his, but he did not see desire there. He saw fear and his heart shattered.

"I-I don't think I can... I'm sorry..." She dropped her gaze and stepped away from him, but he took her hands in his own and brought them to his lips.

"It's alright, I can wait as long as I know you still love me." His voice trembled, afraid she would turn from him, but she remained in his arms with her face pressed to his chest. The fabric muffling her words as she spoke. "What if I cannot give you another child? I may be useless to you as a wife. How can you still love me?"

His arms tightened around her, praying she could feel the love in his heart. "I did not marry you for the children you would give me. Jonathan, Charlotte and Rachel are blessings and I will cherish them always, but I have no need for more than to have you by my side to raise the children we have." He brushed a tear from her cheek with the pad of his thumb, then lifted her up and carried her to the bed. Laying her down, he slid in behind her, cradling her body close to his own. Kissing her hair, inhaling her soft citrus scent, his hand slowly stroked her arm. He would give her more time. He only prayed it would not be too long.

Noah smiled as the woman beside him marveled at the sight before her. Merveille was a wonder, nestled in the trees, its vine covered facade seeming to have grown rather than being built by the hands of men. Claudia's hand gripped his as she spoke excitedly about the beauty of the manor house. "Such a lovely country retreat. The duke must enjoy spending time here," she said as their carriage pulled into the circle drive.

Noah did not feel the need to correct her assumptions that the duke resided at Hawthorne Manor. He understood the man's desire to be in this setting where he could live a quiet life with his family. He wished to have the same thing, yet Claudia was not the woman he loved. Could he come to love her over time as they raised their child; only time would tell.

Hawthorne stepped out of the door with his wife on his arm, both smiling in greeting. Noah was pleased to see the duchess looking so well. The color had returned to cheeks, no hint of the difficult birth or the fever that had ravaged her. Releasing her husband's arm, she moved forward to take Noah's hands, giving them a squeeze. "It is wonderful to see you again, Mr. Reeves." She turned to Noah's betrothed with a bright smile. "Mrs. Reynolds, I am so pleased to meet you. I'm Laura Stanhope."

Claudia dropped into a low curtsy. "A pleasure to meet you, Your Grace," she said stiffly.

"Please, you are a guest in our home. Let us dispense with the formalities. Call me Laura." She took Claudia's hand and led her toward the house as the sound of the children's laughter came from

229

the open door. Charlotte and Rachel ran toward Noah and embraced his legs. It warmed his heart to be greeted in such a way, and he leaned down to return the embrace.

"You must join us in the garden, "Charlotte said excitedly. Her sister was already tugging at his hand.

"Give our guests some time to rest, my little monsters," Andrew scolded. Rachel pouted as she moved back toward her father, her sister following behind.

"But Papa, I want to feed the swan babies." Andrew narrowed his eyes at Rachel.

"Why don't you go ask Miss Greyson for one of the cookies she just made while Mr. Reeves and his lady take a moment to settle into their rooms then we will all take tea in the garden." This seemed to appease the girls, and they happily made their way to the kitchen. Footmen in their burgundy livery quickly gathered the bags and led them to their rooms in the guest wing to wash and change.

They served tea in the garden as promised, and Noah once again marveled at the ethereal beauty of the place. Laura sat in the sun as she sipped her tea and made polite conversation with Claudia. His betrothed seemed rather aloof in her presence, and he decided she was attempting to make a proper impression. No matter how often he spoke of the causal nature of their host and hostess, she remained formal in her demeanor, especially with the duchess.

The duke was assisting Rachel, who had a fishing pole, and she squealed as he waggled a worm at her then watched with rapt attention as he placed the squirming creature on the hook. Noah stood back as Andrew sent the line into the water. "Will you try, Mr. Reeves?" the little girl asked as she held the pole proudly.

"It has been a few years since I dropped a line in the water but I'll try my hand at it." He removed his jacket as Andrew had done and rolled up his sleeves before deftly baiting his hook and casting his line beside Rachel. She smiled up at him and then she asked if he fished when he was little, bringing the memory of days by the lake with Lily. With pant legs rolled up, he would stand in the water waiting for a tug on his line while she would sit on the bank and talk over her latest disagreement with her father or the poor treatment the man showed his mother.

It seemed in the end that her father sold her off into an equally difficult marriage, though the elder duke had at least provided for her. He supposed that was one small comfort. He was brought out of his musings when Rachel drew in an excited breath. "Papa, it moved." Her father placed a finger on the line and, sure enough, it dipped again. He told her how to pull to set the hook and bring the fish toward the bank as she giggled and shouted.

Once they pulled the fish from the water, its tiny body glistening, she called to her mother, who hurried to her side. "My goodness, what a grand fish," she beamed as Rachel held up her catch, no longer than a man's hand. The size did not matter. It was her first catch, and the girl lifted her chin with pride as she showed it to her sister. Charlotte wanted no part of the slimy creature and Rachel continued to hold it in her face until the other girl complained to their father.

"Rachel, you know your sister does not care about such things. No need to torment her. Now, let's send the fish back to its home." She nodded and allowed her father to remove the hook and release the little thing back into the water, where it happily splashed and swam away from the bank. Noah turned back to find Claudia still seated in the shade of a large birch. She was looking over the edge of her teacup, following her gaze, which was fixed on the duke and his daughter.

It was a lovely scene, and he knew she was likely imagining her own child and the moments such as this they would share as a family. For the child, he would make every effort to be happy.

Claudia was watching the duke as he doted on his little girl. Seeing him in this setting, he was even more handsome than when he was dressed in his finery. His dark curls spilled over his forehead and she tensed as she watched the duchess reach up and push them aside. He took her hand and brought it to his lips as she gave him a discreet smile.

After sitting with Laura Stanhope, she found the woman lacking in the regal air one would expect in a duchess. It must be difficult for Andrew to have her out in society, likely why she had been told during tea at Lady Weatherly's that she rarely appeared in London. She understood what they expected of a lady, despite her own humble upbringing. With Noah joining the man in business, she would offer to be his hostess in town. That would easily lead to other opportunities.

Another man came toward the group from the house, shining brown hair with a handsome face and fine clothes. He bowed to Noah and the three men spoke for several moments as the duchess lingered nearby with the children. The stranger reached over a tugged at a loose curl from the woman's simple braid and she gave his arm a playful swat as she laughed, calling him a brat.

"What will our guests think of you treating me so?" she said in a teasing tone.

"It will not surprise them since you are the one that is a brat." Claudia noted the resemblance in their features, though their coloring was different. It confirmed her suspicions when the duchess took his arm and brought him toward her.

"Mrs. Claudia Reynolds, may I present my brother, Robert Parsons." The man bowed, giving her a cordial smile.

"I suppose we will see one another from time to time since my brother-in-law and I will be in business with your future husband." Claudia had recalled Noah mentioning the man. He had inherited the shipping company from his father, and the duke had joined the venture after marrying Parson's sister. It was doing quite well, and she hoped that soon, Noah would gain greater wealth and standing by joining them.

Parsons was also staying for the weekend. Apparently, he had remained here to look after his sister while the duke was away. At dinner, the conversation flowed, like the wine, from one subject to another as the staff served one wondrous dish after another. Her eyes drifted to the duke where he sat at the head of the table, his wife to his right, flanked by her brother. Claudia sat to the duke's left with Noah to her right and she was pleased to be so close to Andrew, as he had asked her to use his given name.

She longed to reach out and brush his broad hand, wondering if he was feeling the pull between them as she did. He focused his attention on her as she spoke, his glorious smile ever present. She knew he was hanging on each word she spoke, as he seemed to ignore his wife while she chatted with her brother. She was loath to leave his company when the men retired to Andrew's study to discuss business and enjoy a drink while they relegated her to the parlor with the young duchess and the children who wished to entertain them.

The nurse brought the baby in and Laura sat with him in her arms, often looking down at him in wonder. Claudia did not understand the appeal of babies. They fussed and spit up and ruined one's body. She would much prefer to be the woman men longed to bed while their wives dealt with the children and the household. That being said, she had spent too many years working in the pub and being pinched and propositioned by men without the coin to better her circumstance.

She had thought Ezra would be her salvation, then Noah. Yet she longed for this life of wealth and leisure. She was certain she could entice Andrew now that the birth of his son had scarred his wife. With an heir, he was free to satisfy his own desires, and Claudia was happy to accommodate him.

An hour later, the men joined them in the parlor and the duke quickly went to look at his son, holding him up in the air as the child cooed. He knelt down beside his wife and brushed a kiss on her cheek before turning to Claudia. Was he attempting to make her jealous? She lowered her lashes, glancing up at him seductively, and he held her gaze a moment before turning back to his son. She smiled inwardly at the exchange, certain he was already making overtures.

As everyone retired, Noah walked her to her room, laying a chaste kiss on her cheek as he bid her good night. She returned the gesture and stepped into her room without her usual pleas to join him in his bed. Her plans were changing. Mayhap she would snare a duke and would no longer have need of Noah. He was a sweet man, handsome for his age, but he could not compare with the magnificence of the Duke of Hawthorne.

Chapter twenty-six

The following day, Noah invited Claudia to ride with him to the village for a visit with his aunt. She had balked at first, saying it would be rude to leave their host. However, when the Duke asked to accompany them, she decided it would be alright. When the duchess said she planned to join them as well, Claudia expressed her concern.

"Andrew, do you think it would be wise for her to travel after her ordeal?" Claudia asked. "It seems she should be resting." The duke looked at his wife, who was giving Claudia a rather annoyed expression.

"Mayhap she is correct, my darling." He cupped her cheek as he looked down at her, his voice gentle.

"I have been resting for weeks. It is time I looked in on things at the infirmary and I..." Andrew held up a hand.

"You are not stepping foot in the infirmary. You would tote linens and scrub floors as soon as you arrive. It is too soon," he said, his tone stern.

"But I.."

"No, I will not have you injuring yourself further. I will speak to Dr. Shaw and have him come visit when he is able. We will allow him to decide." Laura threw up her hands as she let out an exasperated huff. Turning on her heel, she stomped back into the house, leaving them all staring after her. Claudia lay a hand on Andrew's arm.

"You are only looking after her best interests even if she does not appreciate your efforts." He placed his hand over hers and thanked her.

"It has been difficult," he said hoarsely, then stepped away to mount his horse. The three of them rode out, Noah leading as Claudia remained back to speak with Andrew. It warmed his heart to see her concern for the duke and duchess, and he felt himself open to her a bit more.

The weather was fine and in no time they were at Minerva's door, where she embraced him. The children were all introduced to Claudia, and they were invited in for lunch. Andrew excused himself and made his way through to the kitchen, where he greeted Ginny with a warm smile, snatching a roll from the tray she carried to the table. She chastised him half heartedly as he went out the back door, leaving his coat over a chair. The sound of the axe striking wood quickly reached his ears as the young man set to work.

Claudia gave his aunt a scathing look. "You have the duke splitting wood for you? It seems you have several boys here that would be better suited to the task." Minerva did not bat an eye as she looked back at his young betrothed.

"Andrew comes and does these things for us because he wishes to, not out of duty. Laura lived here for a time and was always a great help and comfort to me. When Andrew courted her, he saw what needed to be done here and gladly began assisting us. Laura herself worked in the infirmary until she was unable due to carrying their child. The duke and duchess are kind and generous, with not only their funds but their time.

Jane approached and bent a knee quickly as she addressed Noah. "Good day Mr Reeves, it is pleased I am to thee... see you." He took her hand with a broad grin.

"That was excellent, Jane. I see you have been practicing." The girl blushed at his praise over the improvement in her lisp.

"I hope to th-see Laura soon to show her."

"I know she would be delighted at the company. She wished to accompany us today but her husband thought it best she wait a bit longer." The girl's face fell slightly, obviously missing the young woman who had become so important to them all.

"Is she unwell?" Jane inquired. Noah patted her hand gently and reassured her.

"All is well. She is still healing, is all. You should ask Andrew." Nodding, the girl turned to go in search of her answers.

Andrew mopped his brow as he leaned against the axe handle. Having removed his waistcoat and cravat while he worked, his muscles were warm with the pleasant ache of hard work. He had needed this time to exert himself and clear his mind. He wondered if he had been heavy-handed in not allowing Laura to join them, yet he worried so for her. Inviting Jane to ride back with them and spend the night if Minerva agreed; he hoped it would ease the girl's mind and bring a smile to Laura's face.

He noted a tension between Laura and Claudia during the times they were together. Laura was trying, but the other woman seemed overly solicitous toward him, where she barely spoke to her. He had not thought too much of it until Claudia had intervened today. He would like to think the lady spoke out of concern, but he felt a ripple of unease in her presence.

A movement at the corner of his vision had him turning to find Claudia approaching from the kitchen door. Her eyes seemed to move over him as she handed him a cup of water. Her gaze dropped to his mouth and her tongue darted out to moisten her lips. He thanked her and downed the cool water thirstily. He expected her to go, but she stepped closer, bringing the heavy scent of lavender to his nose.

"You are an impressive man, Andrew," she said in a breathy voice, making him quirk a brow at her. "Seeing you in your shirt sleeves, lending your assistance," she paused, grazing her fingers over his arm. "I can see what strength of character you have." She paused for a moment, leaning still closer. "Do you not long for the delights of London?"

The tone of her voice had him questioning what sort of delights she was speaking of. He recalled the words of Noah's man, Benning, "I question if the young lady has a true heart." The man had said no more while they were alone, but his motivation was clear. He was enlisting Andrew's opinion of the situation. Later in the evening, Benning asked after the dowager -duchess. "It is a wonderful thing to see the major with someone he is so fond of." Again, the man said nothing more.

"I have found little to interest me in London, though that may change soon," he said with a sly smile. She looked up at him through her lashes.

"I am pleased to hear that, Your Grace. I am certain with your presence, London will be quite engaging indeed."

Noah stepped into the yard, causing the pair to step away from one another. Andrew could see the slight lift of the man's brow as he approached them, taking Claudia's arm.

"I wondered what was taking you so long. My aunt is eager to become better acquainted." Claudia nodded and moved back toward the house, giving Andrew a quick glance over her shoulder. As Noah opened the door for her, he gave Andrew a look. Not jealousy, but disappointment. Slamming the axe down into the stump before him, Andrew picked up his discarded waistcoat and cravat. After donning the items, he leaned in the door and bid farewell to Ginny, who was bustling about the kitchen. He wished to speak to Dr. Shaw before he returned home and the hour was growing late.

Dinner that evening was strained. The children had eaten earlier and Robert had left for London earlier in the day, having much work to see after being away for a fortnight, looking after his sister in the duke's absence. Noah and Laura would glance at one another across the table with tight smiles as Claudia and Andrew carried on a lively conversation punctuated with laughter and light touches. After dessert was served, Claudia leaned in to Andrew as she admired the signet ring he wore, bringing his hand closer to her eyes to better admire the intricate design. When Andrew squeezed the woman's fingers, Laura abruptly rose, nearly toppling her chair. "If you will excuse me, I believe I have had enough for one day."

As she swept from the room, Claudia brought a hand to her chest. "How rude," she murmured, then turned her eyes back to Andrew, who was looking after his wife's retreating form.

"We will, of course, understand if you wish to excuse yourself," Noah said, giving Andrew a pointed look.

"Yes, forgive me, I shall return momentarily."

"Take your time," Noah said, turning his gaze on Claudia. "I believe we should retire early so that we might make an early start tomorrow."

"But we are to stay another day and the duke was planning to show me the grounds in the morning. They have an orangery on the property and I am eager to see it."

"I believe we have overstayed our welcome," Noah said briskly as he rose and held out a hand to assist her.

"The duchess is being overly dramatic. It must be the aftereffects of her difficulties from the birth."

Noah pressed his lips together in a hard line, but said nothing more than he escorted her toward the stairs. Before turning toward the guest wing at the landing, raised voices could be heard from the other direction and it startled them when a door swung open and the duke strode out scowling. The duchess appeared at the door and saw the pair on the stairs, then quickly pulled the door shut with a sharp click.

Noah shook his head, saddened to see the loving couple having difficulties, and that Claudia was likely the cause. Harmless flirtation was not uncommon between men and women, yet this had not seemed harmless. Claudia may be a widow, but she remained naïve in the ways of the world. He would need to speak to her about her behavior this evening, as he was certain she did not realize how her behavior might be misconstrued.

Turning over once again as sleep eluded him, Noah could not escape the memories of the night Lily had shared this bed with him. The soft knock on the door startled him from his thoughts and he padded to the door quickly, concerned something was amiss with Claudia. He only hoped she was not attempting, yet again, to coax her way into his bed. Instead, he found Laura in her nightdress, an

241

ornate shawl pulled about her shoulders and her auburn locks plaited for the night.

"I am sorry to disturb you so late, but have you seen my husband?" Worry furrowed the young woman's brow, and she looked as though she might weep at any moment. "He did not return to our room after -er-a disagreement and..." a soft blush came to her cheeks as she was aware they had been seen arguing earlier.

"I am afraid I have not, my lady. Have you looked in his study or asked the staff?" He asked, pulling on his night rail.

"No one has seen him and I... I knocked on Mrs. Reynold's door but she is absent as well." Her words hung in the air, her pain at what she was suggesting, clear in her eyes. Noah's heart sank at the sight and he embraced her like he would a child as her shoulders shook. Then she spoke, her words muffled in the linen that covered his chest.

"I believe I know where they might be," she sniffed.

Pulling her away and looking down at her, he said, "Leave it to me."

Blood thundering in his ears, Noah made his way along the path. He had hastily donned a pair of breeches and a shirt after Laura told him about the couple's possible whereabouts. He wanted to call Andrew out for the callous way he was treating his wife. Did he not see what a priceless gift she was in his life? He thought him a better man than this. Slowly he opened the door to the orangery so as not to alert anyone to his presence. He prayed this was a misunderstanding, but at the sound of muffled voices, his hopes vanished.

"Andrew darling, I knew from the first that you wanted me," Claudia whispered.

"How could I not, and yet I do not know how we can be together?" Andrew was holding her close in the dim light of the half moon that shone through the window at their backs.

"You are a duke, surely you can do as you wish."

"It is only…" Noah moved closer to better hear the exchange. "I do not wish to raise another man's child." Claudia looked up at him in surprise. "Benning told me you are carrying Reeve's child. No matter my feelings, I could not abide having his child under my roof."

Noah's mind reeled at how completely he had misjudged the young man. He was ready to rush forth, but Claudia's words stopped him cold.

"Then there is nothing to keep us apart, for I am not with child. Forgive me, but I was afraid of being cast out and so I lied. Noah had been so far in his cups he realized he had not bedded me and so I did all I could to secure my future, but that was before I met you, my love. There is nothing holding me to him. I am certain the courts would grant you a divorce since Laura can no longer bear children. I can be yours." Noah watched, frozen to the spot as Claudia raised up on her toes to kiss him.

Andrew grasped her arms and pushed her away, turning toward the dark corridor of the building. "You may show yourself now," Andrew said into the shadows. Noah emerged from his hiding place, confused and angry as he watched the color drain from Claudia's face.

"Is this true?" Noah asked. "After all that I have done for you, you lied to me, allowed me to believe that we…that you were…" His eyes lifted to Andrew's face. "And you, how could you do this to

243

Laura?" He turned at the light touch on his back and found the duchess standing behind him with a look of contrition.

"Please forgive our little ruse, but we were concerned for your welfare," Laura breathed.

Claudia cried out, "No, what is the meaning of this? Andrew, darling. Tell her you want me." The duke stepped away from her, moving to his wife's side as she took his arm. Turning to Noah, he gave a shrug.

"Benning had his suspicions and made me aware of them when I was in London." Turning to Claudia, he added, "Your behavior since your arrival only heightened my own suspicions and now you have admitted your deception." Turning to his wife, he smiled lovingly, "Now that we have done our part to assist our dear friend, I believe we should give them their privacy and take some for ourselves." He swept her up into his arms, "You should not be wandering about in the night air my darling. Let us get you to bed." He kissed her forehead and strode toward the door, leaving Noah to deal with his betrothed.

Claudia turned her watery gaze to him. "How vile of him to toy with my emotions in such a way. I lost the baby only a sennight ago, but I thought we could have another. You seemed so happy that I did not wish to dash your hopes." She grabbed onto his arm as she continued to plead, but he had heard the truth. The whole thing had been a lie to snare a prosperous husband, yet when the enticement of being a duchess dangled before her, she was quick to drop the facade.

"I cannot believe a word you say Claudia, there is nothing left but to end our betrothal," he said as she fell to her knees with racking sobs.

"Please Noah, you must understand. I was afraid of being turned out. I never would have done such a thing otherwise. You were slipping away." She clung to him, but he pulled from her grasp.

"You have no more feelings for me than I have for you. I would have seen your future secure, mayhap not in as fine a style as a duke may have, but my intentions were honorable toward you and you have made a mockery of them. He walked away with ground-eating strides as she continued to follow him toward the house, crying and calling his name until he rounded on her.

He took her by the shoulders, giving her a hard shake. "I was kind to you. I allowed you into my home and you repaid me with lies. You have cost me the greatest treasure of my life, one I can only pray it is not too late to recover. Now get out of my sight," he spat, releasing her from his grasp.

"But where shall I go?" she cried.

"I will arrange for transportation to London with a letter telling Benning to give you fifty pounds to assist you in finding lodging. Take your dresses, jewelry and belongings. They are yours. I ask you to never darken my door again."

Andrew stood in the parlor where the elderly butler had directed him. "My staff are gathering her things as we speak and a carriage is waiting to return her to London, if that is what you wish," he said solemnly. "I apologize again for misleading you, my friend."

Noah stepped closer, taking his hand. "It is I who should apologize for believing you to be a rake. Oddly, I was far more

245

disturbed to think that you could hurt your wife in such a way than to be concerned about Claudia's betrayal." He bowed his head, pinching the bridge of his nose for a moment.

"If she had been the woman you love, I am certain I would lay dead on the floor of the orangery at this moment. Though I should like to give you my blessing if you wish to court my mother." The young man's blue eyes were alight with mischief as he looked at him. His lips quirked up in a smile.

"That apparent, is it?" Noah asked. Andrew only nodded before offering one of his finest mounts to take him to London.

Chapter twenty-seven

With Thea, her sister-in-law, chaperoning Julia to the theater that evening, Lillian found herself in a hired carriage, not wishing to be recognized in her coach with its ducal crest. Sitting in the darkness, she clasped her trembling hands together as the wheels clattered over the street toward Barrington's townhouse. They had arranged this meeting the day before, after she had seen Noah and Claudia walking arm in arm in Hyde Park. He had not even looked at her as though what they had shared meant nothing to him, and it had caused her to accept Barrington's proposition.

She was unattached; she reminded herself as the house came into view, her heart tracing. As a mature woman, if she desired the company of a handsome man, that was her affair. After all, why should men be the only ones to enjoy a dalliance? She had been faithful to her husband, and what had it brought her? Nothing but heartache as he went about with other women as he pleased.

It was time she embraced her position and take what she wished. Except it was not Barrington she wanted. Noah's face came unbidden to her mind, but she pushed it away as the carriage stopped and she quickly made her way to the door. Barrington himself answered at her knock as, at her request, he had given his staff the evening off.

He did not wear a coat, only breeches and a white silk shirt open at the neck, and she shivered as his fingers danced over her nape as he removed her cloak. His cologne smelled of sandalwood and citrus, a fresh masculine scent that tickled her senses. He laid a gentle kiss on her neck and seemed to inhale her own rosewater before leading her to a salon at the end of the hall where a small table was set for two.

Candles burned around the space, sparkling off of crystal and silver. He had set a light supper out and he pulled out a chair for her, then filled her glass with rich red wine. She took a large swallow to calm her thundering heart as he sat across from her.

"I have waited so long to have you alone like this, my darling. I am overjoyed that you finally agreed." He reached out, taking her hand and turning it to kiss her palm. The action sent a wave of warmth through her belly and below and her lips parted on a small gasp. He smiled at her reaction, his eyes darkening with desire.

They ate quietly, and she watched his elegant movements as he cut his meat or brought his goblet to his lips. She knew he was well versed in the art of seduction. There were many stories shared by ladies in secluded salons that had shared an illicit moment with him in a garden or a secluded alcove, and Lillian felt her anticipation building.

After they finished the meal, he filled her goblet again and led her to a gold velvet chaise that sat in the corner of the room. Sitting behind her, he slowly released her chestnut curls from their pins as he ran his fingers through the silken strands. He hummed in approval as he pulled the waves from her shoulder, trailing kisses down her neck to her shoulder.

"You are a rare combination of strength and beauty, my sweet. I know you will be a wonder to taste." His voice was deep and rough as he lay her back on the pillows that adorned the chaise. Leaning down, his dark brown eyes hooded as he took her lips, only brushing it with his own at first, then angling his head to deepen the kiss. His

248

hand was in her hair, pulling her in, and she opened to allow his tongue access to her mouth. He tasted wine and berries, and she brought her hands up to his nape, sliding her fingers into his hair.

"My sweet Lillian," he whispered, his voice husky. She pulled back for a moment, reminded of Noah calling her his sweet Lily. "Don't pull away sweeting, kiss me again." His hands were possessive as they roamed downward to her waist, then back up where one cupped her breast. The other was working at the buttons down her back.

She attempted to lose herself in the kiss and yet her mind continued to conjure images of Noah, as he loved her. Tears stung her eyes, and she pushed the marquess away as she attempted to right herself. Bringing an arm about her shoulders, he attempted to coax her back, murmuring words of endearment. "Do not be nervous, I will bring you only pleasure. Husbands too rarely satisfy their wives, but I promise you this will be different."

She pushed him away as she rose to her feet. "This was a mistake, I should not have come." She was patting her hair, though it was beyond fixing. She needed her cloak. Barrington's powerful hand came around to grip her wrist and turn her to face him.

"Where do you think you are going? Do not toy with me, Lillian."

"I apologize... I cannot do this. I thought it was what I wanted, but I see now it was a mistake." Her voice trembled as she fought for control, attempting to pull from his grasp.

"Your mistake is believing I will allow you to leave here without giving me what you promised," he said, his eyes burning into her as his grip tightened.

"How dare you…" Lillian's voice rose with her anger at the man's rough handling of her. Not since her father had a man dared to raise a hand to her. Bile rose in her throat as those feelings of helplessness closed in on her. Her eyes locked with his and she could see he had no intention of allowing her to leave. Resigned, she accepted what she must do.

Noah had ridden at first light, leaving the letter to be carried by Claudia back to London. Andrew and Laura had seen him off, the duke giving him words of encouragement. "Speak your heart. If she feels for you what I believe she does, she will hear you." He looked down at his own wife, the love between them once again clear.

He had stopped only to rest and water his horse, a fine chestnut stallion that reminded him of his own trusted mount of years ago when he was a young soldier. He knew he would arrive before Claudia's conveyance, a single rider traveling faster than a larger carriage. Stopping first at his home to change mounts, giving the stallion a well-deserved rest. He also informed Benning of the events of the weekend and his wishes for handling Claudia.

His friend preferred the idea of sending the girl off with the clothes she arrived in; he promised to carry out Noah's wishes. Mounting the steps two at a time, removed his mud splattered clothes and washed. Once he deemed himself presentable, he stepped to the chest beside the large window at the back of the room to retrieve the velvet pouch tucked in the corner of the top drawer and placed it in his coat pocket.

Now standing at the door of Hawthorne's London residence, he drew in a deep breath and knocked. Jennings, the young butler, opened the door and ushered him into the parlor, where Julia and an older, rather robust woman sat with their tea. Lillian's daughter rose with a bright smile and greeted him fondly. "What a pleasant surprise you are, Mr. Reeves." She motioned toward her companion. "May I introduce my aunt, Theodosia Rawlings."

He bowed quickly, receiving an appraising gaze and a nod. Noah had no time for social graces and immediately stated his purpose. "I wished to speak with your mother on a matter of great importance." Julia's aunt seemed amused as she raised her eyebrows.

"Goodness, it must be a matter of life or death. What could it be? Certainly you could let us know as my sister-in-law is not currently in residence."

Noah's heart sank at her words. He would simply have to await her return. "When do you expect her?" he asked anxiously.

"I am afraid she has left me in the care of my aunt as she wished to return home," Julia told him as she held out a cup of tea for him. He ignored her offer as he paced the small room.

"She left you during your season?"

"Yes, it was rather strange to me as well. She left a note two days ago, but she would not elaborate on the circumstances of her desire to depart."

Bowing to the ladies, he made a hasty exit. He would follow Lily to the ends of the earth if need be to prove himself. That she had left her daughter was worrisome. He could not imagine what would make her leave in such a way. He would have to travel to Hawthorne Manor.

Lillian looked around at the musty room, the furnishings covered to protect them from dust. She had not set foot in this house since her father's death, though she had ensured that it remained in her possession. The tenants would continue to work the land, and Noah's parents had remained in this small house by the stables until their deaths.

They had loved each other and after Mrs. Reeves passed, her husband had only lasted another six months. What would it be like to spend years with the person you loved by your side? She would never know. Noah would marry someone else tomorrow and she would remain alone.

After meeting with the caretaker, Lillian had made her way to the stable master's house. She had no desire to enter the manor house that held only painful memories. This place was different. She had sat at the long kitchen table as Noah's mother prepared a meal or laughed with the family as they shared tea and a freshly baked roll.

She could almost hear their voices as she brought their faces to mind. They had been her family, not the cruel man that had sold her to the duke to fund his own selfish needs. Her Mother had been a loving woman, yet years of mistreatment had left her hollow and unable to protect her child.

Lillian thought of her own children, how she had built a wall around her heart so that no one could get close enough to cause her pain again. It was too late for Jonathan, but she had allowed Andrew and Julia in and she would not push them away again. She had also opened her heart to Noah, given him all of her and he had thrown it away to marry another.

That night she lay in the bed she had made with linens stored at the manor, staring out at the window that was once her own. She wondered if he ever watched it, if even for one night he had longed for her as she had for him. Tears stung her eyes, and she dashed them away, determined not to shed another for the man.

The sound of hoofbeats on the packed earth woke her. She did not know when she had finally dozed off or how long she had been asleep, but there was no reason for anyone to be arriving this night. She prayed the few footmen at the manor would deal with any intrusion, after all. Why would someone come to this small house when the larger manor house sat close by?

She heard the rattle of the door latch and froze, hugging the covers tightly about her. Again there was a rattling, followed by the creaking sound as the door swung inward. Lillian eased herself from the mattress, praying there would be no sound from the old bed frame, and reached for the candlestick on the table beside her. Creeping to the door, she held the heavy pottery over her head, waiting for the intruder to attempt entry to the room. She could hear heavy booted footsteps moving about the place gradually becoming louder as they approached. She held her breath as the knob turned, her trembling fingers grasping her crude weapon, ready to strike. As they entered, Lillian cried out and brought the candlestick down toward the man's head, her aim off slightly as the object glanced off of his shoulder.

"Bloody hell," the man yelped in surprise as she dashed past him. She felt a hand grasp her arm, and she screamed as she fought, twisting and clawing as terror consumed her.

"Let go of me, you bastard," she bellowed as the man wrapped an arm around her waist.

"God's teeth, is that you Lily?" She stilled. The voice was familiar despite being hoarse.

"Noah?" she asked in astonishment as her eyes adjusted to the dim light of the moon coming through the window. "What are you doing, sneaking about here?"

"Me? This is my home. What in blazes are you doing here? I thought to find you at Hawthorne Manor." He released her, bringing a hand up to rub his bruised shoulder. All she could do was stare at him, still at a loss as to what he was about. Reaching out, Noah guided her to sit beside him.

"Julia said you left a note; that you were going home. What are you doing here?"

"I...well, this is home. Or it was once." A tear slid down her cheek as she looked around her. "Wait... why were you speaking to my daughter?" Then realization dawned. "You brought her...your wife here?" Her lips pressed firmly together as she suppressed the urge to cry anew. She scrambled from the bed, evading his hands as he reached out. She ran to the door, thinking to go to the manor house, escaping the pain of seeing him with his new bride, but he caught her easily in only a few strides.

He turned to her and said, "I have no wife."

Lillian blinked up at him owlishly, unable to fathom what he meant. "Please let me go," she pleaded.

"Not until you hear what I have to say." As she tried to pull away again, he grabbed her hand. She cried out in pain and he immediately released her.

"What is it? Are you injured... I'm sorry Lily I didn't mean to hurt you." She laughed at his words, not a giggle, but a hearty laugh that echoed off the walls of the cottage. He could only stare at her in astonishment, certain she had lost her mind. Then her laughter died and her eyes fixed him to the spot.

"As if that makes a difference. The pain is the same. All of you with your words and anxious trying to tear me down until there is nothing left. Well, I am still standing and this is no longer your home. The estate is mine and I want you gone at first light." She stormed from the room, running across the yard to the manor house and disappearing inside.

Taking a deep breath, Lillian paused in the hallway as her heart thundered in her chest. Just as she regained her composure, the back door crashed inward, slamming against the wall. Noah stood there, chest heaving, and Lillian took a step back, preparing to run. In an instant he had her, pulling her toward the library where she had dismissed him from her life years before.

He dropped her into a cloth covered chair; the dust swirling up, making her sneeze. Tugging an ottoman forward, he sat in front of her, blocking any escape as he took both of her hands with greater care. The light from the window illuminated her skin, and he brought her right hand closer to his face as he noted the red, swollen knuckles, drawing in a pained breath.

"Did I do this?" Lillian shook her head.

"Barrington," she said with a small shrug. She could see the flash of anger in his eyes.

"I'll kill the bastard," he growled. Despite the seriousness of the moment, Lillian chuckled.

"Actually, it was my fault. Although it was the man's face that did the damage, I was the one that struck him." Noah raised a questioning brow at her. "Quite certain I broke his nose, though it served him right believing he could have his way without my consent." Noah brought her bruised hand to his lips, brushing a kiss over the tender flesh.

"That's my little Lily," he said with a wry smile.

"I am not…" His mouth stopped her words, kissing her deeply. She intended to fight him, then seemed to forget why she wished to as the feel of his mouth intoxicated hers. When he pulled back, he was smiling at her.

"I know, you are not little and you are not mine. Though one of those things is within my power to change." Lillian searched his eyes, unsure of what he was saying. He was to be married and yet he was here with her.

"I realize there is no way for me to take away the pain I have caused you," he began. "After the war, after losing young Reynolds, I could not find a way forward. Drinking to excess most nights, hoping to find oblivion, but it could not take the pain away. I had taken his widow in, feeling I was in his debt and after one of those drunken nights, I woke to find her in my bed. I thought... Well, you can imagine what I thought, and so I offered for her.

"I had never thought to find you again, yet there you were. Still beautiful, still my Lily. Believe me when I say that you are the only

256

woman I have ever truly wanted. I had planned to break the engagement, provide Claudia with some security and ask you to be my wife, but she told me she was carrying my child." He paused, taking in Lillian's pained expression.

"It was all a lie. She climbed into my bed, but I never touched her, not even after she told me I had. I could not bring myself to share her bed. Her lies would have tied me to her for the rest of my life, had it not been for your son and his wife."

"How did they...what did they do?" she asked in surprise.

"Suffice it to say that they got the truth of it from her and I will forever be in their debt. So now that I am free to do so, I wish to ask; would you marry me, my sweet Lily?" He pulled the bracelet from the pocket of his mud spattered coat. "I realize this is not the traditional ring…"

Lillian took his face in her hands as tears gleamed in her smiling blue eyes.

"Nothing would make me happier than to be your wife."

Epilogue

Noah stood in the church, his heart swelling as he took in the sunlight that shone through the stained glass windows, casting their various hues upon the white flowers that adorned the sanctuary. It was a beautiful sight, but could not compare with the woman at his side. She smiled up at him as he held her small hand in his.

"Any regrets?" he asked in a whisper.

"Only the years we wasted. The ceremony did not matter, only that I was finally your wife." She turned her tearful gaze to her daughter, dressed in white silk and pearls as she recited her vows to the man she loved. Charles Bartlett's face beamed as he looked down into her soft blue eyes and repeated the words spoken by the priest. As the young couple exchanged rings, Noah recalled standing before the anvil in Gretna Green as the blacksmith clergy pronounced him and Lily man and wife nearly a year ago. They had not wanted to wait, having wasted so many years already, and like two love-stuck youngsters, they had run off to Scotland.

When they returned to share their news, they were greeted with smiles and warm embraces. Andrew stood beside him now, holding his wife close at his side with young Jonathan sleeping with his head on her shoulder. Their daughters stood near their aunt, smiling in pretty white dresses with pink flowers adorning their hair. This was his family, not made but found, and he imagined it would please his parents to see him finally with the woman he loved.

The wedding breakfast was a lavish affair, held at Hawthorne's London residence, and he raised a glass to toast the happy couple as they shared a kiss. Parsons Shipping was expanding with his assistance and he was enjoying the time he spent with Andrew and Robert in the offices, once again feeling young and excited with each new venture.

Finding a quiet moment, he led his wife to a secluded corner, where he took her hands in his. "You have made me happier than I ever dreamed, my darling." He kissed her lips softly, but noted a slight frown as he pulled away. "What troubles you?" he asked

"I am only sorry that I can not give you children." He gave her a reassuring smile.

"You have given me a son and daughter and grandchildren. They are yours and I am glad to hold them in my heart. Besides, this way I have you all to myself," he said with a wolfish gleam in his eyes. He was leaning in to kiss her when he felt a tug at his coattails and turned to find Rachel holding her toddling brother's hand.

"Grandpa, it is time for the cake." He scooped up little Jonathan as Lily reached out to take Rachel's hand.

"So it is, my dear lady, so it is." Smiling at his wife, they all walked back to the dining room for a piece of wedding cake.

***Thank you for reading. The greatest gift you can give an author is to share your opinion with others. Please take a moment to leave a review, It will be greatly appreciated.

If you enjoyed Lillian's story but missed book one, pick up your copy of No Desire to be Noble and read Andrew and Laura's love story from the beginning , available only on Amazon as an e book or paperback amazon.com/dp/B09K9RSTR5

***Can't get enough of the Stanhopes? Book three is coming in Spring 2022

It's time to hear Rachel's story as she and her sister Charlotte embark on their own adventure in London.

An anonymous letter leaves Rachel wondering if her father, The Duke of Hawthorne, has been lying to her all her life. With the help of her sister and a mysterious young man, she goes in search of the truth. At the end of this journey she will find answers that will change her life forever.

Also By

The Noble Love Series

Book I

No Desire to be Noble

Book II

Her Price for Nobility

Book III

Coming in Spring 2022

Acknowledgments

First I would like to thank you, my readers. It has been wonderful to hear from you and how well my story has been received.

I have been fortunate to have the assistance of my talented siblings along the way. My sister Kathi, graciously reads along as I write, keeping me on track. My brother Dave has created beautiful covers that make it well worth picking up the paperback.

My friends deserve a huge hug for their willingness to read my work and spread the word, helping me to reach more readers. A special shout out goes to Denise and her daughter Jacqueline (who is also my fabulous daughter -in-law) for going above and beyond, helping me navigate the world of social media.

I would especially like to thank my husband Tom for being supportive and patient as I pursue my dreams. You mean the world to me.

About the Author

Amy lives in a small town in Michigan where she and her husband raised four children and are now enjoying their first grandchild. Being an avid reader it was always a dream to write her own stories, scribbling in notebooks for years. The publication of her first novel *No Desire to be Noble"* lit a fire that resulted in this book and the story isn't over. Book three will be coming in spring of 2022 along with her first contemporary romance *Cinnamon Kisses.*

When not writing, her family continues to keep her busy. She also enjoys traveling when the opportunity arises or cheering on their favorite Michigan teams. She continues her work as a medical coder with evenings and weekends spent dreaming up new ways to make her readers fall in love.

Keep up with new releases and extra content by joining her mailing list at http://amycuriston.com

You can also follow her on Goodreads and on facebook under author amy curiston

Made in the USA
Monee, IL
04 April 2022

94095462R00156